D1637038

VHR
PRESS
VINE HILL ROAD PRESS

Also by
M. L. Doyle

Fiction
Master Sergeant Lauren Harper Mysteries:
The Peacekeeper's Photograph
Canceled Plans (companion short)
The Sapper's Plot
The Ranger's Revenge (Spring 2014)

Nonfiction
I'm Still Standing;
From Captured Soldier to free citizen, my journey home
With Shoshana Johnson
(Touchstone, 2010)

A Promise Fulfilled,
My life as a Wife and Mother, Soldier and General Officer
With BG (Ret.) Julia Cleckley

Romance as Louise Kokesh
The Limited Partnerships series
Part I - Charlie
Part II - Luke
Part III - Wolf
Part IV – Derek
Limited Partnerships Omnibus

*To Jeanne
all the best*

The Peacekeeper's Photograph

by
M. L. Doyle

VHR
PRESS
VINE HILL ROAD PRESS

While the author has attempted to present a realistic view of
military life, liberties were taken for literary purposes.
This is a work of fiction and should be treated as such.
Any similarities to persons living or dead, real or imagined,
is purely coincidental.
That's my story and I'm sticking to it.

Edited by Gale Deitch
Cover design by EarthlyCharms.com
Author photo by Chad T. Jones

DEDICATION

For the men and women of
the 364th Mobile Public Affairs Detachment,
Fort Snelling, MN
and all others who answer the call to serve.

In Bosnia, we can and will succeed because our mission is clear and limited and our troops are strong and very well prepared. But my fellow Americans, no deployment of American troops is risk free, and this one may well involve casualties. There may be accidents in the field or incidents with people who have not given up their hatred. I will take every measure possible to minimize these risks, but we must be prepared for that possibility.
President Bill Clinton November 27, 1995

One

Mud covered my boots, splattered my uniform and served as an unavoidable annoyance every single day of our Bosnian deployment. Like a constant, unwanted companion, everywhere I stepped, I found more of it. After spending the day in a remote farm field, thick clumps of the brown sludge, gunk that looked more like something you'd see in a baby's diaper and equally as gross, completely covered what had been spit shined boots only a few hours before.

I opened the door of my trailer and held onto the frame for balance as I kicked and scraped my boots against the steps to get rid of the mud. As bad as the clumpy, wet stuff was, dried out, the mud turned to a fine dust that wrecked equipment like my video camera, computer and M16. So, like every time I walked in my door, I took my time, working to free my boots of as much mud as possible.

Finally, I stepped inside the trailer, glanced toward Delray's cot where it sat tucked next to the wall, and saw her feet. The hot pink color on her toenails almost glowed from across the room. The night before, she had borrowed my nail polish and given herself a pedicure. I wore the same color on my toes. Wearing combat boots every day made things like that more important; painting your toenails, wearing pretty underwear, girly things, reminders of your femininity.

The sight of those hot pink toes resting there on her cot made me grit my teeth and kick the trailer door closed. I thought she was asleep. She knew that if I ever caught her napping in the middle of the day, she would catch hell.

"Get your ass up, Delray," I said.

I didn't raise my voice. Just said it like I meant it and assumed she would scramble up and make an excuse.

I hefted my Betacam onto the edit table, pushed aside the keyboard and mouse and propped the tripod against the wall. When I took my Kevlar helmet off, I had that momentary feeling of lightness that happened each time the weight was removed from my head, as if, without the heavy lid, I'd lose my tether to the ground. I pulled my M16 from where I wore it slung over my back and stuck it in the weapons rack by the door, then ripped the Velcro closure of my flak vest open and just let the damn thing slide down my arms onto the floor with a hollow thud. I sighed at the shock of frigid air on my sweat soaked BDU jacket.

My video editing equipment and Delray's graphics computers were the reasons we rated an air-conditioned trailer. Delray liked to keep the place almost refrigerator cold and I let her.

By this time, with the noise I had generated, I figured she would have been up and mumbling an excuse for why she'd been lazing around. Sleeping during the duty day? Are you kidding me? When I looked toward her rack, she still hadn't moved. I took a step toward her, ready to say something, to give her the dressing down she deserved but then stopped, my words caught. Something wasn't right. I stared at her frozen feet until her unnatural stillness fully registered.

In that moment, the air conditioning felt too cold. I finally noticed the foul air in the small trailer. A familiar cloying stench I'd smelled before. Here, in my temporary home, it was ugly and intrusive. I shuddered and moved toward her.

"Virginia?"

I leaned over her shelving unit and saw her face for the first time. "Holy shit."

I stumbled away until my back hit the wall. My chest heaved. I struggled to breathe. I heard a noise that sounded like a whimper, then realized it came from me.

My gaze flew around the trailer, focusing on the computer desk, my cot on the other side of the trailer, back to the computer desk, on anything but Specialist Virginia Delray. When my breathing slowed, I knew I had to get confirmation.

I inched toward her cot, preparing myself for a better look. Most of her body had been hidden by the make-shift closet she had fashioned from old wooden crates. Her entire face looked bloated and grayish white, except for her lips, which were blue. She barely looked human. More like a wax museum horror display, a freaky mannequin with short bleached blonde hair spiked wildly around her head. Her eyes bulged open with little red specks of blood dotted throughout the whites. She wore her PT uniform, the one issued for physical training sessions, a grey hooded sweatshirt jacket, with big black letters that spelled Army across the front, and grey sweatpants. Her shower shoes, a cheap brown terrycloth towel and her sleeping bag sat bunched up at the end of the cot, as if she had kicked and fought. Her hands were at her throat and I could see blood and gunk under her fingernails. They were jagged and broken.

A yellow safety reflector belt, issued as part of our PT uniform, cut deeply into the flesh around her neck like a garrote. Usually we wear the belt draped diagonally over the shoulder and then clipped on the side at the waist. Someone had used the belt like a tourniquet, cutting off Delray's blood, her breath, her life.

I stood staring at her for what seemed like hours but was probably only seconds. Gentle rain tinkled against the roof. A group of people walked by outside the trailer, one laughing loudly, several others joining in. I wanted to shout at them to shut up. Didn't they know what had happened here? Obviously, no one knew. My pulse slammed in my temples. I must have been holding my breath, because when I finally did inhale, I got a strong whiff of that rank smell tinged with urine and realized she must have pissed herself in the struggle.

That's when it finally registered that Virginia had been

murdered.

Closer to her cot, the fetid air held the familiar sickly sweet odor that coated my nostrils and made bile rise in my throat. An image flashed in my head of when I had smelled that odor for the first time, at the mass grave mission I had been sent to record. I'd videotaped soldiers in white paper overalls and surgical masks, using small spades and brushes to painstakingly reveal sixty-two men and boys, piled on top of each other in a trench outside a small Bosnian town. They were strangers, those dead people, but the indignity of their disposal never left me. Neither did the smell.

Specialist Virginia Delray was no stranger. She was my soldier. My responsibility. While we weren't friends, far from it, I didn't think her the type of person who could rouse such a violent response from anyone. She hadn't deserved this.

She would not have liked the wax-like appearance of her skin. She liked to compare her tan with my naturally brown color. Holding her arm next to mine, she would smile and say in her Mississippi, tinged accent, "I'm almost as dark as you, Sergeant Harper."

"No one will ever mistake you for a sistah, Specialist Delray. Give it a rest."

I shook my head at the memory, then swayed, almost losing my balance. I had been standing there stiff, my knees locked, my fingers curled into fists. Taking a couple of shaky steps back, I leaned against the wall again. It reminded me of how I felt, staring down at that mass grave, powerless in the face of evil and sickened by what we were capable of doing to each other. My thoughts spun out of control until they landed on what to do next.

My legs felt too stiff and heavy to carry me, but I forced them to take me back to the desk. I had to move, had to report this.

I put my flak vest back on, put my Kevlar back on my head, and picked up my weapon from the rack, settling it across my back. At the door, I turned and looked again at those hot pink toenails. I opened the trailer door, took in a deep trembling breath of fresh air and went out to report that Specialist Virginia Delray lay murdered in my trailer.

Two

After repeating myself twice, the provost marshal still refused to believe me.

"She's dead?"

"Yes, sir. Murdered."

"How do you know it was murder?"

Major Chuck Purser always spoke slowly and quietly. Even when dispatching the Quick Reaction Force, he sounded like he was placing an order for lunch. I thought my news of a murder would finally spark a reaction from him. It didn't. My hands were tightly clasped behind my back, but I couldn't stop them from shaking.

I had made the long walk to the provost marshal's office in a daze. People passed me, said hello, but I couldn't bring myself to speak to them, to tell them what I'd found. It felt intrusive for everyone to know what had happened to Delray.

Major Purser still refused to move.

"She was strangled, sir. You should come look for yourself."

"Did you touch anything?"

"No, sir," I said, while thinking, *Touch anything? Why would I want to touch anything?*

The thought of touching her turned my stomach again. I swallowed loudly. My look of impending sickness finally set Purser in motion.

He pushed himself up, called for his sergeant, still not raising his voice, and slipped into his battle rattle, his helmet and flak jacket loaded up with gear. He wore a nine-millimeter strapped to his thigh and a long, heavy looking baton hung from his belt. We walked at his calm, easy pace, back to my trailer.

I stayed outside while Purser and his NCO went inside. The image of her laying there, the red dots in her eyes, those pink toes, left me shuddering. My teeth rattled together as if I were cold, but sweat bathed my forehead. My rapid breathing sounded loud under my helmet. Purser and Walker weren't gone long.

"I'm sorry you had to see that Sergeant Harper," Purser said, his face crimson.

I exhaled like a tire going flat, realizing I had held a fool notion that he would tell me I had been mistaken, that I had imagined it all in my head. But I hadn't been mistaken.

As the provost, Purser had probably seen a lot of bodies. Maybe that explained his reluctance to follow me here. He knew exactly what finding a body would mean from start to finish.

"Your first name is Lauren, right?" he asked.

"Yes, sir."

"I'm gonna go call CID down in Tuzla now. Tell 'em to get up here as soon as they can. That's likely to be a couple hours. Sergeant Walker will stay here to secure the area. You might as well go relax somewhere," he said. "Just let Sergeant Walker know where we can find you."

Watching him walk away, no one would ever guess he intended to report a murder. I saw reluctance written in his slow stride.

He'd told me to relax, but that wasn't going to happen. The more I sat around, the more I'd be thinking about Delray and those hot pink toenails. Work was the only thing to do on McGovern Base. Work might help clear my head of my final image of her. First, I had to tell my boss what had happened to my soldier.

= = = = = = = = = =

My desk in the crowded headquarters tent was in the section of the Tactical Operations Center reserved for the General's special staff. It sat among a sea of desks where coordination of our role in the NATO peacekeeping mission took place. I had no privacy, but in the months since arriving in Bosnia, I'd grown accustomed to the lack of it. Deployments offered little in the way of quiet or alone time.

As the ranking public affairs person on camp, I served as the official spokesperson for the local commander. There were piles of queries from press agencies that required my response, but I pushed them all aside. I needed to speak to my boss, so I made my own call to my higher headquarters in Tuzla, a medium-sized city located two hours to the south of Camp McGovern via a pothole-riddled road.

Colonel Neil McCallen commanded the media operations center in Tuzla, where the U.S. Division for the NATO Peacekeeping force in Bosnia-Herzegovina had their headquarters. Driving that horrendous road, down and back again, had been a weekly mission of mine to meet with him and receive his command guidance.

McCallen and I have been together many years on many deployments in many parts of the world and we were of the same opinion when it came to Specialist Delray. The young soldier laughed more than she complained, could tell a good tale and could get herself invited to events someone of her rank had no business attending. She was a constant pain in my neck. My hand shook as I reached for the phone and punched in the number to call McCallen.

My gaze strayed to the corner of my desk, to Delray's half-empty coffee mug and a notebook she had left there. Delray often left half-done things lying around; coffee cups, doughnuts, sandwiches minus a bite or two. I'd given her grief about it, but it had done little to change her habits.

"Delray, my desk is not your garbage area."

"Sorry, Sergeant Harper," she'd say, smiling. "I wanted to save it for later. Better not to waste it, don't you think?"

Now, as I stared at her coffee mug, her voice echoed in my memory. It was a waste. A waste of the worst kind. I picked up her mug, dumped the remains of the coffee in the trashcan, wiped the inside with a napkin and stuck it in my drawer with the rest of my coffee things. Her notebook would be full of scribbles I couldn't read, doodles and small sketches she constantly worked on. I opened the notebook and randomly flipped through the pages.

"What the hell has she been up to?" I gripped the phone speaking to no one in particular, listening to the clicks and hisses on the line. The ringing on the other end signaled the call finally went through, but the static I heard forecasted trouble on the line.

"Media Operations Center, this is Sergeant Wilson, may I help you sir or ma'am?" The standard greeting spewed out so quickly and mechanically, I wouldn't have understood it if I hadn't heard it a million times.

"This is Harper. I need Colonel McCallen."

"Hold one."

Waiting for McCallen to come on the line, I continued to sift through Delray's notebook. Unintelligible scribbles filled page after page. In the margins, sometimes covering the scribbles were random sketches; a deftly drawn picture of a soldier, his face gleaming in sweat; the outline of a humvee, someone waving from the passenger seat. On one page she'd scribbled the name Mark repeated over and over, no spaces between the names, some printed, some written in a cursive scrawl as if she'd been trying out different styles of handwriting. Near the last page she'd sketched the image of a rose, the petals full and healthy, three fat drops of water trickled down from the petals as if recently watered.

The randomness of the sketches held as little meaning as her scribbles. I flipped through the pages anyway and thought about the other pressing issues I had to face.

The Vice President and a large entourage of elected officials were scheduled to visit McGovern in less then a week. The camp commander had an upcoming interview with *The Washington Post*, and so far, the news that a BBC reporter and his videographer were missing somewhere in Brcko, the small city nearby, hadn't been picked up by the news masses yet.

Before finding Delray, all of those things seemed imminently important. Now, even the Vice Presidential visit felt like a bother I wished would go away.

I groaned and leaned on my elbows over the desk, hunched around the handset, when Neil finally picked up the phone. He sounded out of breath but upbeat.

"Hey, what's up now Harper? Delray giving you a hard time again?" he joked.

"Sir, you have no idea."

He must have heard the strain in my voice because his voice turned serious.

"Report," he said, followed by a loud burst of static.

"Delray was murdered, sir."

"Say again. You're breaking up."

I hunched further into the phone, pressing it to my ear. "She's dead, sir. Delray is dead." I repeated loudly. Sudden quiet settled around the TOC, a warning that everyone heard me. A quick glance up confirmed that I had everyone's attention, like it or not.

"This connection is terrible. Stand by," he said. "I'll call you back."

The line went dead. I hung up and sat staring at the phone, my hands clasped tightly together, knuckles white, willing the phone to ring with a static-free line. I could still feel everyone's gaze, heard murmurs around the room, a few moved closer as if they wanted to ask me what was going on. I focused on the phone, hoping everyone would leave me alone. Several minutes ticked by.

Our phone lines were notoriously bad. Sometimes you could pick up the phone, dial and it wouldn't ring. Other times, you could dial and hear the static right away, a sure sign that conversation would be impossible. Neil would get through. I just had to wait it out.

My body jerked in surprise when the phone finally rang.

"Harper, here."

"Lauren," he said, relief in his voice. "Did you say she was murdered?"

"Strangled. I found her about thirty minutes ago. She fought. It must have been horrible." I stopped, took a deep breath, trying to control the tremble in my voice. Her final moments of terror evident in her horror-filled eyes and the bloody gunk under her nails. I groaned into the phone.

"Okay," he said, calm, assured. I needed that assurance from him. "I'll issue the press release and see that her family is notified from here. I'll see if I can get on the same flight with the CID team going up, but if not, I'll take the one that leaves here at zero seven tomorrow. We'd get there around zero seven forty-five."

"The sooner the better," I said, embarrassed by the quiver in my voice.

"Lauren," he paused, and cleared his throat.

"What is it?"

"Lauren, you said you would kill her."

"What? When?

"That Colton kid, remember?"

"Oh that," I said. "But I was just angry. I didn't mean anything by it."

Two weeks earlier, twenty-one year old, Kenneth Colton, from Memphis, Tennessee, died in a vehicle accident. I issued a press release announcing what happened, but withheld his name until after family notification. Withholding the name is Army policy. Policy every public affairs soldier should know. When I left the command post for only a few minutes, Delray answered a call from the *Associated Press*. She gave them his name, age and hometown. The AP put the information on the wire and instantly, every newspaper, radio, and television station in the world ran with it. A NATO soldier had died. It was big news.

The accident victim's parents were divorced. The military notification team had been able to reach his father immediately, but his mother had been out of town when they tried to locate her.

She learned about her son's death when she came home and found TV cameras and reporters camped outside her house.

"I swear to God, I will kill that stupid little girl," was what I'd said when I told Neil about it later over the phone. Several people in the TOC had heard me. Considering my mood at the time, I'm sure they all believed that I was capable of it.

"You were pretty angry," he said.

"Well, so were you."

"Yes, but I don't show it like you do."

I chuckled. "Yes, Colonel McCallen with ice in his veins. And me with my uncontrollable temper."

"Your temper did get the best of you that day. And I have to ask, where were you today?"

"Are you asking me if I have an alibi?"

"Yes, and I won't be the last one asking, Lauren. Where were you?"

"Out on a shoot. When I got back at fifteen hundred, I found her." The direct questions made me uncomfortable and my responses rang defensive in my own ears. Why should I feel guilty?

"Who were you out with? Anyone that can corroborate your story?"

"The EOD team. They were demining a farm field nearby using a remotely controlled tank to rollover the mines. We left about zero seven hundred and I stayed with them all day. Every few minutes something would explode. I got some great video...wait," I stopped. "You think they will suspect me."

"Look, I know you couldn't have done something like that, but they're going to ask questions. You need to be prepared for that. Someone killed her. Who did it?"

The million-dollar question. No one got on or off McGovern without a NATO ID card. The murderer had to be someone with access to the camp, which could be anyone of almost three thousand people. Most people knew that I didn't think much of Delray as a soldier, but I couldn't believe anyone would think I killed her.

"Well, I was out on a shoot all day. Besides, I may have a temper, but I'm not violent or anything. I just get a bit loud. That never hurt anyone."

"Okay, so if you were out all day, you have a solid alibi."

"*If* I was out?"

"You know what I mean."

"No, sir. I don't." I rested my forehead in my palm as I hunched over the phone, shocked to see a teardrop hit the desk. I sniffled and bit my tongue, determined not to cry. Delray, the petite southern belle, had annoyed me daily. I was twice her size. Most of my days were spent carrying around heavy video equipment and at thirty-seven, I was in the best shape of my life. Add to that, I'm a black woman with a temper. If McCallen thought people might think I did it, I could be in trouble. McCallen tended to be right about most things. Damn him.

"Don't get worked up about this needlessly, Harper. We'll sort it out if we have to. I'll be there as soon as I can."

By the time I hung up, I felt limp with dread. That poor, stupid girl. I could hear her laughter, see her throwing her head back in mirthful abandon. I had threatened to kill her in a moment of frustration. I remembered one of my mother's wise sayings. One she repeated to me often in her day. "A black woman with a hot temper ain't looking at nothing but cold, hard trouble."

My mother, one of the smartest women I'd ever known, worked hard and died too young. Like McCallen, my mother's words of wisdom usually rang true. I had to hope this time, just this one time, she could be wrong.

Three

Several minutes after my call with McCallen, I still sat hunched over the desk, thinking about Delray's family. I wondered how they would take the news. They lived in Mississippi—both parents, a younger brother who had plans to join the Army like his big sister, and a younger sister who, according to Delray, thought planning for her eventual wedding held the key to her future happiness. Delray had a boyfriend back home that she often whined about missing. That, and the fact that she liked honey on her oatmeal and drank her coffee with two heaping teaspoons of sugar and a lot of milk reached the extent of my knowledge of her personal life. Delray often told me her family worried about her. She wrote to them. My guess is she sent letters filled with reassurances about her safety on this peacekeeping mission. She probably promised them she would be okay and her leadership would keep her safe. Her murder would be a terrible shock to them.

Knowing I couldn't just sit there and brood, I booted up my laptop and started drafting Delray's family a condolence letter. It was too soon to write it. Too soon after finding Delray, my emotions too raw, but it gave me something to do. Waiting around for McCallen to show up would only drive me crazy.

Thinking about the grieving family, my thoughts shifted to my mother. I resembled my mother, at least that's what all of my relatives told me. I couldn't see it. We had the same dark brown skin, the same thick hair that tended more toward curly then kinky, the same dark brown eyes, but I never thought we looked much alike. We did have the same work ethic. Neither of us could sit still for long. She raised my sister and me alone, working two and three jobs at a time, never resting.

I had just graduated from college when my mother died. I was twenty-four, my sister only sixteen. They would have put Loretta in foster care if I hadn't taken over her guardianship. I had just begun my career search and had hoped to land a reporter position but was willing to do the grunt work, to sit at a news desk or take an assistant producer job at a small town TV news station, the way most TV news careers started. I put those plans on hold. Loretta couldn't become just another African-American child in the foster care system. A friend suggested I talk to a recruiter and after listening to the sales pitch, the decision seemed simple. I joined the Army. It hadn't felt like a sacrifice, although Loretta sometimes tells me she felt guilty at the time, for being my burden. As my dependent, she moved with me on stateside assignments until she graduated from high school and I never felt an ounce of regret for my decision.

"I'm in college now," Loretta said to me. "You don't need to take care of me anymore. Take care of yourself."

The thought of Loretta made me want to call her, hear her voice, assure myself she lived.

I sat staring at the phone, thinking of making the call, when I glanced up and saw Brigadier General Hank Paterson, the camp commander, headed toward me, his aide Captain Keith Griffin in tow. I stood up and went to parade rest; my feet shoulder width apart, hands clasped behind my back at the waist, my eyes directed straight ahead.

He stopped a few feet from my desk.

"Master Sergeant Harper, I'd like to speak to you for a moment."

He pointed to a spot on the floor in front of him, indicating he wanted me to move there. I complied, wondering what he wanted.

He took a step closer, inches from me, clearly invading my space and using his six foot, three inch, two hundred ninety pound bulk to intimidate me. My curiosity factor went up another notch.

"I'm sorry to hear about your soldier, Sergeant Harper," he said. People were milling around the TOC and Paterson used his command voice as if he wanted everyone in the room to hear, and they did. They all stopped what they were doing and watched us.

"Thank you, sir" I said.

"I considered Delbert one of my soldiers, you understand. She was your soldier, but she was still under my care and part of my Army family."

I wasn't going to point out that he had gotten his family member's name wrong.

"Yes, sir."

"A good leader is one who brings everyone home unharmed," he bellowed.

So, he blamed me for this? "Yes, sir," I repeated, clasping my hands tightly behind my back, wishing he would wrap this up and move on.

He stepped to the side and put his hand on my shoulder, placed his thumb just above my clavicle near my neck and slowly squeezed until it hurt. It might have looked like a comforting gesture, but looks are deceiving. From hours of self-defense classes, I knew his thumb pressed near a pressure point that could instantly bring me to my knees. He must have missed the exact spot purposefully in order to hurt me. His intentions seemed apparent in his pointed glare and the tiny quirk at the corner of his mouth. He not only meant to inflict pain, he was enjoying himself.

"We're going to find out who did this thing, Harper. And I expect your full cooperation in this." He kept squeezing. I had no idea what to think. I shifted my eyes quickly to Captain Griffin to see if he understood the situation, but he stared at his clipboard, purposely avoiding my gaze.

I pressed my lips together, about to whimper in pain, then took a deep breath and met his stare, hoping my gaze communicated my anger.

"No one wants this killer more than I do, General," I said through clenched teeth. "No one."

He kept the pressure on for a few seconds more, staring me down and waiting for me to blink. I stared back. Finally he released the pressure, smiled and patted my shoulder in what I'm sure looked like a casual gesture.

"Good, Sergeant Harper. Very good." He glanced around the room at everyone watching.

"Carry on," he commanded and strode way, his little officer minion following behind.

I stayed at parade rest, watching him leave, then released my hands from behind my back. "Jesus H. Christ" I mumbled to myself. My shoulder and the side of my neck were almost numb. I shook out my arm and rolled my head around. It provided no relief.

Paterson had an interview scheduled with *The Washington Post* the next day. I should have told him that by tomorrow morning the media would have received the press release announcing the death of one of his soldiers. McCallen's release would indicate CID's intent to conduct a full investigation of the death, with no mention of murder, but it wouldn't take the press long to figure out something serious had happened. We should have discussed how we would handle questions about it, but my shoulder hurt too much, and it pissed me off that it hurt.

I'd had countless communication planning conversations with Paterson in the past. I thought we had a good relationship, the kind of relationship a PAO should have with a commanding officer. Something had changed.

Whatever the reason, I decided Colonel McCallen could deal with the General when he arrived. I hoped that would be soon.

= = = = = = = = = =

Wooden walkways snaked around the camp, connecting living quarters and working areas in hopes of keeping everyone out of the mud. The trailer park I lived in formed a small branch off the main line of walkways. Two-and-a-half hours later, with Sergeant Major Jenkins from CID in the lead, our entourage made a racket on the raised wooden sidewalks as we headed back to my trailer.

Chief Warrant Officers Ramsey and Santos introduced themselves as soon as they arrived. Ramsey told me Jenkins would collect and analyze the forensic evidence, while Ramsey and Santos conducted the investigation. The two of them walked behind me on the way to the trailer. I felt their eyes on me the entire journey.

Due to the size of the CID team, Colonel McCallen had lost his seat on the Black Hawk flight. My disappointment cut deeper than I imagined. I felt alone, surrounded by the investigators, a couple of MPs, a CID photographer and a handful of officers from headquarters who were there for nothing other than curiosity. McCallen would have been a friendly face in the crowd. My loneliness and dread increased as we got closer to the trailer, our hollow steps on the walkway reverberating around us. The last thing I wanted was to go back in that trailer.

Standing on the bottom step, Jenkins opened the trailer door. In that position, the floor came up to about chest level. He leaned his head in and looked at the dried mud tracks on the floor, his head turning back and forth from the computer desk to Delray's cot as he scanned the trail of my muddy boot prints across the floor.

As soon as he opened the door, the foul odor wafted out. I wrapped my arms around myself and planted my feet, further determined not to go back in.

Jenkins went up a couple of steps and then turned and motioned the MP with the camera to come forward and take some pictures. The photographer clicked off a few, then stepped back so Jenkins could go inside.

They entered one by one, slowly, like something dangerous lived in there, the flash of the camera going off constantly. Then I heard Jenkins. "This is a crime scene!" He shouted. "If you are not part of my immediate investigative team, get out now!"

The officers from headquarters came trooping out then. They mumbled that he didn't have to yell and took their leave of the trailer. I felt gratitude that Jenkins had done that. It made me feel violated to have them all in there gawking at Delray.

It had already been dark for about an hour by then, but the camp floodlights illuminated the entire area. The usual Bosnian weather surrounded us, a thick wet heat with nasty grey blanketing clouds that just hovered over your head and spit at you all day. The Bosnian weather made it easy to understand why the war had gone on for as long as it had. The incessant grey, depressing conditions seemed excuse enough to continue killing each other.

I stood outside the trailer in the spitting rain, listening to the investigators talking, speculating.

"She fought back pretty hard I'd say." It sounded like Jenkins. "Judging from the evidence under her nails, whoever did this will have some fairly deep scratches."

I had thought that too, looking at her bloody nails.

"How long has she been dead?" Someone asked.

"Not sure," said Jenkins. "But I'd say several hours at least. Looks like she was coming from the shower, so figure maybe from about six or seven this morning?"

I hadn't left until seven. What if I'd gone back to the trailer for some reason? Say I'd forgotten something like an extra tape or batteries for the microphone. It happened often enough. I might have walked in on it, might have been able to help her. I shivered, and wrapped my arms tighter around myself.

When Jenkins came near the open door, I took the opportunity to question him. "I'm not going to be able to get any of my things for a while am I?"

"No," he said, "Not for at least a day or two, Sergeant." He looked down at me like it shouldn't be a problem.

"Can I at least get a change of clothes or things I'll need for the night?"

"No, sorry," he said, in an attempt to placate. "It's all evidence,

Sergeant. I can't let you take anything."

"Nothing?"

"That's right."

My cot and sleeping bag, a change of uniform, my camera. I hadn't considered that all of my belongings would become evidence. I wanted a shower, wanted to wash that rancid odor out of my memory. The thought of not being able to wash made me feel a bit panicked.

"Look, I don't want to be difficult, Sergeant Major," I said, trying not to whine. "Can I at least have my toilet kit? It's sitting right there."

I pointed to the black backpack sitting open on top of the wooden crate by the door. Jenkins glanced at Ramsey who absently nodded his head. Jenkins picked up the bag and rooted around in there. He pulled out my shower puff, my shampoo and conditioner. He checked the pockets, all of them, one by one, looking for some excuse to keep it from me. Finally, he handed it down to me.

"Thanks," I said, and turned to leave.

"Wait a minute," Ramsey said.

I stopped, with a sigh, thinking he had changed his mind and would take my bag back again.

"Can you take a look in here and see if there's anything missing? Anything that might be wrong with the room?"

My breath caught in my throat. I did not want to go in there to see her and those hot pink toenails. I did not want to smell that smell again.

Ramsey, standing in the door of the trailer, saw my hesitation.

"We need your help, Sergeant Harper. Just a quick look."

He held his hand out, like he wanted to help me up the stairs. I took the steps slowly, ignoring his hand, and stepped into the trailer, With Ramsey, Santos, Jenkins and the photographer in there, the crowded trailer could barely accommodate me. I stood in the doorway and looked around them.

"Everything looks the same as when I left this morning," I said.

"What time was that?" Ramsey asked.

The foul odor reeked stronger now. My shallow breaths weren't helping. I covered my mouth and nose with my hand and swayed, feeling dizzy. Santos steadied me, then handed me a small jar of mentholated rub.

"Under your nostrils," he said.

My hands shook as I took the jar. The pungent ointment made my nostrils burn but presented enough of an olfactory distraction to cover up the odor partially. I wondered if I'd ever be able to eat again. They all watched me, sympathetic looks in their eyes, except for Ramsey. His blue eyes were icicle cool. I shivered.

"I left around zero six hundred to take a shower. When I came back from the shower, Delray wasn't here. I'd assumed she went to shower herself," I said. "I dressed, grabbed my gear and went to meet the EOD team. Everything seems the same as I left it. Even my towel there," I added weakly.

The dry towel, draped over a hanger, hung from a nail next to my cot. Right next to that nail, sat anther nail where my reflector belt should have been. My reflector belt wasn't there. I clenched my fists, trying to stop the sudden trembling. I switched my gaze to the other side of the trailer, to the nail near Delray's cot, where she hung her reflector belt to keep it handy for early morning PT. Her belt hung there, light glinting off the reflective material.

The door of the trailer gaped open. The air conditioner cycled full blast, but the frigid air wasn't what had me feeling wobbly. My reflector belt wasn't where it should be, but I knew exactly where to find it. Around Delray's neck.

"Oh God," I mumbled.

"Are you alright?" Ramsey asked, those frosty blue eyes not missing a thing.

"I, my, ah, reflector belt," I said, hating how frightened I sounded. "It's gone."

Ramsey took a step toward my cot, pushing himself past the photographer.

"Where do you keep it?"

"On that nail there," I said, pointing. I dropped my arm quickly to cover my shaking, then wrapped my arms around my chest. I wanted to tell someone to turn the air conditioner off, but couldn't force the words out between my clenched jaw.

Ramsey looked at the empty nail, then over at Delray's reflector strap. He motioned for the photographer to take pictures. The click and whir of the flash unit sounded loud in the trailer.

"Okay," Ramsey said. "Anything else?"

I looked around the edit desk, at Delray's computer area, and where her stuff sat neatly folded in her crates. Ramsey stood in front her cot. I knew if he moved a step away, I would be able to see her pink toes. I couldn't see them, but their image still haunted me, burned there the way a flash is still visible behind closed eyes.

I wanted to get out of there, wanted to gulp clean fresh air, but something felt off kilter and it took me a minute to figure it out through my freezing brain. I was responsible for the expensive equipment Delray and I used. The Army had entrusted the editing gear, the cameras, even the furniture we used, to my care by way of my signature on a bunch of forms. It amounted to a couple hundred thousand dollars worth of stuff. It became habit to visually inventory the trailer each time I came back and something was missing.

"Her camera," I said. "It's not here."

"What did it look like?"

"It's in a large black bag with a shoulder strap. It holds a couple of lenses, the flash unit," and I pointed to the crime photographer's bag.

"Like that one," I said. "Only a bit bigger."

"Okay," Ramsey said. "Anything else?"

"No, everything else seems the same as when I left this morning," I said.

Ramsey moved in front of me, a hand on my arm. He must have been able to feel the way I trembled through the fabric of my uniform.

"Are you alright, Sergeant Harper? Should we get you to a medic?"

I wondered why he thought I needed a doctor, then I glanced down at myself. My arms wrapped around my body like a straight jacket, my knuckles white. My entire body felt stiff, like it does when you've been out in freezing cold, clenched up like a fist, a fist that will never relax again. Somewhere in my addled brain, I knew I was in shock, but I didn't want to see a doctor.

"No, I'm okay. I just need to get out of here," I managed to say.

He stared at me for a long moment, deciding.

"Okay, Sergeant," Ramsey said dismissively. "We'll call you when we need you."

I almost ran out of the trailer. On the walkway outside, I used a light post for support as I stood panting, trying to slow my heart rate, gulping in fresh air. For once, I felt grateful for the cleansing rain.

It took a while, but I finally calmed down, and realized I couldn't leave. There was nowhere else to go. I decided to stay, just in case. In case of what, I didn't know, but somehow I just couldn't leave, not with Delray still in there.

Soldiers walked back and forth going about their business, taking surreptitious glances aimed at the trailer where they knew one of their own lay dead. I got plenty of looks as I stood there.

After a few minutes, Ramsey and Santos left the trailer in the direction of headquarters, ignoring me.

I'm not sure how much longer I stood out there in the rain, watching people come and go. The photographer left, but Sergeant Major Jenkins continued his work inside. A team of soldiers showed up with a stretcher and a body bag. Several minutes later, four of them carried Delray out of the trailer, strapped to the stretcher.

The black plastic bag looked too small to contain a soldier. She couldn't have weighed much more than a hundred pounds.

I drew myself to attention, saluted her and held it as they carried her by me. As the team made their way down the walkway, others stepped aside and saluted her body.

As I watched their progress down the walkway, I noticed an MP walking toward me. He saw me and fixed me with his stare and I knew the investigators weren't wasting any time.

"Chief Ramsey wants to see you," he said.

I sniffled, wiped my eyes with the back of my hand, grateful again for the rain, then slung my backpack over one shoulder and followed the MP across camp to headquarters.

I headed to face my first interrogation in Delray's murder investigation. I could tell from our brief meeting that Ramsey's questioning would be thorough and tough. I had faced tough people before. My drill instructors, the first sergeant who threatened to put me on report for doing exactly what he had ordered me to do, and my mom, who never let me get away with anything. I could only hope that history had prepared me for what I was about to face.

Four

Headquarters was a series of Drash tents connected by tunnels, some rooms larger than others and each room filled with people on phones or sitting at computers. Phones rang, chatter from radios echoed in English, but some Italian and German, a general din of people at work filling every space. We walked past one tent where a group of British soldiers argued with an American Colonel, everyone's voice raised and angry. I heard the name of the BBC news reporter, Hannerty and knew the argument was about his disappearance. I tried to slow down a little so I could hear what they were arguing about, but the MP hurried me along.

Finally, we came to the opening of a small tent where the CID team had set up shop. Ramsey was a big man and seemed to fill up the room. He came over and took my hand in a bone-crushing handshake, those intense blue eyes focused on me. I imagined he could tell I had been crying, imagined those eyes could detect everything I felt. I suppressed a shiver but continued to hold his gaze.

He introduced himself again and the man I couldn't help but mentally label his sidekick, Mr. Santos. Ramsey motioned me to a metal folding chair.

I sat down. The MP stayed by the door, his back to us, obviously there to ensure we weren't interrupted.

"I'm sorry about your soldier, Sergeant Harper," said Ramsey. "My condolences."

"Thank you, sir."

"Mr. Santos will be taking notes for me." Santos, already busily typing away on a laptop, looked over his dark reading glasses at me for a moment.

Ramsey picked up a folder and flipped through it. I recognized it as my 201 file, my personnel records, all my training and experience, every moment of my Army career spelled out in precise military fashion. He closed the folder and fanned himself with it.

"It's Lauren Harper, right?" he asked, his short blond bangs kind of floating up and down to the rhythm of his fanning.

"Yes, sir," I said.

"It's hot in here, do you think?" He took off his BDU jacket to reveal his brown short-sleeved t-shirt. I wasn't hot, still couldn't stop myself from trembling, but considering the whole, there-was-probably-a-struggle thing, I figured I could just clear that little suspicion up right away. I took off my jacket, hung it on the back of my chair, and made sure he saw my scratch-less arms. He tried to be surreptitious about looking. Instead of scratches, he would see the obvious goose pimples that blanketed my arms from shoulder to wrist. I rubbed them with little effect.

He went on about my background for a bit, looking through my files.

"Born in Minneapolis, Minnesota, went to the University of Minnesota and it looks like you're working on a graduate degree. In what?" he asked, looking at me.

"News media studies."

"News media studies," he repeated. "Never married?"

I shook my head no.

"No kids?"

I wish I had a dollar for every time someone asked me those questions. Married? Kids? My lack of both made me abnormal in the big scheme of things, I suppose, but it was tiresome to face the questions repeatedly. I'm sure most people just looked at the uniform and figured either I chose career over family or that I was gay.

"I never knew my father. My mother died when my sister was still in high school. I joined the Army when she became my dependent. I was too preoccupied with caring for her to think about starting a family. I've been involved a number of times, but I've never met anyone I wanted to spend the rest of my life with and I don't want to be a single parent like my mother."

He looked surprised that I revealed so much so easily.

"I'm not a youngster, Chief. People ask me those questions all the time. I don't usually share all the reasons behind my life choices, but I figure, since I'm being questioned in a murder case, I should be honest with you."

He seemed satisfied by that and tossed my file down on the desk.

"You told us about your morning. Tell us about this afternoon. What time was it when you found her?"

"I got back from my shoot just after 1500. I'm sure of the time because that's when the EOD squad has their shift change, at three in the afternoon. We got back to camp; I went straight to my trailer and found her."

"And you came back here immediately to report it?" He stood, peering down at me while Santos typed away. They both watched my every movement. It felt unnerving.

"Yes sir."

"Was anyone angry with her? Anyone consider her an enemy?"

He paced back and forth, never taking his icy gaze from mine. He had great big dimples, a square chin and deep wrinkles around his eyes. It was a fascinating face in an open and honest sort of way. Okay, I'll admit, despite his unnerving stare, he was a handsome man, very easy to look at, and he knew that. I could tell he had used that attractiveness to get his suspects to open up and was using it now, in a subtle way, to make me feel like I should tell all, the way people say more than they should on a first date.

"She was my soldier, Mr. Ramsey. We didn't hang out

together, so I don't really know if she was having issues with anyone. She never said that she was, but I wouldn't expect her to confide in me."

He stopped pacing and seemed to consider the next tactic. He put his foot on the chair across from me and leaned on his knee, looking at me intently.

"Everyone seems to think highly of you," he said, a smile playing on his lips. "Very professional, they say. A great leader. Good soldier. Articulate. I haven't been able to find anyone to say anything negative so far."

Articulate. In my experience, people only applied that word like a compliment when used to describe African-Americans. We were to feel ultimately complimented because we could speak coherently. It felt more like an insult than anything he'd said so far. I felt my anger flare. I managed to check the angry words, but refused to keep quiet about it.

"Articulate? I wouldn't be much of an Army spokesperson if I couldn't talk, Chief."

Ramsey colored slightly, pressing his lips together. He glanced at Santos then forged on.

"Unfortunately, people didn't seem to have the same opinion of your soldier, Specialist Delray," he said.

Since he wasn't asking a question, I kept my mouth shut.

"What did you think of her, Harper?"

Now that was a question. Problem was, I didn't want to answer it. I sat up straighter, blew out a breath.

"Come on, Sergeant," Ramsey said. "She was your soldier. What kind of person was she?"

"To be honest, Chief, I feel as if I failed her."

His eyebrows went up. "Go on."

I fidgeted. It was hard for me to admit it. She was undisciplined. She'd been working for me for months and she still couldn't write a decent feature story or take a publishable picture. I'd worked with her, tried to edit her stories and give her tips and tricks. None of it sunk in. After a while, it became too time consuming to give her the training she needed. She exhausted me.

I'd avoided giving her assignments that were important, knowing they were beyond her capacity.

"She was young, sir. She needed … constant leadership. I'm afraid I wasn't able to give her the attention she deserved."

"Constant leadership."

"Yes, sir."

He started pacing again, but let the silence stretch uncomfortably. The plastic tent flooring muffled his steps. A slow stab of guilt cut through my gut, the longer the silence stretched. Specialist Virginia Delray had gotten on my last nerve, but her lack of skill as a journalist was my fault. I'd given up on her.

I curled my hands into fists on my knees and squeezed. Ramsey saw my tension. He settled himself on the chair across from me, leaning his elbows on his knees. He invaded my space. I knew his blue-eyed gaze could see my guilt. Instinctively, I wanted to move my chair back. His close proximity was obviously meant to make me feel uncomfortable. It worked.

"Constant leadership, and you didn't give that to her?" He practically whispered my words back at me, the low voice meant to calm. I felt myself deflate, and slumped back into my chair.

"No, sir," I said, and found myself whispering back. "I didn't give that to her."

"So you failed her, you say?"

"Yes, sir."

He smelled like manly scented soap. His gaze wandered over my face as he sat only inches away. Clicks from Santos's keyboard were the only sounds in the room, the whole table vibrating each time he slammed his thumb down on the space bar.

"You feel guilty about that," he said. He put a comforting hand over my clenched fist, speaking in that quiet, intimate voice.

His frosty gaze could see everything, I thought, as if I'd scrawled my feelings across my forehead. His thoughts glared back at me just as clearly. Sympathy and accusation. His belief that I murdered Delray appeared there in the line of his eyebrows and the way he touched me. His manipulative sympathy disgusted me and pissed me off. I moved my hand away from his and sat up straighter.

"For not training her, Mr. Ramsey," I said, no longer whispering. "For losing patience with her. For not making her a better soldier. That's what I feel guilty about."

He stared at me for a long moment, that icy glare back again. He pressed his lips together and breathed heavily through his nose, then stood up and walked toward the desk. He kept his back to me for several seconds, his hands on his hips. Finally, he turned around.

"Okay, let's see what you know," he said, and launched into an endless stream of questions.

========

Five hours later, around midnight, my feet pounded on a treadmill in the gym tent as I tried to run off my tension. A lone soldier dribbled a ball and shot baskets at the hoop in the front of the tent, the ball bouncing off the backboard sounded like a gunshot in the cavernous room. Several young soldiers from the scout platoon gathered in the free weights area, their conversation punctuated by loud laughter. I saw it as a sign of a group that needed to work off their own stress. Their camaraderie gave me a pang of loneliness, reminding me I didn't have anyone in which to confide. I looked forward to McCallen's arrival.

I punched up the speed on the treadmill, trying not to think about it, not to think about anything but my breathing. The t-shirt of my hastily purchased PT uniform was already soaked through. The only luck I had for the day was that the tiny PX on base had a t-shirt, sweat pants and running shoes in my size. My runners slapped against the treadmill, each step in the new shoes reminding me that everything I owned was now evidence in a murder case.

The weight lifters gathered up their things and left. The gym grew quiet, the sound of the dribbled basketball echoed through the space.

The gym was about the only entertainment on the camp and

the first thing built when Americans decided to set up here. They poured a huge concrete slab and put a big white fest tent on top. The open space had served as headquarters and housing for the entire contingent for months. It must have been impossible to sleep. The lights would have been on constantly and noise carried easily in here.

Since then, a civilian contracting company turned the base camp into a sea of tents for living, sleeping and working. Thick walls made of tons of sand, and concertina wire, guard towers, and floodlights surrounded the whole camp. Sometimes, the walls made the camp feel like a prison.

I punched up the speed on the treadmill again, thinking about prison. Ramsey never came right out and said I was a suspect, of course, but it was evident that most of the questions were about my rapport with Delray, any fights or resentments we might have had, our relationship. His questions were all about me and Delray. No one else.

After hours of questioning, he finally let me leave, but promised we would talk again. I didn't look forward to the next time.

The treadmill beeped, then began to slow for my cool down. Hands on my hips, I walked and panted. No matter how far I ran, I would still have to deal with Ramsey and his investigation.

I left the gym around one in the morning, feeling as if a good long shower would help me sleep. I passed a few people on my way to the showers. The mission ran twenty-four seven so there were always a few people about no matter the hour.

I stepped into the shower trailer hoping for quiet and scorching hot water. The minute I entered, I knew my first wish wouldn't come true.

Three Bosnian interpreters huddled in a corner near the row of sinks. One of them was crying. The other two, one blonde and one with a towel wrapped around her head, were comforting her. They spoke in Serbo-Croatian. I couldn't understand a word. They looked up when I walked in and the one who had been crying pushed the other women aside and pointed at me, her words coming fast and urgent.

"What's going on?" I asked.

There were so many interpreters around camp, most of them women; I had to admit one face sort of blended with the next one. I'd met a few on various missions, but they seemed to change frequently and I rarely saw them around more than once or twice. A few had introduced themselves, but the names were difficult and I never got to know any of them. The media I worked with usually brought their own interpreters if they needed them.

The crying girl was young, petite and pretty with a horrible home-dye job. I assumed she had tried to bleach her short hair stark white but it ended up looking dry and damaged. Her skin was alabaster pale and her huge eyes took up most of her face. She was in uniform, as all the interpreters were required to be. The camouflaged jacket and pants were too large for her but she compensated with wide cuffs rolled up at her wrists and the top of her boots. Her uniform bore her name, *Abdic* embroidered on a fabric nametag and sewn over the left pocket of her jacket, the word *Interpreter* over the right. She wore a red bandana tied like an ascot at her throat, something that was against uniform regulations but tolerated for the interpreters. Influenced by movies like Rambo, many liked to add some cocky flourish to show their special position as part of the American forces.

Abdic had been crying hard for a while; her whole face looked puffy and used up.

"This girl Virginia, she is your roommate, yes?" she asked.

"Yes. Did you know her?" I hadn't ever seen them together, but they might have met while Delray was out on a story.

"We have just to meet yesterday. With the engineers," she said. "I am interpreter for engineers." She went into another bout of crying. The amount of tears seemed excessive for someone she had just met. The other women spoke to her excitedly, sounding as if they wanted her to stop talking to me. I took a couple of steps closer.

"Did something happen yesterday?" I asked.

The question seemed to spark the other two women into more

excitement. The words held no meaning for me, but it seemed clear they wanted Adbic to shut up. I kept hearing what sounded like her name, Mishka, and no, no. But the crying woman forged ahead despite their warning.

She leaned forward and grabbed my hand.

"Yes, me and Virginia," she said. "We saw..." Before she could get another word out, the blonde woman backhanded her. The smack of the blow echoed in the trailer.

"Hey," I yelled and shoved the blonde away. I didn't think I pushed her that hard, but she went flying against the wall and slid down until she sat with her legs splayed in front of her.

"What the hell are you doing?" I demanded, looking down at her sprawled on the floor.

She stood up slowly, warily, fury written in the sneer she wore. The woman with the towel on her head stood in shock with her hands covering her open mouth. Mishka had her hand to her heated red cheek, her tears forgotten for the moment.

With her nose in the air, the blonde said, "This is none of your concern."

"My soldier is dead. If she knows something," I pointed to Mishka, "then she needs to tell me what it is." But the blonde wasn't hearing any of it.

"She is stupid girl that knows nothing."

She grabbed Mishka by the arm and hustled her toward the door.

"Wait," I said, and moved to block their way.

The blonde stopped and stared down her nose at me. "You cannot make her tell you anything," she said, in a slow, soft voice. "We have stood up to people much more frightening than you."

I guessed she was in her early twenties, but her gaze came from eyes that had seen much more than I ever had. She would have been a teenager when the war started. She stood defiant, daring me to do something and knowing that I wouldn't. I stepped aside. She led the group out the door, Mishka still crying.

What in hell did you get yourself into? I thought. Delray had been working on a story about the road construction team in Brcko.

Yesterday, she'd come back after one day of shooting with them and said she wanted to spend another day on the story. I agreed to it, but she'd never made it out with them again. Instead, she'd been murdered. If Mishka served as the interpreter for the day Delray had been with the engineers, she might know if something had happened, what Delray might have seen or done to wind up dead.

Then, like a jump from a sauna into a snow bank, I realized, Miska wasn't crying because she was sad about Virginia. They didn't know each other, had only met a day ago. No, heartache wasn't what caused her tears to flow. Mishka had been crying because she was afraid.

Five

My first instinct was to march back to headquarters to tell Ramsey what happened with the interpreters. Then I thought about the frigid look I would get from him, the questions.

Take a shower. Clear your head. Then decide about talking to Ramsey, I thought, turning the shower on full blast. I was grateful Sergeant Major Jenkins had let me have my backpack. I had signed out a new sleeping bag and cot from supply and set up temporary living space in a women's tent. A sack full of uniforms and underwear I had dropped off at the laundry the day before would be ready for pick up in the morning, so I'd have a change of clothes, but my shower stuff was personal. The makeup and hair products, things Loretta sent me from the States, would be impossible to replace in this remote place.

I took a long hot shower, replaying the conversation with Ramsey in my head, wondering what the heck Mishka had been crying about, what Delray had gotten herself into. "That stupid, stupid, little girl," I said in a whisper. I looked down and saw the hot pink polish on my toes, the color vibrant even in the dark shower. Suddenly, I was sobbing. I sank to the floor, curled into the corner of the shower stall, the water mixing with my tears.

Guilt, like a fist in my belly, had me doubled over. The times I lost patience with her, the hours I spent not speaking to her even though we lived together, simply because I couldn't stand to hear her squeaky voice. The times I questioned her desire when I knew she wanted to soldier. She had been proud of her rank and studied for the Sergeant's exam, studying I should have helped her with. It all came flooding back. Now she was dead.

Good soldiers were people anyone could lead. It was how you handled the slower kids, the ones who got into trouble, who sometimes failed that marked a good NCO. I hadn't killed her, but I hadn't helped her much either. Maybe she would have told me what was going on if she trusted me, if she thought I would listen. I sobbed at my failure, at my damnable impatience, at the loss of her.

By the time I turned the shower off, I was a limp, wet mess. I struggled to get my filthy uniform back on, and went to do the only thing I could think of that would make me feel better.

= = = = = = = = = =

Reading the random graffiti etched on the walls, I sat in a booth in the Morale, Welfare tent, hoping my sister was home. She would have just arrived home from work, getting ready to make dinner. At least that's what I hoped.

"Loretta?"

"Hey big sister!" she said. The smile in her voice released the tension in my shoulders. Then she sucked in a breath. "Oh, my God. It must be two in the morning there. What's wrong?"

I told her, starting with finding Delray, the investigators, the interpreters. Then I told her the hardest part, about my guilt.

"Stop talking like it was your fault she was murdered, Lauren," Loretta said. "How could you know something like this would happen?"

"She was my responsibility. I let her down."

"That doesn't mean you're responsible for her death. She must have been mixing with the wrong people. You know what mom always said. People are murdered because they hang around with people who murder people."

I chuckled at the memory. Our mother repeated the confusing

warning whenever she saw us with someone she didn't approve of and it was difficult to get Lavern Harper's approval. For a time, Minneapolis had been known as Murder-apolis. Most of those killed were young black men, gunned down in the streets over drugs or some petty argument. Our mother often used the violence in the streets as an excuse to be overly protective, and a constant example of how not to lead our lives.

"That's the problem," I said. "I have no idea who Delray hung out with."

"Well, maybe you should find out."

Ramsey had asked me who her friends were. It was embarrassing how little I knew about her. We lived together, yet she was a stranger.

"Okay, my wise little sister. I'll have to ask around. Now, tell me what's good about your life so I can think about something else."

Loretta laughed, then launched into stories about work, shopping, a new boyfriend. Even in those early hours of the morning, other soldiers were in the tent on other phones but no one was waiting in line, so I felt relaxed. When I yawned noisily, Loretta laughed again.

"Girl, you better get your brown butt to bed. You've had a long day."

"I'm tired, but I don't think I can sleep."

"You know what mom would say," Loretta said, chuckling.

"Yep. She'd say two words."

Loretta and I said them together. "Hot milk."

My sister's laughter danced through the phone lines, tugging tears to my eyes.

"I love you, baby sister."

"Same here. Now don't you leave me worrying about you. I'm gonna need daily updates. Email me. You hear me?"

I agreed to her demand, said good bye, then slowly hung up the phone. I'd never liked hot milk, but Lavern Harper's advice was usually golden.

= = = = = = = = = =

A few Bosnian workers were still in the chow hall, mopping the wooden floors with a heavy pine scented mixture, and refreshing the soup kept hot all day and night. The large television in the corner usually blared the Armed Forces Network, but the workers had turned the channel to a Bosnian music video station. A Middle Eastern pop star with dark eyeliner and a Pepsodent smile danced and warbled out lyrics in a language I couldn't identify.

I recognized one of the workers from the Chicago Cubs baseball cap he always wore. He was built like many of the locals, slender but shorter than the average American. He wore his shoulder length, midnight-colored hair pulled back in a ponytail. Thick stubble marked his cheeks and neck. He was sharply handsome, almost beautiful in a magazine model sort of way. Probably in his early twenties, his dark-eyed stare made him look much older. He went through the motions of mopping the floor but paid more attention to the music video on the television.

He glanced over, noticed me watching him, stopped mopping, then pointed to the television and arched an eyebrow at me. I smiled, gave him an okay sign. Instead of showing any approval at my response, his eyes darkened and he quickly looked away, as if resentful that he had to ask permission in the first place.

I shrugged off his negativity and pulled a pint-sized carton of milk from one of many industrial coolers lined along the wall, poured it into a coffee mug and stuck it in a microwave.

A few soldiers came into the mess tent obviously just off patrol, their boots and trousers covered in mud, their faces filthy, their weapons and equipment clanging. They fanned out, grabbing food from various stations, their talk subdued. A couple of them walked over the newly mopped floor leaving muddy tracks in their wake.

Chicago shot angry looks at them. He shoved the mop into the bucket, moved to a side of the serving area, and waited for the soldiers to get their food. He leaned against a counter and watched them move about, gathering up their food, a disdainful look on his face.

I sat down at a table, blew into my milk and took a cautionary sip. It tasted like heaven and I suddenly realized my last meal had been breakfast almost a day ago. It wasn't long before I was staring at the bottom of my mug. I went back to the cooler and poured another mug full of milk.

By the time I was done with the microwave, the soldiers sat eating, their easy conversation low and weary. One of them had propped his M16 against the table. The weapon slowly slid to the side, slamming against the floor, making a loud racket. Every man at the table looked at me, the owner of the weapon with a worried look, the rest struggling not to laugh.

"You know what to do," I said.

"Oh, man" he mumbled, and the rest of the guys pointed and razed him, "Drop, Graham," they teased.

He shrugged, then dropped to the floor and did a couple of perfectly executed push-ups. It was impressive really, because he still had all his gear on, flak vest, canteens, and all the other heavy stuff a soldier wears.

After he did four pushups, I said, "Recover, soldier."

He stood up and went to parade rest. He wasn't mad or anything; in fact he kind of smiled. He knew I could have kept him down there a lot longer. A soldier's life depends on his weapon. You learn quickly that you never ever let your weapon fall to the ground. Graham obviously understood the point.

"Relax, Corporal Graham," I said.

He dropped his hands from behind his waist and stuck them in the armpits of his flak jacket. His squad mates all looked at me nervously, afraid I was going to give them some stupid task to do, even though they were obviously dog tired.

"Were you patrolling in Brcko tonight?" I asked

"Yes, sergeant," he said with a question in his voice.

I got up and walked over to the group, wanting to take some of their tension away and hopefully make them more inclined to talk to me.

"Can I ask you guys something? Off the record?"

I motioned for Graham to sit back down and I started asking questions. If you want to know what happens after dark, you ask the guys who walk patrol. I got them to start telling their war stories, what life was like in Brcko when most people are asleep. First, they told me what they thought I wanted to hear, then they started on the funny stuff. Eventually, they got around to the serious scary stuff they don't write home about, like random sniper fire, minefields and kids who find themselves playing in them.

When it felt right, I asked them if they knew where the engineers were working on their latest road project.

"Sure, we patrolled by there tonight," Graham said.

They told me about the neighborhood, that it was a commercial area, offices mostly, a coffee shop or two. The one who looked the youngest turned bright red and said, "and that one place."

"What place?"

Graham cleared his throat. "There's a whorehouse near there. It looks like a regular bar, but it's not."

"How do you know it's a whorehouse?"

"Easy. Universal symbol for a whorehouse, red lights," Graham said chuckling. "Plus, one of our local contacts told us about it. It's called the Weeping Rose, like it's some kind of fancy place, but it's a hole. I wouldn't go in there, even if we could."

"How do you know it's a hole if you've never been in there," another solder ribbed him.

"I don't have to go in to know, fool," Graham said, turning to me. "Dudes going in there in the middle of the night look shady to me. Prostitution is illegal here, but no one seems to care. As far as I know, the place hasn't even been searched; at least we've never been given that mission. Not since I've been here."

It was hard enough to restore law and order in a war-torn country. Maybe prostitution was low on the priority list. Something about the name of the place sounded familiar, a gentle tug at my memory, but I couldn't place it.

"When you guys go out, do you bring an interpreter?"

Graham shrugged. "Sure. We have one permanently assigned

to each squad."

"I met an interpreter tonight. Short, young, with bleach-blonde hair?"

"That describes a bunch of them."

"Well, this one was crying. I don't know, but I got the impression she was scared."

The men exchanged looks, the silence stretched uncomfortably. Suddenly, they wouldn't look at me.

There were rules about dating interpreters, but the rules were sometimes impossible to enforce. Maybe one of them had become entangled with one of them.

Graham spoke up. "Ours changed," he said. "The girl changed."

"What do you mean? She stopped being friendly or something?" I asked.

One of the guys at the end of the table stood up abruptly and made a show of leaving, shaking his head as he walked away. Another one followed.

There were just four of us now, Corporal Graham and two privates. They exchanged looks, then, like a group of people who work well together, they seemed to make the same decision at once. They all took furtive looks around, checking to see if anyone else was in the area, then scooted closer to me on the benches.

I leaned into their little cluster. "No one knows you guys are talking to me," I said. "No one needs to know."

The kid sitting next to Graham raised an eyebrow at the corporal. Graham nodded his approval. The young soldier leaned in, his hands clasped in front of him on the table as if in prayer. Dirt lay embedded in the curve of his upper lip. I'd thought it was a mustache at first, but closer inspection revealed nothing grew there but peach fuzz.

"One day, out of the blue, it was a different girl," he said. "The new girl said her name was Velda, like the one before, but it wasn't Velda. It was a different girl entirely."

The three of them waited for my response, eyebrows up, expectant.

"What did she do about her ID card?" I asked. "Wasn't the picture different?"

"That's the weird part. The photo matched her, it just had the same name," Graham said. "Not just the same last name either. The same first and last name. I'd seen both women whip out those cards every time we come on base. They were exactly the same."

"Did your Lieutenant say anything?" I asked.

None of them liked that question. As if by mutual agreement, they got up to leave. I didn't want them to think I would cause them trouble.

"Hey, don't worry about it," I said. "We never had this conversation."

"Have a good night, Master Sergeant Harper," Graham said. They shuffled out the door looking more tired than they had when they came in.

The engineers repaired a road near a whorehouse where sketchy characters hung out. Interpreters randomly appeared with phony ID cards. As interesting as whorehouses and falsified papers sounded, neither thing seemed connected to Delray.

I'd finished my second cup of warm milk long before, but any effect it may have had felt lost in the new information I'd learned. I gathered up my backpack and carried my dirty coffee mug to the kitchen window. Chicago sat behind the food counter, scribbling in a notebook, the pages filled with close Cyrillic writing.

I stared at the notebook he scribbled in and thought about Delray's notebook with her unintelligible scribbles and random sketches. The notebook with the sketch of the rose with the fat drops that made it appear recently watered, or maybe those drops were supposed to represent tears. Like a weeping rose.

When Chicago glanced up at me, I realized I'd been staring, my mouth open. He narrowed his dark eyes at me and winked. I spun away from him and left quickly, the screen door slapping loudly behind me.

Six

D awn was only a couple of hours away, but I figured I had to at least try to get some rest. The lights were out in the tent and as far as I could tell, the other five women were asleep. I used my flashlight to find my new cot in the dark, unrolled the sleeping bag I had left there and figured I'd have trouble sleeping, but apparently didn't. It felt as if I had just closed my eyes when the bleat of someone's alarm made me open them again. The red digits on my glowing watch confirmed the time as zero six hundred.

The dawn brought just enough rain to be annoying. I sprinted, first to the laundry to pick up my uniforms, thankful they opened early, then went to the showers. This time there weren't any crying interpreters there, just one other soldier who sang gospel to herself in a deep throaty voice. I French braided my hair, tucked the end under the braid and secured it with a fat barrette. I cringed at my red-rimmed eyes and wan complexion. Not enough sleep. Makeup wasn't a daily part of my routine, but now and then it helped to cover fatigue. I looked like crap, and the thought of Colonel McCallen's arrival meant a little extra care in my appearance wouldn't hurt.

I took my makeup pouch from a side pocket of my backpack and there at the bottom of the bag, I saw a small blue computer memory card. I recognized it as one that fit Delray's camera.

"How did that get there?" I mumbled to myself. I held it up, staring at it. Delray must have put it there. But when? My bag had been sitting near the door. If someone frightened her, she might have tried to get rid of it quickly. She could have stuck it in a random pocket. Maybe she put it in my bag, knowing I'd be the one to find it.

An image of her terror flashed through my head, making me close my eyes. If she hid this in my bag, she knew at the time she was in mortal danger. The thought of her fear made me shudder. *Oh, Virginia. What were you up to?*

I had to see what was on the chip. I obviously couldn't get back into the trailer to get access to Delray's photo software. If I took it to the TOC, Ramsey might see it, and want it for evidence. He already had everything I possessed in custody. I'd be damned if he was going to get the memory card too. I wrapped it in my fist, and hoped for an answer.

McCallen. He would bring a laptop with him.

I flew through my makeup routine, then dashed back to the tent to put on a freshly starched and pressed uniform and finished by dabbing perfume on my neck and wrists. I still had time to put a coat of polish on my boots and buff them to a glassy shine.

The tiny memory card felt heavier than it should have in my pocket as I made my way to the BUB, the battle update briefing we held each morning. Brigadier General Paterson, made it clear that these meetings should last only fifteen minutes. To ensure we stuck to the schedule, everyone, save the General, stood throughout the briefing. It was an effective way to make sure no one prattled on longer than necessary.

When I walked into the room, conversation dipped. Several people openly stared at me. At first, I figured they were staring because I was a curiosity. My soldier lay murdered. How would I act? When the MP commander wouldn't look at me, I started to get nervous. People I usually chatted with stayed on the other side of the room. No one offered their condolences, or asked about Delray.

I wondered if something had happened overnight. If Ramsey had decided I was a suspect, the MP commander would probably know. I shrugged the feeling off thinking my guilt over how I had treated Delray clouded my perception.

I had arrived early. The General usually strode in at exactly zero seven thirty, precisely as scheduled. I scanned the room to see if all the players were there. The executive officer, Colonel Raybourn, stood discussing something with the MP commander. Chaplain Hirsch, who occupied the other half of the trailer Delray and I lived in, gave me a friendly nod hello. I would be briefing directly after him. There were two British soldiers and three German soldiers in the room. They wouldn't brief, but they came to the meetings to stay updated on the mission situation. Several civilian contractors were there as well as a representative from the State Department and a UN police force representative.

Someone near the door gave the command. "Attention!"

The room snapped to attention as the General and Captain Griffin strode into the room. "At ease," the general mumbled as he took his chair at the front of the room facing a raised platform and a large projection screen. A PowerPoint slide announced the day, the current temperature, and the security classification of the briefing as classified.

As soon as the general settled into his chair he said, "Begin."

The meteorologist stepped up to brief the weather as remaining rainy and cloudy with temperatures in the high 80s. He ended his report by announcing, "I'll be followed by the Chaplain."

Chaplain Hirsch began his briefing by asking for a moment of silence for Specialist Virginia Delray. "A young and vibrant woman whose life was cruelly taken by someone among us. Let us stay dedicated in our duties despite this horrible loss, but also let us stay vigilant for one another so that this terrible thing doesn't happen again to one of our own."

The moment of silence stretched on and I took the opportunity to glance around the room to see what, if any, reaction it the chaplain's words had on others. Most had their heads bowed respectfully but one or two were openly staring at me. Major Townson, the civil affairs officer in charge of the interpreters, directed a cold look at me. I'd only dealt with him in passing and didn't know much about him. Maybe one of the interpreters told him about the scene in the shower trailer. Whatever the reason, his hard-eyed glare felt uncomfortable.

I heard the Chaplain say, "I'll be followed by public affairs."

I stepped to the platform, made sure my slide was ready and began my brief.

"Sir, Colonel Neil McCallen, the Public Affairs Officer in charge of the Coalition Press Information Center, will be here this morning to assist in preparation for the Vice Presidential visit." I used the Vice President as an excuse for calling Neil to help with the Delray situation. I didn't want everyone to know how anxious I felt over her murder and the prospect that the investigators suspected me.

"The reporter from *The Washington Post* will be here at ten hundred hours for your interview. I will be available when your schedule allows to provide pre-interview preparation."

General Paterson interrupted me.

Without looking up, and with his head buried in the paperwork strewn across his table, he said, "No, no need for that. Send Colonel McCallen directly to me when he gets here. I expect him to take over your duties until this other matter is resolved."

"Sir?"

"I suspect you will be tied up with other things, Sergeant Harper," he said. "Just send McCallen here when he arrives."

"Yes, sir," I turned to continue to brief the three points still waiting for explanation on my slide, when the General interrupted me again.

"That will be all, Sergeant Harper."

I hesitated for a moment, then replied. "Yes, sir. Thank you, sir. I'll be followed by the G-1," I said.

I stepped off the platform, my entire body numb, my face burning. Somehow, I made my way through the crowded room, until I found a spot in the back. The briefing continued, but much of it went by without my hearing or understanding it. My hands clenched into fists, I tried to still the rapid beating of my heart. I'd been dismissed in front of the entire staff.

I couldn't look at anyone, so I stared at my boots, wishing I could leave the room.

"Don't sweat it, Harper. He's probably going to chew my ass later too," said Crofton Hawes. Hawes, a civilian contractor in charge of procuring supplies for the camp, controlled hiring of the cooks and cleaners, the laundry folks, the maintenance personnel and all of the food and fuel supplies that were trucked onto McGovern. The huge Texan had a large belly that hung over his ornate belt buckle and constantly had a large plug of tobacco stuck in his cheek. He sported a Dallas Cowboys baseball cap, and carried a plastic water bottle he used as a spittoon.

General Patterson had issued orders prohibiting people from spitting tobacco juice on his walkways and floors. Those who chewed carried around clear plastic water bottles instead. Looking at the three inches of black goop at the bottom of Hawes's bottle seemed far worse than stepping over it on a sidewalk in my opinion.

I nodded my thanks at him. He smiled at me, exposing tobacco chew stuck in his teeth. I tried not to visibly shudder and told myself that it was the thought that counted.

Three or four briefers had finished when Major Townson took his position on the briefing platform.

"Sir, resettlement efforts will begin today in the neighborhood east of Brod. Ten Muslim families are authorized to inspect their homes and assess needed repairs. Tensions in this neighborhood are high."

"Noted," the General said. "QRF and 2nd platoon as back up should they be needed," he said.

"Sir, we continue to have a shortage of interpreters. It was necessary for us to pull permanently assigned interpreters from several sections. Those sections without a permanent interpreter will now be required to come to the pool to request assistance if they need one."

Paterson nodded his head and made a motion with his hand to hurry Townson along. The change seemed convenient to me. If sections didn't have a permanent interpreter assigned, then changes, like the one Corporal Graham and his soldiers told me about the night before, wouldn't be as noticeable. Switching them around meant no single unit would develop an attachment to their interpreter. Interesting.

"Sir, that is all. I'll be followed by Military Police."

The MP Commander took his position. I peeked around the people blocking my view, interested in anything the MP had to say.

"Sir, the CID team has collected quite a bit of evidence but are still processing the crime scene. We are prepared to assist them in their investigation if they require it. At this time, a possible suspect has not been identified."

I could almost feel the attention shift from the front of the room, back to where I stood. A general murmur started, and slowly grew in volume.

"At ease!" Griffin commanded.

Silence settled in the room, but not my heart rate. Standing with my hands clasped behind my back, I kept my head up and focused on the briefing slide, attempting to avoid everyone's gaze. Ramsey may not have thought I was a suspect, but obviously some of my colleagues did. If I wasn't a suspect, why had the general dismissed me?

"Sir, that is all. I'll be followed by the doctor."

Several more presenters did their thing and finally it was over. The fifteen-minute briefing had felt like a lifetime. I took the most direct route to the door, avoided speaking to anyone, and hoped no one would notice how unsteady I walked.

Normally, I would have connected with people for possible stories or media engagements sparked by things I heard during the meeting. The after-BUB social time presented the best opportunity to coordinate things, since everyone you needed to talk to was in the same room at the same time.

Coordination be damned. I didn't want to talk to any of them.

Two pink message slips waited for me on my desk. *The Post* reporter had called to confirm her ten o'clock appointment, and there was a message from a Sergeant Major Fogg of the British contingent, requesting a call back. I ignored both messages and went to the airfield to meet McCallen's aircraft. I was early, but I craved the fresh air. I hoped the walk to the other side of camp would help calm me down after the stares and murmurs I'd heard.

I headed toward the helicopter-landing zone, thankful for the light rain. The cool drops felt good on my face after the heated embarrassment I'd felt. My head down, I avoided making eye contact with the curious.

Captain Griffin, the General's aide, already waited at the LZ, leaning against a tree and flipping through paperwork on the clipboard he always carried. He looked me up and down and returned my salute offhandedly, then went back to looking at whatever held his attention on the clipboard he always carried. He was a short, early-balding man who never said much. I'd seen soldiers mockingly imitate him behind his back, the way he always has his head buried in that clipboard and the way he scuttled after the general. I wondered if he knew that he was the butt of many jokes.

I heard the chopper long before I saw it. The Blackhawk, with its nose down, whooshed toward the landing zone, the rotors pushing rain around in great flashing swirls. The chopper leveled off and floated down, flattening tall grass beneath it. As soon as the runners were on the ground, the door slid open and the crew chief hopped out, doing his landing safety checks. Before the rotors of the chopper slowed, the passengers came out, bent at the waist. They exited, following each other in a straight line to the side of the airfield.

Colonel Neil McCallen was the third man out of the chopper. He had an over-packed rucksack in one hand that he carried as if it was weightless and his laptop computer bag in the other. His helmet covered up his red hair, but nothing could cover the freckles that gave him a youthful appearance. He was wearing the shoulder holster I bought for him in Sarajevo, his name etched in the dark brown leather of the holster under his arm, the straps stretched across his chest and shoulder. He looked up, saw me and started to smile. Before I could even get my salute off, Captain Griffin cut him off and led him a few feet away. I could see that Griffin wanted McCallen to follow him, but McCallen was having none of it.

"Harper!" he called to me.

I went over and saluted him. He dropped his rucksack and returned the salute with a smile and a lingering look as he tried to assess how I was doing all the while telling Captain Griffin what he felt his priorities were.

"General Paterson's interview isn't until ten-hundred this morning," said Colonel McCallen. "Master Sergeant Harper and I will prep him just as soon...."

"The General won't need Sergeant Harper's assistance on this one," snapped Griffin looking at me. "He has an opening in his schedule now."

Colonel McCallen looked at me. Both of us knew he wouldn't win this argument.

Most people would say that Colonel Neil McCallen would be a handsome man if it wasn't for all the freckles and the long deep scar that slashed diagonally from his left eyebrow across his nose, through both lips, ending at his chin. I thought he was handsome because of the freckles and the scar, and just looking at him made me feel better about things.

"This shouldn't take too long, Sergeant Harper," he said.

"Understood, sir," I replied.

It had been weeks since I'd seen him. We talked on the phone almost daily and exchanged emails several times a day. Before becoming a public affairs officer, he had led a Special Forces team and performed combat jumps into hostile places most people never heard of. His last jump, the one that earned him the scar, also busted up his knee and ensured he'd never jump from a perfectly good aircraft again. Being a media hound was not his idea of a proper military career, but he was good at it and we worked well together.

I watched Griffin and McCallen walk away, and then cursed. I'd forgotten to ask Neil for his laptop. I started to run after them, but slowed to a walk, then stopped, when I saw them pass an MP. The soldier was headed my way and I hoped he wasn't sent by Ramsey.

"Chief Ramsey wants to talk to you again, Sergeant Harper," he said.

I wanted to protest, to refuse to go along. The MP waited patiently. When I looked at him, he returned my gaze with a hard, unforgiving stare. I took a deep breath.

"Okay," I said. "Let's go."

It felt as if I trudged through the worst Bosnian mud, the sucking, clinging kind as I followed that soldier him back to the little room where the frost of Ramsey's eyes would bore through me. After what happened at the BUB, spending more time with Ramsey was the last thing I wanted to do.

The walk back to headquarters was like running a gauntlet of gawkers. Like people who can't drive by an accident without thoroughly checking out the wreck, it felt as if everyone on camp lined up to be Lookie Loos. They all knew where I was going. I had a feeling this set of questioning wasn't going to be as friendly as the first. As much as I enjoy being right, this time I couldn't take any pleasure in it.

Seven

The chill in the room felt palpable. Ramsey stood with his arms crossed, lips pressed into an angry line. Sitting in the middle of the desk was an evidence bag, the yellow reflector strap glinting under the florescent light.

Skipping any greeting, Ramsey simply pointed to a chair and Santos started typing. It felt like I'd never left.

The investigator picked up a folder and flipped through it, pacing back and forth. I sat and watched. I ran my tongue over lips that felt dry and chapped. A few more hours of sleep would have helped. And breakfast. I could have used a good breakfast.

Ramsey finally dropped the folder on the desk and groaned, rolling his head around on his shoulders.

"Get much sleep last night, Harper?" he asked.

"No, sir," I replied.

"I didn't, in case you're wondering," Ramsey said. "I hate sleeping on cots. Puts me in a bad mood."

He paced some more, then stopped in front of the table, picked up the evidence bag and dangled it in front of me.

"Do you know what this is, Sergeant Harper?" His hair was still damp from a shower. He looked young and vulnerable with his wet hair and his dimples.

"It's a safety reflector belt," I said.

"Ah, now that's what it looks like, but that's not what it is," he said, pointing at it. "That is a murder weapon."

He shifted the contents around a bit inside the bag.

"You see this? Those initials, kind of etched into the clasp right there?"

I didn't bother to look. I knew they were the L and the H I had carved onto the belt with my pocketknife.

"Your initials," Ramsey said. "Can you explain that, Sergeant Harper?" he asked, as he tossed the bag back onto his desk. He folded his arms across his chest, waiting for an answer.

"Chief, you knew it was my belt yesterday. I told you it was missing from where I kept it."

"That's right, you did," he said. He turned and walked back to the desk. With his back to me, he kept talking.

"What you failed to tell me yesterday, was how much you disliked Delray."

He turned and stalked toward me, taking several slow steps, until he was directly in front of me. He bent down. With hands on his knees, he supported himself. The posture put him eye to eye with me. I tried to hold my ground but shrank from him anyway.

"You didn't like her, did you?" He asked, adding a nasty tone to his question. "You told me about failing her," he put air quotes around failing. "But you didn't tell me you couldn't stand to be around her."

I looked away from the glare of his eyes, pressing my lips together, rubbing my damp palms on my thighs. "It's true. I didn't like her much."

"What's that you say, Sergeant Harper?" he asked, his body tense, his face turning red. He had heard me.

"I said, I didn't like her."

"That's right," he repeated, almost shouting now. "You not only didn't like her. You threatened to kill her, didn't you?"

I squeezed my eyes shut, sorry for the harsh words that had come out of my mouth. For someone in the communications business, the fact that my words were coming back to haunt me felt ironic. There was no way to justify what I'd said.

"I was angry," I said. "I didn't actually mean it."

He straightened, hands going to his hips. His lips made a straight line across his face and those dimples were looking like valleys. "Oh, you didn't mean it. Well, that makes it all better, doesn't it?"

I leaned forward in the chair, dropping my face in my hands. This was going badly. My head throbbed from lack of sleep and lack of food.

"I didn't mean it," I mumbled into my hands.

"Yes, you've said that," he said. He let the silence settle into the room, and then changed tactics.

"You have been in fights before, haven't you Sergeant Harper?" he said, taking up my personnel folder again. "It's not like you've not had a violent history."

I sat up and glared at him. "Come on, Chief. I was in basic training. It was two-against-one. I was defending myself."

"Two-against-one?" he asked.

"I'm not proud of that."

He put my file down, then grabbed a chair and plopped it down in front of me.

"Look, people who live together have arguments," he said, sounding reasonable. "One of them is messy, the other is a neat freak. Resentments build up. Before you know it, two normal, sane people are at each other's throats."

"At each other's throats?"

"In this case, literally." He paused, giving me that icy stare. "It happens all the time, Harper. Married couples, roommates. It wouldn't be surprising news. Most of the time, it's the husband, or the roommate, or the business partner…

"People who get murdered hang out with people who murder people," I said.

"Ha, now that's a good one. Did you hear that, Santos?" he said, turning to look at his partner. "People who get murdered…come up with that yourself, did you?"

"It was something my mother used to say," I said, then clamped my mouth shut, sorry that I'd brought it up. Ramsey was good. It hadn't taken him long to learn my vulnerabilities, my weaknesses. Ramsey's problem was that I was innocent. He simply didn't know it yet.

"But it's true. You mother is right," he said. "Most often people are killed by someone they know. Someone close to them." He leaned in close again. "I think that's what happened here."

"I've been in the Army thirteen years," I said. "Do you have any idea how many people I've shared tents with? How many different rooms I've slept in? There have been plenty of times I've lived with people I wasn't compatible with. A professional soldier can't be picky about things like that."

"Ah, but if you had a choice, you wouldn't have lived with Delray."

"You're right. I wouldn't have," I said, almost shouting. I turned away from him, trembling with the need to get control of my temper. I rubbed my face with my hands and took a deep breath.

"I wouldn't have lived with her if I'd had a choice," I said, calmer. "We had nothing in common. She was young. I found her annoying. But I didn't kill her."

We stared at each other for a long moment. Santos's keyboard clicks stilled. Ramsey stayed silent and stared.

I let him win, glancing at my watch as if bored, thinking that the time Ramsey spent interrogating me, was time wasted; time he could be using to find the real murderer—a murderer who so far, was getting away with the crime. It seemed obvious that Ramsey wasn't ready to look anywhere else. My only option was to get the interview over with in the hopes that, once done, the investigator would turn his frosty-eyed gaze on someone else.

I took a deep breath, let it out slowly and settled myself into the uncomfortable metal chair. For good measure, I threw my arm over the back, crossed one leg over my knee and felt my heart beat slow down a notch.

If he wanted to accuse me of murder, I was ready to take him on.

My newly relaxed demeanor threw Ramsey off his game. He stood, paced long enough to make a circuit of the small room then stopped. Eventually, he slumped back in his chair. He glanced over his shoulder and shared a look with his partner.

"Santos doesn't think you did it," Ramsey said.

For the first time, Santos spoke up with a thick Puerto Rican accent.

"A bad temper does not mean a killer," he said with a shrug. "Me? I have a bad temper. Ask my wife. Besides, no defensive wounds."

"We've only seen her arms," Ramsey chimed in. "She could have scratches in other places."

"We'll know when the DNA match is done," Santos said with a shrug. It sounded like an argument they'd already had.

"Well, she's all we've got so far," Ramsey said, his knee bouncing nervously. "We won't have those test results for days."

While I didn't like their open discussion of me as I sat there, the back and forth revealed they had some doubts about my culpability. That, I felt, was a good thing.

More doubt wouldn't hurt. The memory card was burning a hole in my pocket. I bit my lip, deciding. Giving the chip to Ramsey without knowing what was on it, could be a waste of time. On the other hand, giving it to him voluntarily, especially if there was something incriminating on it, would be better now than later.

I leaned back in the chair, straightened my leg and reached deep into my pocket, my arm disappearing almost to my elbow. Ramsey watched my every move. When I brought my hand out holding the memory card, he raised his eyebrows.

"I found this in my toilet kit this morning," I said. "It was in…"

"That backpack Jenkins let you take yesterday," he said, turning to Santos. "I knew we shouldn't have let her keep that thing."

He spun back around and stared at the small computer card. He stretched a hand to his partner, who had a pair of latex gloves ready. Ramsey snapped them onto his hands, then carefully took the card from me.

"Do you know what's on it?"

"No, sir," I said. "I haven't been able to get to a computer to open it. But I'm sure she deliberately put it in my bag. My bag was right by the door. She could have...."

"She was probably trying to hide it before she opened the door to her killer," he interrupted. He drew the card closer to his face to examine it then his gaze flicked to me. "She may have died for this," he said.

Ramsey waited while Santos struggled into his own pair of gloves, then delicately handed him the card. Santos inserted it in the computer, opened his photo software and we waited for the computer to do its work.

There were over a hundred pictures on the card. As the pictures began to appear, we saw that it had been a typical Bosnian morning, with misty rain and fog. Many of the shots were out of focus and badly framed. I winced at another stab of guilt. She never understood her complicated camera and I'd tired of explaining it to her, her lack of skill evident in almost every shot.

She managed to capture soldiers with shovels as they pushed tar around, a roller going back and forth to level the road. The road project was on a busy commercial street in Brcko. Later pictures showed that the sky had cleared, rare sunshine and blue skies brightened the dreary day. More pedestrians appeared on the sidewalks, kids stopped to watch and ask for candy, their hands out, jostling each other. There were lots of pictures of soldiers with smiling kids—some of them weren't too bad, almost useable.

Then, more than halfway through the images on the disk, she'd captured the picture of a man with a video camera. It was the kind of video I've taken often, a picture of a person taking a picture of me. On the side of the man's camera were the letters, BBC.

"Hey, that's...," and I hesitated, trying to remember his name. "Ian, Ian Tooley, Franklyn Hannerty's videographer," I said. "Their bureau says they haven't checked in for two days ... no three, if you count today."

Ramsey looked at the date below the photo. "Three days ago, would make it the same day this was taken," he said. "Any others of this guy?" he asked.

There were. The first, of Tooley with his eye pressed to the viewfinder of the camera, a smile on his face, enjoying the photo exchange. In the next photo, he wasn't looking through the viewfinder. He had tilted the camera away from him so you could see his whole face as he waved at Delray. Around mid-thirties, he sported that rough, unshaven look TV news folks get in places like Bosnia. He wore a photographer's vest with multiple pockets that bulged with paraphernalia. Tan cargo pants and good hiking boots completed the look.

There were more road construction pictures, more smiling kids, and some with Tooley in them as he shot tape of the same action. In a couple of the pictures, I recognized Hannerty, as he stood off to the side, leaning against a building as if waiting for someone. In one shot, he's glancing at his watch.

The light in the pictures changed as the afternoon progressed. The later shots had more pink and purple hues, shadows crouched over people's faces and the sides of the armored vehicles. Then a series of pictures that made my heart lurch.

Hannerty stood in front of a building. A large window to the right of him was bathed in red light. On the window—Cyrillic writing, along with a picture of a large rose with fat drops of water coming from its petals.

"That's gotta be the Weeping Rose," I said.

"The what?"

"The Weeping Rose. It's a whorehouse."

"How do you know that?" Ramsey asked. He and Santos stared at me, waiting for a response.

"I was talking to some soldiers who patrol that area on the overnight shift. They told me about it and that they've seen some sketchy looking dudes going in and out of there."

"Sketchy looking dudes?"

I shrugged. "That's what they said. Delray had a drawing in her notebook. It looks exactly like that rose. She knew something about that place."

"What notebook are you talking about?"

"It's one she left on my desk. She'd leave her notebooks everywhere," I said, thinking of her irritating habit. "She was never very good at keeping track of things."

I glanced up and realized Ramsey was staring at me. "I want to have a look at the notebook."

"Of course."

The pictures that followed seemed as if Delray had put the shutter on auto and left her finger on the button. The door of the suspected brothel opened, Hannerty and Tooley moved toward the door. Someone in an American uniform stood in the doorway, the faint glimpse of camouflage hidden in shadow. The figure moved further into the doorway and became fully visible.

"That's Captain Griffin," I said, popping up out of my chair. "He's General Paterson's aide."

Ramsey and Santos exchanged a look, then went back to cycling through the pictures. Griffin ushered the British pair inside, and the door closed.

I looked at Ramsey. "Where the aide goes, so goes the General," I said.

"Not so fast," he cautioned. "It's the other way around. We don't know that the General was there. We also don't know why the reporters were there."

"It could have been a meeting," Santos suggested.

"In a brothel?" I asked.

"We don't know that it's a brothel," Ramsey said. "You're basing your assumption on what some soldiers told you.

"Griffin must have found out that Delray had those pictures, or maybe Delray said something to him, tried to find out what he was doing there."

"Speculation, Master Sergeant Harper," said Ramsey. "All speculation."

"These pictures are from the first day of her shoot," I said. "She told me she wanted more material before she could finish her story so she planned to go with them again. That was yesterday. The day she was killed."

"Her camera is missing, you said. We don't know what she may have seen." Ramsey stood up, crossing his arms.

"Whatever she did," I said, "she must have attracted attention to herself or let on somehow that she knew something."

There were still a few more pictures, but nothing more of Griffin or the BBC journalists.

Ramsey stepped back from the desk and began his pacing thing again. I watched him walk the room for a bit.

"We need to find her camera," I said.

He nodded and kept pacing, "Yes, we'll continue searching for it."

"The photos still in the camera could show why she was killed. Maybe even who did it."

"Unfortunately, murder investigations are rarely so neatly solved, Sergeant Harper."

"General Paterson has asked us for an update," Santos said, looking at his watch, "in about thirty minutes. He wants to know the status before his interview with *The Post*."

"Right," Ramsey said.

They did some silent communication that I interpreted as meaning they would ask the General just what he and his aide, or maybe just the General's aide was doing in a brothel at the edge of the town of Brcko around the evening hours of the day the British journalists went missing. I wished I could be in the room when Ramsey said the word brothel to the General.

"I want you to stay on base, Sergeant Harper, until further notice," said Ramsey.

"Does that mean I'm officially a suspect?"

"That means I order you to stay on base, for now at least."

"Roger, sir." I stood up to go and he picked up the evidence bag.

"Did you think we wouldn't find out about the threat?" he asked. One eyebrow went up and he maximized those dimples again.

"I didn't mean it, for Pete's sake," I said. "It was just a stupid thing I said in frustration."

Ramsey's icy glare had softened, his blue eyes red rimmed and tired looking. I didn't like him much, but I wanted him to find Delray's killer.

"All right," he said, "you can go. But don't leave the camp, and let me know if you hear anything else about this."

"Of course, Sir," I replied, but he had already turned his back to me.

"Mr. Ramsey," I said. He turned to me again, irritated that I was still there.

"Do you have any idea how long her body will be....I mean, I need to make arrangements to ship her home. I should be able to tell her family something, shouldn't I?"

"I don't know, Harper," he replied, dismissively. "Check with the mortuary team."

I left wanting more than anything to find Colonel McCallen. He would be tied up with the General at least until after the interview.

I decided to go see the chaplain to start planning Delray's official memorial service. Since the chaplain was also my next-door neighbor, I wondered what he might have heard from my trailer early on the morning Delray was killed.

Eight

My cot sat against the thin wall that joined the chaplain's side of the trailer to ours. While lying in my rack on countless nights, I heard people knocking on his door in the wee-hours of the morning. He always seemed willing to listen, and people poured out their problems to him.

In the four months I had been on the camp, we had had one suicide. Maybe it was from being so far from home, the horrible weather, or maybe it was because here you carried your weapon everywhere you went and the ammunition to go with it. No matter the reason, the event affected everyone on base, some more than others.

After the suicide, the chaplain's trailer filled with men who came one by one to claim that it had been their fault for not noticing how troubled the soldier had been. The dead soldier's lieutenant, a fresh-faced kid straight out of West Point, had sobbed and prayed and sobbed some more, and the entire time, I could hear the chaplain's patient voice, his Brooklyn accent identifiable through the thin walls.

Black and yellow police tape draped the door on my side of the trailer along with a huge "Do Not Enter" sign. Even when the tape and the sign were removed, I doubted I could ever live in that trailer again.

As always, the chaplain's door was open. A fact I was grateful for now.

"Chaplain Hirsch?" I called from the bottom step.

He turned from where he was sitting at his desk, his glasses pushed up onto his forehead. He lowered the glasses to his nose and peered at me, then his face lit up in recognition and concern.

"Master Sergeant Harper, my poor child," he exclaimed, as he leapt up from his chair and came to the door, his arms stretched out to provide the comfort he assumed I needed.

Chaplain Hirsch was the only Jewish Chaplain I'd known in all my years in the military. He was tall and silver haired, and even when he spoke seriously, it was easy to see that life was a delightful adventure for him. Since I never went to chapel, the only times I'd heard him speak had been during the one or two minute invocations he gave before ceremonies or special occasions. Judging from those short exposures to his preaching he was brilliant and bombastic.

He kept repeating, "My poor child, my poor child," as he took my hand and closed the door, leading me into the trailer. He almost pushed me into a chair as if I were too frail to stand, then he sat across from me, patting my hand the entire time. He was offering the words in a caring way, his eyes sparkling with intense sensitivity, but his words and his actions seemed so overblown that I was struggling mightily not to laugh.

"I'm so glad you came to me, Sergeant Harper," he said. Only it came out Sah-gent Hah-par. His accent, so charming and foreign to my Midwestern ears that, even if I hadn't already known it, I would have easily determined that Hirsh was from Brooklyn.

"Virginia was a beautiful girl, just beautiful. Who would do such a terrible thing to her?" he went on.

"It is terrible, sir," I said.

He pressed my hands together in his and gave me the full intensity of his dark eyes. Pure kindness radiated from his face, from the soft look of his eyes, to his sympathetic smile, his emotions real, no sign of fake sentiment. His warmth made me believe that he felt genuine sympathy for what I might have been feeling in the wake of her murder.

I understood then why so many people went to him. He was there for me as he had been for so many others. He kept patting my hand and waiting for me to speak, and I felt I could sit there for as long as I needed and he wouldn't flinch.

"I don't know what will happen with her now," I said.

"Oh, I see," he said. He explained that the mortuary team would prepare Delray for transport as soon as the investigators released her body. Delray's family would be notified by a casualty assistance team in the states.

He looked at his watch and mentally calculated the time differences.

"I'm sure they've been informed by now," he said. "The casualty assistance officers will help her family with all the arrangements. Delray can have a full military burial."

There were so many little things I hadn't had a chance to think about. Funerals, wakes and obituaries. I wondered if her boyfriend knew about her yet. Delray's belongings in her quarters back in Germany, the cat she sent back home when we learned we were deploying to Bosnia. The traces of her life left behind.

"Chaplain Hirsch, were you here yesterday morning?" I asked. He was already shaking his head before I finished the question.

"Wednesday mornings I hold a prayer session for headquarters at zero six thirty, which of course you wouldn't know since you have never been to any religious service of any kind since you have been on this camp," he said as he wagged a finger at me with a smile. "Yes, I know about your absence. I keep track of these things, Sergeant Harper and I'm not the only one who does," he said, pointing up to the Record Keeper in the heavens.

"Now, Virginia, she would come to the prayer sessions very often and was always at chapel on Sundays. Such a nice girl, she was," he said shaking his head. "Come to think of it, hardly anyone came to that prayer session on Wednesday. I remember because I wondered if anything was wrong. The General and his aide almost always attend the service and when they weren't there, I waited a few minutes just in case they were busy, and I thought there might be some new crisis going on that I hadn't heard about yet."

He brushed off the General's absences, with a flap of his hand.

"I'm sure they were busy with something. But to think that she was right here being murdered and if I hadn't been off leading a prayer I might have been here to help her. It's just too much to be believed," he said.

"The General and Captain Griffin always go to your prayer service?" I managed to get in.

He nodded his head. "Oh yes," he said. "Whenever they get the chance." He peered at me. "Why would that surprise you?"

Evidently, my disbelief was evident in my expression. The General's barring seemed opposite of anyone pious or religious even in a passing way. I couldn't conjure up an image of him on his knees in prayer, to carve out the time, however short, for silent reflection. After my encounter with him yesterday, perhaps silent prayer was exactly what he needed. This morning in the shower, I discovered a large black and blue mark on my collarbone that felt sore to the touch and would match the General's thumbprint.

"Now, Sergeant Harper, when would you like to have the memorial service?" he asked. Military tradition required a memorial service so the Army family could mourn the fallen no matter where in the world they died.

I shrugged my shoulders. "I don't know, sir. Whenever you think it appropriate I guess."

He was nodding his head again and patting my hand.

"Don't you worry, Sergeant Harper. My aide and I will arrange everything. Of course, you should prepare a little something to say about her. And find one or two people who knew her and liked her to say a few words also." He finally released my hands and turned to his desk, looking for paper and a pen to start making a list.

He prattled on as he planned.

"She always liked to sing *Go Tell It On The Mountain* during service," he said. "Such a beautiful, clear voice she had."

I had no idea Delray could sing. I would never have known what song she liked. I had been unaware that she went to a prayer service most Wednesday mornings and wouldn't have known she was Baptist if I hadn't seen her dog tags. I had been working with her for a year in Germany before our unit was deployed to Bosnia and we had shared our trailer for four months on this mission, and I didn't know her at all.

That knot of guilt returned. How could I have been so self-absorbed?

"We might as well have the service on Sunday morning," he said, continuing his planning. Then there was a knock on the door and I took it as my cue to leave.

"Chaplain, I'll be ready to speak, and I'll find a couple of others who want to speak on her behalf. Just let me know if there is anything else you need me to do," I said, moving toward the door. He looked up from his writing and fluttered his hand at me.

"Of course, of course, but you don't have to rush off," he said. "It's first come, first served around here, you know. It has to be." He smiled again, his natural joy for life undiminished in spite of the death of the young girl with the clear voice.

I opened the door of the trailer to a young soldier. He looked familiar and then I remembered he was the driver for the commander of the engineer company, Sergeant Steele.

He looked surprised that the door had opened, as if he had been about to walk away. He was damp from standing in the rain. Mud completely covered his boots and the lower half of his pants. He was carrying a SAW, a huge complicated machine gun usually given to either the biggest guy in the unit or the one who needed to show he had the biggest balls. In Steele's case, it had to be because of his size because they didn't come much bigger. Steele was not just tall. Broad shoulders, massive chest and hands that looked surprisingly gentle, were all oversized.

He had been crying. His large black eyes were swimming in a sea of red. The redness stood out against his coal dark skin. He looked down and away when he saw me, embarrassed that his tears were so obvious.

The chaplain told him to come in. I walked down the steps to get out of the way. When the chaplain saw that it was Steele, he jumped up from his chair and came to the door.

"Sergeant Steele, I'm so sorry for your loss," he said.

I wondered what he meant and then the Chaplain stopped me.

"Sergeant Harper, this is Sergeant Marcus Steele. You do know him, don't you?" he asked, looking from me to Steele. Steele shook his head and said, "No, sir, she didn't know about me."

"I didn't know what about you?" I asked him, starting to get annoyed about all the things I didn't know.

"Why, Sergeant Steele and Specialist Delray..." said the chaplain, and he shifted his gaze from Sergeant Steele back to me. "They always came to the prayer service together." He continued to look at me as if I should get it by now.

What? They were friends? I thought.

The chaplain threw his hands up in frustration. "They were dating, Master Sergeant Harper," he exclaimed. "Dating. Well, as much as young people can date in this place."

Standing next to him, Steele towered over me, his arms gently resting across the top of the massive weapon he carried. He shifted his weight from foot to foot, avoiding my gaze.

"I wondered why you hadn't come to see me yet, Sergeant Steele. Come in, come in," said the Chaplain, leading the soldier into his trailer. Steele followed Hirsch inside, glanced down at me for a moment, then closed the door.

I stood stiffly, staring at the door, my mouth hanging open. Delray had always talked about a boyfriend back home in Mississippi. I tried to remember if she ever said anything about Steele. Maybe the fact that he was black stopped her from telling me, afraid I would have an opinion about her dating a black man. Then I remembered that page in her notebook, the name Mark repeated until it filled the page. It was a shock, no doubt about that. Maybe she wanted to avoid letting me know she was cheating on the boyfriend back home.

Then I settled on the truth. Delray didn't tell me anything about her life, her pursuits or her dreams because she didn't think I'd care. Would I have cared that she had a regular appointment to attend the midweek prayer service? Doubtful. As long as she got her job done, showed up on time for her other duties, her personal pursuits were tiny blips on my radar. I'd been too self-absorbed to learn the most basic things about her, too self-absorbed to understand her as a human being and those failures extended to my ability to be a true leader to her.

She often prattled on at times, telling me this and that, but I was usually busy doing something, or tried to tune her mousey voice out. The only things I ever talked to her about were her assignments, her work, or to ask if she had cleaned her weapon lately, done the required PT training, or inventoried her equipment.

I had decided early on that I didn't like her and would never relate to her and it now seemed evil, shallow and thoroughly rotten of me to so easily dismiss someone I barely knew.

Shame and guilt washed over me. It wasn't dreadful enough to be a bad NCO. I had to be a rotten person as well. I could have cried, but that seemed like a self-indulgence of the worst kind, a reason to hate myself even more if my tears stemmed from the fact that I'd finally come to a full realization of how much I sucked as a human.

I couldn't go back and get to know Delray. It was too late for that, but I could get to know her killer. Delray was practically a stranger to me.

I planned to get personal with the guy who took her life.

Nine

As I walked in the direction of headquarters, I heard the pounding of running feet on the wooden walkway coming up behind me. I moved to the side and out of the way as six, then seven, then eight soldiers rounded the corner at full sprint, their helmets, weapons and other gear clanging and bouncing with the rhythm of their speed. One of them spoke into the radio clipped to the shoulder of his gear. "We're on the move. QRF Able out."

The Quick Reaction Force in motion meant there was trouble somewhere. Probably something to do with the resettlement efforts Townson predicted at the morning BUB.

Resettlement played a major role in our peacekeeping mission. Returning people to the homes and farms their families had owned for centuries, homes they lost when forced out during the war was supposed to mean a return to normalcy, a return to peace. More often than not, the practice of moving families out so the rightful owners of the property could move back in, stirred trouble. Sometimes riots broke out. Calls for the QRF happened when the threat of violence felt imminent and an immediate and decisive show of force became necessary.

The soldiers ran past me while others came from different directions in the camp, all heading to their vehicles parked in a row near the gate. The four humvees and an M1 Abrams tank all stood ready to go. Soldiers climbed onto the tank and disappeared through the hatch and in seconds the engine fired up, and the noxious smell of the fuel wafted toward me. One soldier crawled up to stand in the turret, his goggles lowered onto his face. The rest of the soldiers jumped into the armored humvees. Two lead vehicles and the one in the rear had fifty caliber machine guns mounted in the turrets.

Soldiers pulled the gate open and the convoy of vehicles drove through, probably short minutes from when they first received their call. Black smoke and the smell of the tank fuel drifted through the air long after the tank rumbled and clanked out the gate at the front of the convoy.

Normally, I would have tried to go with them. I would have run for my camera and tripod and tried to hitch a ride in one of the humvees or tried to get someone else to take me out to where the resettlement was going on. Soldiers helping to resettle families, soldiers helping to stop a riot, soldiers working in a quick reaction force, they were all the kinds of stories I was there to tell, but now I wasn't allowed to leave the camp. I had no idea how long my confinement would last.

==========

When I got to the general's office, I saw McCallen standing near the door, talking to the reporter. He excused himself from her and came over to me.

"I'll be a few more minutes," he said. "You look..."

"Like crap. Yes, sir. I know."

He laughed. "That's not what I was going to say. Give me a few minutes and we'll go talk."

I grabbed a nearby chair at an empty desk, sat down and then noticed the General and Captain Griffin standing nearby.

"Holy crap," I said to myself.

General Paterson had his hand on Captain Griffin's shoulder, discussing something with him. The General looked relaxed and natural, just having a little chat with his aide. That's how it appeared anyway. I could almost feel the pain inflicted by the vice-like grip on Griffin's shoulder.

Griffin stood with his back to me, but I could see his right leg trembling, his left shoulder, the one the General had his grip on, hunched up near his ear. The clipboard Griffin always carried slowly slipped out of his grasp.

I stood, picked up receiver of the phone on the desk in front of me and held it out to him.

"Captain Griffin, a call for you," I said.

Both men turned in my direction, startled that I was there. The interruption had the desired effect. General Paterson released his grip and Griffin took a little step backwards as if he lost his balance for a second. The General patted Griffin's arm a couple of times, shot a look in my direction, scanned the room quickly, and retreated into his office.

Griffin stood there until the General moved out of sight, then he turned to me and stumbled a little on the loose flooring as he walked to the desk where I stood, his hand out to take the phone.

I pushed the chair toward him.

"Here," I said. "Sit down." I hung up the phone and cocked my hip onto the side of the desk.

"Why did you hang up on them?" he asked, refusing to take the chair, his eyes red and swimming, his face regaining some of its color.

"There wasn't any call," I said. "I just knew you needed...well, I've had that hand on my shoulder recently too, sir."

His wrinkled brow and clenched jaw slowly relaxed as he realized I understood what had just happened to him. He tossed the clipboard down on the desk and opened his mouth to say something, but thought better of it. Deflated, he plopped down into the chair, doubled over to put his face in his hands. I stood looking down at him. I glanced around to see if anyone else watched but everyone in the room was busy dealing with the QRF situation.

"Why does he do that?" I asked.

Griffin took a deep breath, rubbed his face with his hands a couple of times, then sat back in the chair and looked at me. He was in his late thirties and a little pudgy around the middle. He covered the loss of his hair by wearing it mostly shaved but you could see from the shadows that it would have been black and gray and growing only on the sides. He looked dog-tired with bags under his eyes and a sallow grey color to his skin.

"I'm not sure what you mean," he said. He cocked his head to the side and looked at me with a dare in his eyes. Would I talk about what the General had done? I took his dare.

"I have a black-and-blue mark right here," I said, pointing to my collarbone. "And I got it from your boss."

We had a little stare-down contest. Griffin let me win. He glanced around the room while he marshaled his strength to get up and walk away.

"Next time you say there's a phone call for me," he said standing, "I expect there to be a caller on the line, Sergeant." He turned to leave but I grabbed his arm.

It pissed me off, this attempt to pretend that nothing had happened. I initially felt sympathy for Griffin. I wondered how many times and in how many other ways the general made his aide quiver in agony. Like an abused spouse, Griffin pretended it hadn't happened, that I hadn't seen it.

"What other things are you covering up for him?" I asked.

Griffin looked down at my hand on his arm and slowly brought his eyes up to meet mine. Through clenched teeth he said, "Remember yourself, Sergeant."

I released his arm and waited to see what else he had to say.

"You are the closest thing to a suspect CID has right now, Harper. The General could have you sent to the detention facility as the investigation progresses. So far, that hasn't been necessary."

A threat, and a weak one at that. Ramsey didn't have anything to charge me with, and from what I knew about the investigator, I doubted he would arrest anyone until he was ready, no matter what the general said.

I wanted to say something about the pictures, but I figured Ramsey hadn't talked to him about it yet. I kept quiet about them. The story the images told wasn't clear, but if they meant trouble, I was sure the general would throw Griffin to the wolves if he needed to.

"I've spent some time with Chief Ramsey, Captain. He seems to know what he's doing. I have every confidence he'll find who the real killer or killers are." I paused for a second then threw in, "Sir."

There could have been a slight flicker of worry, a little tightness around the mouth, a creasing in the forehead but I wasn't certain. He kept his eyes locked with mine then gave the room a quick survey. With a final glare, he picked up his clipboard and walked away.

I sat down and thought about what I had just witnessed. Was Brigadier General Paterson in the habit of abusing his aides? Did he have a history of such activity? And what, if anything, did any of that have to do with the disappearance of the BBC team or Delray's murder?

Wrestling with the puzzle left me feeling clueless. I barely noticed when Colonel McCallen finally arrived. He had his laptop and rucksack in his hands again.

"Take me to my quarters will you?" he said. I asked him where he was staying.

A smile brightened his face. "Apparently, I'm going to Disneyland."

I stood up and raised my eyebrows, "Oh, la de da!" I led him out of the headquarters complex.

Ten

Congressional delegations, ambassadors and United Nations representatives often visited our base when they wanted to see, first hand, what international peacekeeping is all about. Travel in Bosnia, however, takes time. Highways are nonexistent. Most roads present a series of hazards to dodge like massive potholes, horse drawn carts, slow scooters, bicycles and pedestrians who seem oblivious to the dangers of walking two abreast alongside the road. Even if you could travel via helicopter, a visit to McGovern usually meant at least a one-night sleep over.

The camp designated a group of trailers to accommodate the many special visitors we received. We called the cluster of trailers Disneyland.

"How did you get keys?" I asked McCallen as we walked in that direction.

"I told Bishop I needed to check out where the Vice President's media operations person was going to stay. He knew it was bullshit but," McCallen shrugged, "space everywhere else is short, so he gave me the keys. The CID team took the last open tent."

I smiled, thinking that Ramsey and Santos slept in uncomfortable cots in tents, while McCallen had the luxury of VIP accommodations.

I had never been inside one of the Disneyland trailers and I wondered what they looked like. The sign on the door said Suite #5. McCallen handed me his laptop then went up the steps and unlocked the door. I followed him inside.

"Holy mackerel," I said. "This is the life."

The trailer, twice the size of mine, had an honest-to-goodness queen-sized bed in the middle. I laid his laptop on the desk, took off my helmet and then plopped down on the bed, giving it a bounce. I smiled at the thought of sleeping on a bed again. When I looked up at McCallen, he smiled at me.

"Too hard for my taste," I said jumping up, regretting my impulse.

McCallen dropped his rucksack on the floor and took off his helmet, dropping it on the desk with a thud. The shiny mahogany desk came equipped with a comfortable looking leather chair. A sofa, coffee table, end tables, lamps and wall-to-wall carpet, completed the trailer's elegance.

"I haven't seen carpet in months," McCallen said.

He walked to a door that looked like a closet and opened it. "You've got to be kidding."

I went to look myself.

We stood in the doorway admiring the view of the private bathroom, with sink, shower and flush toilet. "Man, oh man" I said.

In the real world, one could expect to find a few hours or a few moments in a day to spend alone. On McGovern, private moments, even when engaged in the business of natural bodily functions, were impossible. Someone sitting in the stall next to you would ask for toilet paper or talk at you through the walls. Having a personal bathroom was the stuff of dreams.

"I wonder if General Paterson's trailer has one of these."

"It probably does," said McCallen.

I glanced up and saw the two of us framed in the mirror above the sink. McCallen's short-cropped flaming hair, his freckles and pale skin, stood in stark contrast to my dark brown coloring. For a moment, our eyes met in the mirror. I looked away quickly. He chuckled and stepped back from the door. I moved to the sink, wondering what was funny and decided my hair, a frizzy mess surrounding my face, would make anyone laugh. I ran a little water into my hand and smoothed it over my head to try to tame the curling tendrils.

"You look like crap," I whispered to my reflection. I smiled at the luxury of having a mirror then remembered the image of the two of us standing together.

"You shouldn't be here," I said, staring at my reflection.

"Are you talking to yourself in there?"

"Just admiring the accommodations," I said, stepping out of the small room.

McCallen shrugged out of his shoulder holster and dropped his flak vest on the floor.

I leaned my M16 against the wall and took off my flak vest. Our eyes met again, my stomach did a nervous flip. I couldn't look at him. I paced around the room, pretending to check out everything. For years, especially in most recent months, I'd made it my business to avoid being alone with him. Delray had been a useful unsuspecting tool in that mission. Now she was gone.

"I'm sorry about all of this Harper, you finding her like that," he said. "How are you doing?"

To anyone else, I would have said I was okay. I couldn't lie to McCallen. "Frankly, sir. I'm kind of a mess."

"You don't look a mess. You look great, actually. It's good to see you."

I could feel the heat in my face. I smiled back at him. "I could blame you for all of this, you know, sir. If you had given me that transfer I requested, I wouldn't be here."

He chuckled. "I couldn't let you go, Harper. I needed you with me. On this deployment, I mean."

I started to feel warm. I went to the air conditioner and cranked it up a couple notches. Then I went to a window, parted the blinds and looked out, anything to keep from looking at him, at his grey eyes. I brought up the subject I usually used when the tension grew too much.

"How's Michelle and the boys?"

He leaned back onto the desk and crossed his arms, his wedding ring glinting in the soft light from a nearby window. "They're fine."

"When is she due?" I asked, even though I knew the answer.

He looked down, a crimson blush working its way up his neck. "Around three months."

I opened drawers in the nightstand, fiddled with the lamp, cycling through the three different light levels. A wooden locker in a far corner had so far, been ignored. I went to it, opened it, closed it. After that, I searched for something else to occupy my attention. I glanced at McCallen. He clenched his jaw, but the desire in his eyes burned me from across the room.

"Oh God," I sighed, frozen in place. "This is not good."

"Lauren," he said, standing. "Let me be here for you."

"You are here, sir," I said weakly. "I appreciate you coming," That sounded so lame. I opened my mouth to say more but didn't know where to begin. I couldn't tell him that I needed his strength, or that I felt totally and completely alone. I couldn't say that I already carried a heavy bucket of guilt about Delray. I didn't need another one to balance me out. Instead, he told me what he couldn't do.

"I couldn't stay away," he said.

"Please, don't talk like that."

He took a step toward me and hesitated. Even after all the years we'd worked together, our physical contact had been restricted to handshakes for congratulations and pats on the shoulder in encouragement. The prospect of touching him in any way was enough to make my mouth dry.

He started to speak and then stopped, his hands curled into fists. I could hardly breathe.

I looked at the door, knowing I should leave. When the tension built like this in the past, leaving had always been the best option. For years, leaving had worked.

Dim light slanted in through the blinds on the windows and he stood in the wash of the light. Subdued tapping on the roof meant the rain had started again.

"Damn it, Lauren," he said, shaking his head. "I know you're about to walk out. Don't. Just, don't."

He opened his arms and gestured with his hands for me to

come. "No one could fault me for giving you a hug under these circumstances. You need a hug. Hell, I need a hug."

He made it sound so innocent. I couldn't go to him and yet nothing could stop me. I took another long look at the door.

Then I moved toward him. It was just a hug, but with each step, I knew nothing good would come of it. I always like to think I'm in control. I was in control, complete control when I stepped into his embrace.

I wrapped my arms around his waist and buried my face in his chest. His arms came around me. He lowered his cheek to the top of my head. We stood there, while he rocked me gently right and left, his body coiling around me tighter and tighter.

"I can only imagine how horrible it must have been for you," he said in a husky voice. He smoothed a strand of hair away from my face. "The way you sounded on the phone, it broke my heart. I was frustrated when I couldn't get here last night."

"You're here now," I said.

"Yes, I'm here now."

I closed my eyes and relaxed into the warmth of his body. My job is to be a leader, to have the answers, to know what to do next. The tension of the last day began to dissolve. I wanted to melt in his arms, to cry like a child. His embrace seemed to absorb my fears and anxieties.

Then, slowly, subtly, the comforting feel of his warm hug became more electric. The calming warmth grew charged with longing. My head swam with need. I felt breathless. I could smell his aftershave and the crisp outdoors in his clothes. Our boots touched and I wondered how and why he could want me when there was nothing sexy about how I looked or where we were.

The awareness that I had never touched him before made me weak with wonder. I had dreamt about what it would feel like to lay my head on his chest, to feel his arms around me. We fit just as I imagined we would. He moved slowly, tightening, pressing me closer. Then, he took in a long shaky breath, and moaned, a deep rumble in his chest.

It was too much. With a gasp, I looked up at him. A mistake.

He gazed down at me, surprised that we were suddenly eye-to-eye, closer than we'd ever been. His lips parted, and his hand moved to the back of my head and I let him cradle me there for a long moment, staring at him, amazed by the light of his eyes, the freckles scattered across his nose and cheeks, and that scar, the angry line that made me want to heal his wound. His gaze roamed my face.

I should have stopped him when he bent down to kiss me. I should have backed away and run as far as I could, but I stayed, frozen, waiting for what he would do. He slowly slanted his mouth over mine, brushing back and forth, not kissing me yet, just testing, holding my gaze as his lids lowered and opened lazily, checking that I was still there and with him until his tongue cautiously met my lips, seeking an invitation to go further.

With a sigh, I parted my lips and closed my eyes, giving in, arching my back, pressing my chest into his, allowing his tongue to make a full exploration of my mouth, the first slick glide of our tongues together so intense it sucked my breath away. I wrapped my arms around his neck, stretching, seeking. I touched his face, my hand sliding up to grab his hair, clenching a handful in my fingers. His facial stubble rubbed my cheek and I enjoyed the lemony taste of him, the sense of him surrounding me felt overwhelming. He trembled under my hands and the sounds of his response, of our rising passion filled the small trailer. His desire amplified mine like a lighted detonation cord on a sparking path toward an explosion, unstoppable in its rapid charge forward. He grabbed a fistful of my hair and clamped his mouth on mine tighter, drawing me into him, drawing away all my defenses.

He broke the kiss, panting my name.

"Oh, Lauren. Lauren."

Then he kissed me again, making me moan and tremble as he devoured me, his tongue dancing with mine drawing me further into abandon. When our boots touched again, I remembered where we were. We were in uniform, on an overseas mission. I was kissing my commanding officer. I was his sergeant, and everything about this was wrong.

I pushed hard against his chest and he released me, stepping back. I moved quickly out of his reach, panting. He came back toward me, his mouth open in surprise. His lips swollen and raw.

"Please," he said, in a desperate whisper.

I wanted more than anything to go to him. His eyes were shining, his breath ragged. He stretched his arms out to me again, ready to say something more, but I took another step back and he checked himself. He clenched his fists, dropped his arms and stood stiffly. He closed his eyes and shuddered as a bright blush washed up from his neck to his face making his scar an angry white line. When he looked at me again the pleading in his eyes was even worse. I knew I didn't have the willpower to resist him if I didn't retreat.

"I have to go," I said and spun around to leave.

"Wait, Lauren. Just, damn it. Don't go."

"I can't stay. I need time."

I moved to the door and grabbed for my flak vest, flinging it up overhead to thrust my arms through their holes.

"In the mess tent for lunch," I said, and risked a glance back at him. He stood rooted in the same spot, his chest rising and falling, his eyes burning into me. He turned away and nodded his head.

"Okay," he said, in a strained voice. "In an hour."

Eleven

I left Disneyland feeling used up. I needed to be alone. I moved down one walkway, then another, turning where the walkways turned, passing several people. Many I knew, but I only nodded recognition and avoided conversation, keeping my eyes to the ground. Someone tried to stop me to talk, but I lied.

"Late for a meeting," I said, and kept walking.

The rain felt like a shower with bad water pressure, annoying and with little effect. I was glad it rained. Sunshine and good weather would have made my mood even worse.

Eventually I came to the motor pool in the far corner of the camp. Row upon row of humvees, tanks and wrecker equipment, pickups, Bradley fighting vehicles and five-ton tractor-trailers all lined up neatly in order.

The unspoken secret around camp held that the motor pool was lover's lane. After the midnight shift rolled out, there weren't any official reasons to go into the motor pool, so lovers found an empty humvee or pickup truck and the privacy they sought. I hoped that I could find some privacy here in the daytime as well.

I went to a back row, found a five-ton and climbed up into the cab. The long unobstructed seat promised the comfort I needed. I took my weapon off my back, pulled my helmet off, rolled both windows down and enjoyed the feeling of the breeze and the sound of rain in the confines of the cab. I lay down across the seat and closed my eyes.

Behind my eyes, I saw Neil standing there, his arms

outstretched to me. All of my defensive maneuvers I used over the years had failed me. I had known where my feelings would lead. My desire for him had motivated me to ask for a transfer, to demand it. He'd denied the request. I could have gone over his head, but I hadn't. The truth, that I really wanted to stay with him, tasted bitter.

Turning off my feelings for him overstretched my capacity for self-control but it seemed clear it would be up to me to resist. He'd been unwilling to help.

Most of the soldiers I worked with over the years were married. The pay and benefit incentives in the military almost encouraged it. They married young, they married their high school or college sweethearts and they made babies right away. Then as they got older, they started looking around. Temporary duty travel or TDY as we call it, became a desired mission. Sometimes married soldiers and government civilians took their rings off when on TDY, and like a trip to Las Vegas, lived by the creed of what goes on TDY, stays on TDY.

I found the attitude disgusting and had never, in all my years wearing the uniform, engaged in any of that. I held the belief that if a man cheated on his wife, then nothing would stop him from cheating on me.

Then along came Neil. I had come close to breaking every rule I had ever set for myself. When I looked at him, I felt things I couldn't talk about out loud.

His wife and children made him off limits, now and forever. Even if he chose to leave Michelle, which I knew he would never do, I wouldn't want any part of him, not after he left her.

Not to mention that a romantic relationship between an officer and anyone in their chain of command violated the Uniform Code of Military Justice. Strictly forbidden. If caught, we could both lose everything. It would be the end of both of our careers.

That left only one thing to do. Get over it. I had to turn off the feelings I had for him and marshal on.

I thought about all that as I lay there on the seat of the five-ton. The blessed privacy allowed me to relax. I lay back on the seat, threw my arm over my eyes and spent a great deal of time mentally kicking myself, for my inappropriate feelings, for my neglect of my soldier, for everything. My feelings of disgust with myself were exhausting. Eventually I must have fallen asleep.

I woke to the sound of voices outside the truck.

"No, let go. You are hurting me," I heard a woman say. She had an accent and I figured she must be one of the interpreters or one of the workers around the camp. She sounded like she stood very near the truck I occupied. I didn't want to be seen there. A senior NCO shouldn't be hiding out and sleeping in the middle of the day, but I kept listening to see if she needed help.

"I'm sorry. I'm not trying to hurt you." It was the very deep voice of an American man. He had a thick southern accent. "But you have to tell me what you saw," he went on. "Don't you know you could be in danger?"

I tried to sit up a little to see if I could spot them. I peeked over the dashboard and scanned the area but couldn't see anyone. Then I heard footsteps in the gravel and suddenly they were right next to the truck. I quickly ducked back down out of sight.

"I told you all that I know," she said. "I look for my sister. I tell Virginia I look for my sister the other day. She say she will help. These women, they know what happened to her, to my sister. I am sure of this, but they not say. They afraid. And now Virginia," she stopped, overwhelmed with crying. That's when I recognized her. I had heard that crying before from Mishka, the interpreter with the short, dye-damaged hair.

"How was Virginia helping you?"

"She help me look for Mila, for my sister. Mila was interpreter here, but she never say for who. She just bring home money and she say she make good friends and people that help her to maybe to go America. Mila want so bad to go to America. Then one day she no come home. We ask and we look but she is no where."

There was a fresh bout of crying but the man encouraged her.

"I know this is hard but you gotta tell me," he said.

I tried to look again and I still couldn't see anything over the dashboard. I scanned the area and realized that if I moved just a little I could see a reflection in the truck's side-view mirror. There they were. She leaned against the truck and a soldier stood in front of her. He had his hand, large and dark skinned, on her shoulder and I could see part of his weapon. It was a SAW. Sergeant Steele. He wanted to know what happened to his girlfriend. I wondered if I should reveal myself, but worried that my showing up would cause Mishka to keep quiet. I stayed right where I was, listening.

"Then I hear Mila is again with the Americans. And I think maybe she like it here more than home. Maybe she not come home no more. So I get job here too, to see if I can find our Mila."

She moved away from the truck and started pacing. Her footsteps crunched on the gravel. I glanced at my watch and knew Neil would be waiting for me in the mess tent. He would just have to wait.

"I get job and come here. I ask for girl named Mila and I am introduced to girl name Mila but she is not my sister, she is not my sister." She started crying again and Steele wrapped her up in his arms and comforted her. It couldn't have been too comfortable with that huge weapon between them.

"Who was she then, if it wasn't your sister," he asked.

She pushed herself away from Steele and started walking again. "She is that bitch," she said angrily. "That bitch that work for Civil Affairs. But I saw her ID card. It say Mila Dravic, just like my name, like my sister name, but she not my sister."

Steele watched her pace back and forth a bit then asked, "When you started working here, did they give you an ID card that had your name on it?"

Hmmm, good question I thought. I wondered that myself.

"No, not my name is other girl name. But they say is easier and is too much paperwork and I must wait for many months if I do not use other girl's name."

"Who told you this?" asked Steele.

"This Civil Affair Officer, this Major Townson. He hire all the girls. He say I use other girl name, I start right away. I no use other girl name, it will be long time to start. I need to find Mila

88

now I think, so I use other girl name."

Major Townson was under a lot of pressure to keep the interpreter pool stocked, but this sounded like something far beyond just personnel troubles. Civil Affairs units had the job of working with local community leaders and governments, deciding what building and civic projects we would take on. I'm not sure why they were in charge of interpreters. It appeared to be an additional duty. If Townson had set this system up as a way to rapidly get replacements, he had to know he would be caught eventually. When he left, after a year of deployment, someone else would take over for him and discover his illegal system. How did he think he'd get away with this?

"How many other girls are using different names," Steele asked. Another good question. After almost half a year on this camp, I had only a vague guess at how many interpreters there were working on the base, let alone any of their names.

"I don't know," Mishka said. "But I know five girl here, they not use own name. But there are many more, many more girl I think."

She moved so her back was to the truck, then slid down so that she sat out of site of the mirror. Steele put his hand on the truck and leaned down over her. I could see his face now. His dark skin glistened from the rain. He glanced around to see if anyone was watching and I was afraid he would somehow see me in the mirror, so I ducked down again. I must have moved too much because I made noise. I hoped only I could hear it but I heard Mishka gasp and stand up.

"Someone is here," she whispered.

Steele shushed her and the gravel shifted as he crept up to the door of the truck.

Damn, I thought. I couldn't be found here.

I quickly lay down on my back, my face turned into the seat, threw my arm over my head and hoped it covered my name and rank.

His light steps in the gravel stopped by the window. He paused there for a minute and I tried to picture what he would be seeing. I took long slow breaths in and out, to simulate a deep sleep. I wasn't the first person to take a daytime nap in an empty truck. To Steele, I hoped I would look completely harmless and unrecognizable.

After a short pause he returned to Mishka. He must have told her to keep quiet because all I heard after that were their steps leading away. I gave it a few seconds more to be sure they were out of the area and slowly sat up looking all around. They were gone. I gathered up all my gear and got out of there.

Twelve

By the time I got to the mess tent, the lunch service had nearly ended. No one stood in the chow line. I scanned the tables to see if I could find Neil.

We ate well on McGovern. The big Texan, Crofton Hawes, hired and managed the kitchen staff. He purchased most of the meat, produce and fruit locally so meals were fresh and flavorful with plenty of choices.

A handful of American supervisors ran the kitchen, but the people who did most of the real work were Bosnian locals. Soldiers protested when they learned that many of the workers in the kitchens earned a measly $1.75 an hour. Hawes had argued that while the pay seemed low to us, it was twice what they could earn outside the camp.

He was right. Many of the people pushing brooms and serving food, had advanced degrees, were former businessmen, scholars and government workers. The jobs on base were the only jobs around in the war-ravaged country, so people fought for them, no matter how menial.

I noticed Hawes standing in the back of the food service area talking to the young Bosnian who had been watching music videos the night before. Hawes towered over the young man, his face red and angry. The Bosnian, with his ever-present Chicago Cubs baseball cap and a toothpick stuck in the side of his mouth, stood relaxed, almost disdainful of anything Hawes said, even as Hawes poked a finger at him. Chicago glanced up at Hawes, shrugged his shoulders, gave him a triumphant smile and sauntered away.

Hawes sputtered powerlessly. Glaring at the young man's back, Hawes hitched up his pants and slammed out the backdoor of the kitchen.

I knew Hawes didn't speak Serbo-Croatian, so the Bosnian had to understand English. The night before, Chicago had used sign language to communicate with me. Maybe he tried to hide that he at least understood English. I wondered if the little guy with the magazine-model face had something on Hawes, something that would allow him to show utter distain for the Texan's anger.

I ruminated on that as I picked up a plastic tray, a plate, and silverware and moved down the chow line. Comfort food. After the morning I'd had, I craved comfort food. I grabbed a grilled cheese sandwich, a bowl of chicken noodle soup and poured myself an iced tea. Then I looked around for Neil.

When I spotted him, I froze. "Oh no," I mumbled to myself.

McCallen sat in the back of the room at a table with Ramsey and Santos. My last interview with the two investigators had been an unpleasant one and I had little desire to see either one of them again so soon. I stood there hesitating, wondering what they had been talking about, and wanting to back away, when Neil saw me. I shook my head no, but he raised his arm and waved me over. Ramsey and Santos both swiveled around to see who had drawn his attention. I felt trapped. I walked toward the table, the hair on my arms standing rigidly as I felt Ramsey's eyes follow me all the way to my seat.

When I reached the table, I glanced at McCallen, attempting to communicate my dread. Instead, the brief glance directly into his eyes felt like an electric jolt, bringing back the vivid memory of his lips on mine. He must have felt it too. A wash of emotion swept up his neck to his cheeks. I felt a searing heat in my face and a cold sweat broke out on my forehead. Too obviously, we both tried to look anywhere else but at each other. Our discomfort must have flashed across our faces like neon lights.

I moved to take a seat next to Neil on the bench and, as if he were afraid to touch me, he slid a couple of inches further away. I set my tray down and put one leg over the bench, then glanced at Ramsey.

A slow smile spread across his face. His frigid eyes flashed from me to Neil and back again, then to Santos. *Holy crap*, I thought, as I put my other leg over the bench and sat down. The investigator hadn't missed a single moment of our reactions. The cocky smile on his face told me he thought he had learned something valuable.

"Gentlemen," I said, trying to keep my voice steady.

They greeted me more or less in unison. An awkward silence followed. I filled it by taking my helmet off, shrugging out of my weapon and laying it all on the floor under the table. When I glanced up, Ramsey's icy gaze lanced through me. I had to look away and busied myself with crumbling crackers in my soup, taking a bite of my sandwich.

I hadn't had a chance to tell Neil how much trouble I faced with these two. I couldn't look at him, but he must have sensed my nervousness. I watched his hands under the table, as he prepared himself. He stretched the fingers of both hands out as far as they would go, then slowly clenched them into fists and repeated the motion a couple of times. Next he would take a deep breath in and let it out slowly. I had watched him perform the relaxation routine scores of times. He used it when he faced a difficult interview or confrontation. Sitting across from Ramsey and Santos, I needed McCallen to be centered. I needed his help.

"So," Ramsey began with an obvious pause, "how long have you two worked together?"

McCallen had finished eating, his tray pushed to the side, a half-eaten hamburger and a pile of fries sitting forgotten on the plate. He casually put one elbow on the table, appearing relaxed and conversational. Ramsey and Santos continued eating.

"About six years, isn't it Sergeant Harper?" Neil asked. I nodded and noticed from the corner of my eye that Neil's complexion had returned to normal. I wished I felt as calm as he looked. I could still feel the cold sweat drying on my forehead. I couldn't wipe it away, afraid my hands would shake.

Ramsey took a bite of his lunch. "Six years. That's a long time for an officer to stay in one place." A pause left room for McCallen to explain further, but he kept silent. That forced Ramsey to reveal that he already knew more than he pretended.

"Oh, but you haven't been in the same place that whole time, have you?" he challenged. His eyes turned on me, "Didn't you follow Colonel McCallen to Germany when he left Fort Hood?"

I made a show of chewing to give myself time to answer. I had followed Neil to Germany because I admired him as an officer, because he respected my ability to lead and because I had a huge crush on him, but I wasn't going to tell Ramsey any of that.

"As I'm sure you know, it's not unusual for a commander to hand-select his First Sergeant," Neil responded.

"It may not be unusual, but is it wise?" Ramsey asked, "I mean, the relationship between a commander and his first sergeant is a very, ah, intimate one, wouldn't you say, Colonel? Especially when the first sergeant is an attractive, single female."

Neil fidgeted with his shoulder holster, then hooked his thumb there, staring at Ramsey.

"And what century were you born in?" he asked incredulously. "Are you implying that men and women can't serve together without something inappropriate happening?"

Ramsey glared from me to Neil and back again. He put his silverware down and leaned toward Neil across the table. He almost hissed his response.

"I'm not implying anything, Colonel McCallen. I'm saying I think something inappropriate *is* going on between you two."

He wiped his mouth with a paper napkin and threw it on his plate, glaring at me.

"At first I thought she might have done it out of a fit of temper. She does have a temper, you know. And she's admitted, quite candidly, that the victim wasn't her favorite person." He was enjoying himself, making a joke of it and watching my reaction.

"But now, after seeing the two of you together, well, this is rich." His smiled widened. "Something is going on between you two," he said teasingly.

I glanced at Santos, the person who had believed in my innocence before, but he wouldn't look at me. Evidently, he'd had a change of heart.

"What if Delray knew about this relationship?" Ramsey went on. "What if she threatened to end your careers? That leaves a pretty darn good reason for you to kill her."

My heart stopped for a moment. Seconds ticked past before I remembered to breathe. Just as I opened my mouth to make a lame denial, Neil laughed. He shook his head, looked at Ramsey, laughing as if the accusation was the most ridiculous thing he'd ever heard.

"Okay, Mr. Ramsey," he said sarcastically. "Good luck proving that."

McCallen kept chuckling. I tried to smile, but it probably looked more like a grimace. Suddenly Neil stopped laughing and glared at Ramsey, deadly serious. "And I suggest you check your facts before you start making unfounded accusations. I'm a married man."

"Oh, I'll check my facts, Colonel. And I think I'll find what I'm looking for."

"And what if the answer is in something you aren't looking for, Chief? What if you miss finding the real killer while you're so busy trying to prove my NCO is a murderer?" This time, Neil's cheeks flushed in anger, the furious wide scar that slashed across his face, a harsh marker of his intensity.

I felt gratitude for his defense, but knew that Ramsey's suspicions would affect McCallen too. Even the hint of a scandal would put a permanent smudge on his career.

"Sometimes we think we know people, but we really don't have any idea what they are capable of," Ramsey said.

"I know what Master Sergeant Harper is capable of."

"I'll bet you do." He flashed that nasty smile again, as if he knew a dirty little secret.

"Our investigation is still in its infancy," Ramsey said. "We have a lot of evidence to process, like the murder weapon that belongs to your Sergeant here. There are some confusing bits we have to sort out, but I've assured General Paterson that we'll solve this one."

"And Harper is your only suspect?" Neil asked, a note of disbelief in his voice.

"I didn't say that," Ramsey directed a charming smile at me. His dimples and the gleam in his eye made him seem very likeable and not at all as dangerous as he proved to be. "Other suspects may be revealed in time."

"What about those pictures? Did you show them to the General?" I asked.

Ramsey shrugged as if they were nothing. "Not yet. But frankly, I don't see that the pictures have much relevance."

"Chief," I pressed. "They show that Captain Griffin had motivation to kill her. He's with two journalists who are missing. The woman who took a picture of him with the missing journalists is dead. What more do you want?"

"It is an avenue we will pursue."

"What if I told you that Delray promised to help one of the interpreters look for her missing sister?"

Ramsey and Santos exchanged a look. Santos took a small notebook and pen out of the pocket on his sleeve.

"What interpreter?" Santos asked.

"Abdic was the name on her uniform. I think Mishka is her first name. She said she worked for the engineers."

"And you say she and Delray had some kind of agreement?"

"Yes. Well, I'm not sure. All I know is that Delray told her she would help her. The interpreter said her sister had worked as an interpreter here too at one time, but then disappeared."

I glanced at Neil. He stared intently at Ramsey, his anger evident in the straight line of his lips.

"Thank you, Sergeant Harper," Ramsey said. "You see? We are pursuing other lines of investigation. We are. But here's the deal. I like you for this one. You had the means—the murder weapon and the strength to overwhelm her. You had the opportunity— you lived with her and we have witnesses who say they heard you threaten to kill her. Now quite clearly, you have the motive— a desire to protect your career and your secret, adulterous affair. The magic three," Ramsey shrugged again.

"You are insinuating that her motive is to protect a relationship with me!" Neil poked a finger into his own chest. He had come here to help. Now, whether the chargers were true or not, he faced the possibility of criminal charges. Adultery is a crime under the UCMJ. His career would be over not to mention a threat to his marriage. The whole thing was a mess. "You're barking up the wrong tree, Chief," Neil pressed. "You're wasting your time."

Santos cleared his throat noisily.

"The victim had quite a bit of flesh under her fingernails," Santos said. "We have hair and blood samples. The forensic evidence should be solid proof. Sergeant Major Jenkins has already left to deliver the evidence to the lab in Germany, but it could be a couple of weeks before we have complete results. I suggest we relax until then."

"We do have some results back," Ramsey said. "If the flesh under her fingers nails belongs to the killer, then the killer's blood type is O negative." His smile widened. "Isn't that your blood type, Sergeant Harper? Kind of a rare one too, isn't it?"

His smug grin made my skin crawl. Every soldier in the Army has fingerprints, blood type, dental x-rays, and DNA samples on file. I had hoped all of that information would prove me innocent. So far, that wasn't working out well for me.

Ramsey checked his watch. "You think you know someone, whether or not they're trustworthy. I've been doing this job long enough to know that looks can be deceiving. The right person, properly motivated, can do things you'd never imagine. I'll trust in the evidence."

"For a man who trusts the evidence, you're sure leaning heavily on innuendo," Neil said sarcastically. "Just how do you plan on finding proof of an affair that isn't happening?"

Ramsey picked up his tray to leave, ignoring the question.

"We'll obviously need to have you in for questioning sometime today, Colonel McCallen. We'll send an MP to find you. But for now, it would seem you two have much to talk about." Ramsey left, Santos following silently behind him.

Neil watched them walk to the front of the mess tent, his eyes narrowed and intense.

When they walked out, he looked down at the table and his shoulders slumped. "Holy shit," he mumbled. He looked up at me shaking his head. "Holy shit, Lauren." He put his elbows on the table, brought his hands up in front of his face, folded as if in prayer, closed his eyes and leaned his forehead there. "Holy shit."

I wanted to put my hand on his shoulder, to comfort him, but I knew we would never touch each other again.

"I'm so sorry, sir. When I saw you sitting with them, I didn't know what to do. I haven't had a chance to tell you what's been going on."

He took a deep breath and let it out slowly. "Well, I guess you'd better start."

He slid a little further away from me on the bench, turned so he faced me and settled in to listen. As bad as the impromptu interview with Ramsey had gone, what I had to tell McCallen was much worse.

Thirteen

I told Neil about finding Delray and how she'd looked, the bloated face, the bulging eyes and her blue lips. I unburdened myself, exposing my shock and fear.

"That smell. I will never forget that smell," I said, shuddering. "The poor kid."

Sitting there telling him what happened reminded me of one of the reasons I admired him so much. I had watched him listen to people for years. He listened intently, absorbing every word, his skill in listening allowed a person to share more than they'd intended.

I spewed out everything. As I talked, the remaining lunch crowd cleared out and most of the tables sat empty. We couldn't go to the TOC, with all the watchful eyes. We definitely couldn't go back to Disneyland. I couldn't trust myself to be alone with him there again. So, we just stayed where we were. I did most of the talking.

I told him about that first confrontation with Mishka and the other interpreters in the shower trailer.

"She seemed petrified," I said.

"Petrified of what?"

"Whatever it is, I know it has something to do with what happened to Delray."

"Based on what?"

"Her fear. It reminded me of the look of terror on Delray's face. What or who was Mishka frightened of?"

I told him about finding the photo memory card and that Ramsey had allowed me to see the pictures of the BBC team with the general's aide entering what we assumed was a brothel.

"A whorehouse? The general's aide was in a whorehouse," he said.

"The Weeping Rose."

"It makes sense. Hannerty and Tooley were investigating a story. Something about claims that, since the NATO forces arrived here, prostitution in the region has increased. They allege that the tens of thousands of soldiers brought here are making prostitution a growing industry, but what the hell would that have to do with the general's aide?"

"They were investigating brothels? It doesn't make sense."

In that brief pause in the conversation, we naturally looked at each other. The moment our eyes locked, I felt that physical charge run through me again. I tried to shake it off, but I'd lost my place. I couldn't turn away. We sat for a minute, staring at each other, his green eyes searching my face.

"I'm sorry about what happened in my quarters," he said, shaking his head. "I never expected anything like this to happen. I mean, I never..."

He stopped and looked down, taking a deep breath. "That's a lie. I've always, well, for a long time anyway, I've..."

"It's okay, sir. You don't have to explain."

"Do you remember the first exercise we ever went on together? That trip to Thailand?" he asked.

I smiled. It had been hot as Hades, a straight month without a day off, long hours that left us exhausted but one of the most memorable and enjoyable missions I'd ever been on. Most of that enjoyment had come from working with the new public affairs Major with the red hair and the unforgettable scar on his face.

"Ramsey was right, about the intimacy thing," he said, unable to look at me. "I actually spend more time with you then I do with Michelle. Even when we're not deployed, the hours... But, that's no excuse for what happened."

As far as I could tell, Michelle was a good person, a loving mother. A typical officer's wife with her blonde salon hairdo, slender frame, perfect manicure and Anne Taylor wardrobe. I had never heard him utter a complaint about her. She seemed the complete opposite of me. I couldn't imagine her in uniform, firing a weapon or wearing combat boots.

"I need some ice cream. Want some?" I asked him, getting up.

"Vanilla," he said.

I took my time going to the cooler. I searched through the boxes and found a vanilla and a strawberry single serving. I walked back to the table and this time took a seat opposite him. By this time we were the only ones in the dining tent, save for the workers who were restocking refrigerators and generally cleaning up.

We busied ourselves pulling off the covers to find little wooden spoons. We sat like that for a while, eating our ice cream, thinking about things. When I glanced up, he sat staring at me. I wondered how long he'd been doing that. He cleared his throat.

"Was that everything?"

I shook my head no and continued. I told him about the General and the bruise on my collarbone and about watching the General do the same thing to Captain Griffin.

"Wow. And Griffin tried to pretend nothing happened?"

"I wasn't surprised by that. Would you want to admit that your boss was abusing you, physically abusing you?" I shuddered. "Griffin must be going through hell."

"I don't know. I just spent the morning with the two of them. He seems like the typical General's aide... exhausted, stressed, and nervous all the time," he shook his head. "The only people who want to be a General's aide are people who want to be a General."

I realized that's exactly what Captain Griffin would want, to be a General someday. The selection to serve as an aide alone would be a significant item in Griffin's career file. The relationship between an aide and the general officer, more like a marriage, is one of mutual benefit. The aide works endless hours for the general and in turn, learns what being at that level of leadership means. It's also a relationship of extreme loyalty. If Paterson habitually abused his aide, Griffin would never report it.

"That kind of ambition," I said and shrugged, "might make someone do extraordinary things, maybe illegal things." I let the sentence hang.

Neil looked doubtful. "That's a big leap. You saw Griffin in a picture. They could have been meeting with community leaders or something, and invited the BBC to join them."

"Why would they meet with the BBC without telling me?" It was my job to arrange such things, to find out what the news agencies wanted, to anticipate what their line of questioning might be.

"Why would they arrange to meet with the press without telling me and why would they meet with the press in a whorehouse?"

"You keep saying 'they'. The only person you saw in the picture was Griffin, right? Maybe he went alone. Without Paterson"

"Okay, let's say he was alone. The same questions apply. If it was an official meeting, why would he meet them in a whorehouse and why wouldn't he have talked to me about it before hand?"

"Maybe he didn't want anyone to know he was meeting them....not even the general."

I thought about that for a second, finishing my ice cream. "There's really only one reason to meet with the press in secret and that's to feed them something as an anonymous source."

Neil nodded his head. "So he meets up with them at a brothel to tell them what? That prostitutes are working there? That soldiers are using the services of the local ladies? What?"

"I don't know, but I think it's a question that needs to be asked, don't you, Sir?" I was trying to find some way to alter the direction of the investigation. My efforts felt pointless.

"Obviously Ramsey is still concentrating on you. I figured he would find out about the threat you made against Delray," McCallen said. "Still, that's a pretty weak thing to hang an investigation on. Hell, *I* wanted to kill her after that piece of work. Besides, the DNA evidence will clear you."

"I kept telling myself that too, but we lived together. She borrowed my stuff all the time. My nail polish, my lotion. She even used my hairbrush sometimes when I wasn't looking. Said she liked it better than her own. My DNA, my fingerprints, it's not hard to imagine that if they're looking for trace evidence, they will find it all over the place."

"But Ramsey's idea of a motive, there's no evidence of that." Then Neil looked at me and raised an eyebrow. "Is there?"

I felt my face burn. I couldn't look at him. I buried my face in my hands.

"Lauren?" Neil asked, sounding worried

I couldn't look at him but I had to tell him.

"I keep a journal, sir."

How could I tell McCallen the things I had written in my journal? Ramsey would find it and browse my innermost thoughts. He would soon find evidence that I, at least, had indulged in impossible fantasies about my commander. Knowing Ramsey would be reading those thoughts made my skin crawl.

It took McCallen a second to realize what the journal meant. The full ramifications came slowly, but eventually, what my written words could mean to him and even to his family, set in.

"Oh, Lauren."

"I'm sorry. It's habit. I've kept a journal since I was ten."

"Lauren, what were you thinking? What did you write about?"

I met his eyes, and saw the fear there. His career, his family, everything at stake. I feared to tell him, but I had to. I owed him that.

"I sure wasn't thinking it would be used against me in a murder investigation!" I stopped and took a deep breath. "But I wrote quite a lot, sir, I've written quite a lot about how I feel about you. I've been writing about it for some time. What else could I do with those feelings?"

The look of shock on his face sparked my temper.

"I wrote, for example, Sir, about asking you for a transfer," I said, heatedly. "You turned it down."

At the time, I knew his reasons weren't about executing the mission. He turned down the request because he wanted me to stay with him.

The flush that washed up his face again confirmed that I had been right. He opened his mouth to speak, to deny the feelings maybe. His shoulders slumped and his eyes softened.

"Nothing, nothing would have ever come of this," he whispered.

"Don't you think I know that? I've always known that. That's why I tried to go, but you wouldn't let me!"

"Did you speculate in your journal about how you thought I felt? What do I say to them when they question me?"

"The truth! You can call it admiration. Call it whatever you want. We never acted on it and we never would."

From behind me, I heard someone say, "Would never do what?"

Neil's eyes shot over my shoulder, but I didn't need to turn around to see who had asked the question. I recognized that unmistakable accent. It was Chaplain Hirsch and I wondered just how much of our conversation he had heard.

Fourteen

Most people would have felt embarrassed to insert themselves into a clearly private and intense conversation, but the Chaplain was not most people. He bustled up to the table as if invited.

"I'm sorry to be interrupting, but am I ever glad to see the two of you," he said excitedly as he sat down next to me and across from Neil. "You are Colonel McCallen, aren't you? I've been so busy with everything I haven't had a chance to come and find you."

His mouth kept going, while he picked up a napkin and put it in his lap, fiddled with his silverware and plates. His ceaseless talking gave Neil and me a chance to catch our breath and re-group. We sat up straight, realizing how far over the table we'd been leaning, both of us exhaling loudly. The tremor in my hand surprised me. I tried to relax and look as natural as possible, and probably failed.

"Again, I know I'm interrupting, and I am sorry about that, but we really need to discuss the memorial service. I spoke with the investigators and they say they will release her body tomorrow. She should be on her way to her family very soon and I wanted to be sure that you were aware of that. I've been so busy, I've barely been able to leave my trailer," he continued.

"It's alright, Chaplain Hirsh. I should have brought the Colonel over to meet you earlier."

The chaplain reached out his hand, rising from his seat. They shook hands, Neil looking Hirsch in the eye.

Even though Hirsch hadn't said anything about what he must have heard as he arrived, I got the impression the chaplain knew everything, as if our actions were imprinted on our foreheads like a scarlet letter.

"It's a pleasure to meet you, even under such difficult circumstances."

The chaplain crushed crackers into his soup and began to eat noisily. Neil and I exchanged glances while Hirsch looked down.

"Have you invited anyone to give a eulogy for the memorial service?" Hirsch asked me.

"To be honest, no I haven't. I assumed Colonel McCallen would say a few words."

"Of course," McCallen replied.

Hirsch inhaled his food, barely allowing time to chew and swallow. I never realized that a chaplain could have a busy, stressful schedule, but Hirsch obviously had things to do and the need for food wasn't going to get in the way.

"I took the liberty of asking Sergeant Steele if he wanted to say something," Hirsh went on. "But he said he would prefer to sing. They used to sing together, you see. I think that's how they became involved."

At the mention of Steele, I realized I hadn't told Neil about him. Considering the way he questioned Mishka, he might have some useful information. I also had to put talking to Major Townson on my list of things to do. What was he doing with the interpreter pool and how long did he think he would get away with the name changing game? Steele must have thought it had something to do with Delray's death, or he wouldn't have been questioning Mishka.

Hirsch prattled on about memorial service plans. Then he stopped and sat looking at me.

"I realize you two are under a lot of stress; this murder, the investigation, all the questions…it's all so very upsetting. Not to mention you still have a mission to carry out here." He raised his bushy eyebrows and suddenly became very still, as his intense eyes went from one of us to the other. "You should be supporting each other, but you've got to remember that emotions have a way of becoming skewed, confusing at times like this. Don't let this tragedy and the upheaval it causes be an excuse to do things you otherwise wouldn't do. Do you understand?"

My suspicions were correct. He could see everything.

"Most importantly, don't let the stress harm the friendship you have, not to mention your professional relationship." The chaplain looked back and forth at us through squinted eyes that were wet and red rimmed.

Part of me wanted to accept his explanation that stress and the unusual circumstances were what drove us to that kiss. In honesty, I knew it wasn't the truth. We kissed because we'd been playing a long drawn out game of flirtation. My attraction to McCallen fed his ego. His desire for me fed my own. The impossibility of it excited us, and if I were brutally honest about it, the game had gone on for so long some kind of physical manifestation seemed inevitable. I'd fantasized about it too often.

Granted, if I had known that one kiss would have given Ramsey a motive to pin on me, I never would have done it. But still, I couldn't honestly say I was sorry, only grateful that I had stopped it and we hadn't gone any further.

I glanced at Neil, who stared at the table. His cheek jumped from his clenched teeth.

"Well, I will leave you two now," Hirsch said, collecting his tray and standing up.

"Master Sergeant Harper, my door is always open to you. And to you of course Colonel," he added.

"Thanks Chaplain," Neil said. "It was good to meet you."

"If you need any help writing your eulogies for Sunday, let me know. I can help with this sort of thing as well." I watched Hirsch walk toward the front of the mess tent with his tray, and then saw the MP step in the door, his eyes scanning the tent. When his gaze landed on us, I sucked in a breath. He walked toward us. "Colonel McCallen, sir?"

I looked at Neil and saw his forehead drawn into a frown as he glared at the young soldier.

"I'll be right with you." His tone of voice halted the soldier who hesitated a moment then turned his back on us discreetly as he waited.

Neil turned to meet my gaze. "Holy Christ," he whispered.

"Sir, I am so sorry."

With a heavy sigh, Neil stuck his helmet under his arm, picked up his tray and stood from the table, resigned.

"Don't apologize for this, Harper," he said in a quiet voice. "You're right. I could have signed those transfer orders. I chose not to. I couldn't let you go." He stepped over the bench and shot a look at the MP.

"You should make a stop in the TOC to see if there are any queries we need to handle. The Vice President gets here in a few days."

"Roger, sir," I said.

He stood there for a long moment looking down at me, his eyes softly scanning my face, the affection there making my heart ache. In an instant, the look disappeared. He turned his attention to the MP's back, steeled himself for the interview, and marched off.

"Let's go," he ordered as he passed the MP, who obediently followed behind.

I slung my weapon over my back, grabbed up my helmet and tray, and followed them. One of the Bosnian workers was standing there watching the whole scene. He wore a white paper cook's cap on his head, a clean white coat, and a red and white bandanna tied like an ascot around his neck. Thick rubber kitchen gloves covered his hands that held the handle of a mop propped against his shoulder. The man stood frozen, openly staring as if in the front row seat of a drama.

McCallen dumped his trash and stuck his tray in the kitchen window, then put his helmet on, slipping the chinstrap into place. He glanced at me over his shoulder, his green eyes hooded by the helmet. Then he turned and walked out, the MP following behind. The screen door of the tent slapped shut and their boot steps marked their progress away.

That room, the questions. I knew exactly what McCallen faced and it made me feel sluggish with worry. I finally shook myself into action and moved to dump my trash, but the Bosnian leaned his mop against the tent wall, hurried over, held his gloved hands out for my tray, and smiled at me.

"*Biti voljan,*" he said.

You don't always need to understand the words to understand the sentiment. It seemed obvious that he knew I wasn't feeling at my best. He had salt and pepper hair, a well-trimmed thin beard and mustache, his stature slight and short, his eyes clear and knowing. He looked to be around mid-fifties, but judging age was difficult, since the war added years to people's faces. Most locals appeared far older than they were. I wondered what horrors this man had seen.

I handed him the tray, wishing I could talk to him. "Do you speak English?"

He hesitated for a second, as if he didn't want to admit that he understood. Something made up his mind and he exaggeratedly nodded his head, almost in a long slow bow, a smile slowly spreading across his face. His teeth looked starkly white behind the dark mustache and beard. "Yes" he said. "But please, I was not trying to listening in." He took my tray and turned to add my dirty dishes to McCallen's.

"My English is, um, rusty. Not since I teach at university."

"What did you teach?"

He turned back to me but his eyelids drooped sadly, his mouth a small frown. He shrugged in an exaggerated way. "Mathematics," he said, laughing. "But, here I teach disinfecting and how to clean floors." He shook his finger at me in a playful way, "I am very precise floor cleaner."

I laughed with him and he patted my arm, happy that he had turned my serious face into a smiling one. I glanced over his shoulder and saw Chicago and another young man in a white paper cap. They stood close to each other, their shoulders overlapping, their heads touching, whispering.

"These are two of my students," the man said with pride.

"They have no papers to prove they are almost graduating. Everything in here is," and he spread the fingers of both hands in front of his face like a small explosion, "is gone. Is no more papers. So we come here and we work, we earn money." Again, the exaggerated shrug.

The young men whispered to each other, their gazes not missing a thing. The one in the paper cap gave me a small smile, laughing at my lack of understanding. Chicago narrowed his eyes at me, his mouth quirked up in a cocky grin. After seeing him with Hawes, I had no doubt he could understand the conversation, and I speculated that he probably heard many things hanging out in the mess tent. Things people wouldn't realize he understood. I felt uncomfortable under Chicago's gaze.

"What is your name?" I asked the older man.

"Bojan, Bojan Cosic. Once upon a time, I was Dr. Cosic," and he smiled. "And you are Master Sergeant Harper."

"Exactly," I said, holding out my hand for a shake, but he held his hands up, covered in thick rubber gloves.

"Well, anyway. It was nice to meet you, Dr. Cosic."

"You have a nice day, Sergeant Harper." He promptly turned to pick up his mop and went back to work on the floors.

I left thinking about a professor with no options but mopping floors. For a moment, it felt as if my personal drama with McCallen didn't compare to what had happened to so many other lives in this country.

Fifteen

The heart of base operations, the TOC, usually beat with a rapid rhythm, but for late afternoon, an unusual quiet settled over the large room. Most of the people working had probably been at it since zero six hundred. After more than seven hours at work already, most were in need of rest, but they wouldn't get it. A typical day meant fourteen to sixteen hours, many of them filled with tension and high-octane demands. Even when off shift, the stress never abated since any emergency could disturb a brief respite in an instant. On McGovern Base, no one completely relaxed on or off duty.

Commanders and visiting officials insisted we should take days off to relax and unwind. It never happened that way. In the months since my arrival, there had been only two days that I hadn't worked, but I didn't consider a debilitating case of the stomach flu relaxing.

I went to my desk where Delray's hand-written sign in big block letters read, PAO. She'd used a bit of an artistic flare making the letters look almost Cyrillic to match our location. I stared at the sign for a long moment, thinking about her creative side, the way she often doodled, making tiny sketches in the margins of most of her notebooks. Such a waste.

I dropped my helmet on the desk and shrugged out of my weapon, picking up a stack of pink message slips. The press release McCallen issued about Delray had generated a flurry of phone calls with questions, most of them asking for details about identity and the circumstances of her death.

The headquarters in Tuzla would decide when to release the details, but it wouldn't be long before the media horde would start speculating. If you didn't keep feeding the beast, eventually it would bite you. Undertones of cover up and conspiracy would loom and things that could have been resolved with a simple answer, no matter how unpleasant, could turn into a monster of a controversy. Feeding the beast usually helped to keep the monster tame.

Once the press had her personal information, they would be after Delray's family, wanting reaction, asking about Virginia's history and picking at the fresh and painful wound. I hoped her family would get another day of peace to grieve before that happened.

I returned some of the phone calls. Yes, the death was under investigation. Yes, CID was gathering evidence. No, I couldn't give out the soldier's personal information. The answers I gave only sparked more questions, but I had to give them something. Soldiers on the street would talk, rumors would fly; the media tended to find out these things. They were hungry for a snack at least.

I called *The Associated Press*, *The Times* and *The Washington Post*, a *CNN* intern who sounded like she was fifteen, and a *Fox News* editor who poked and prodded me for more information.

"I'm going to call your bosses in Tuzla. We have a right to know," he barked.

"You're welcome to do that, sir, but as I told you, it is Army policy to withhold the name of fallen soldiers until twenty-four hours after the family has been notified."

"How are we supposed to know when the twenty-four hours is up?"

"Tuzla will issue a follow-up release with the details," I said.

He grumbled his displeasure again and hung up unsatisfied. I took a long deep breath, leaned my elbows on the desk and put my face in my hands. They were talking about my soldier. My roommate. And if Ramsey had his way, a press release would go out that had my name on it. I could almost draft the damn thing myself.

McGOVERN BASE, BOSNIA-HERZEGOVENIA - Murder charges have been filed against a soldier accused of killing a fellow coalition peacekeeper. The accused, thirty-seven-year-old Master Sergeant Lauren Harper, of Minneapolis, Minnesota, is a public affairs specialist stationed at McGovern Base. Harper is charged with ...

The vision so clear, I could almost feel the paper cut it would give me. The worry and tension made me feel weary. So much could go wrong. Disaster so near I could feel it hulking over me like a physical presence. Charges against me, suspicion of my relationship with McCallen, my career, McCallen's marriage.

With my face still buried in my hands, I groaned with the weight of my fears.

Then someone noisily cleared his throat.

I looked up at a very large man standing in front of my desk.

"Can I help you?" I asked weakly. I had to lean back in order to look up into his face.

His lips stretched into a smile that failed to meet his eyes as he stared down at me. In a thick British accent, he said, "I'm not sure, luv. Can you?"

His hair stood at attention, cropped in a dark crew cut, with a perfect widow's peak. His nose, wide and bent, had been broken sometime in the past. His full lips, cocked in a smirk, along with the dimple in his chin gave him a devilish appearance. Add his size and the intense look on his face, if I'd met him in a dark alley, I would have turned and walked quickly in the other direction.

He crossed his arms around his massive chest. A large signet ring decorated one finger. He wore his green camouflaged uniform shirt tucked tightly into his crisply ironed pants. Altogether, he was a powerful looking man, and an unhappy one.

I'd been to England several times before, but I figured this guy was from a place most tourists never visited.

"I guess that would depend on what it is you need," I said.

He flashed straight, gleaming white teeth at me in a crooked smile, revealing a broken front tooth half the length of the other. It added to his overall charm. From the stripes on his sleeves, he was a senior non-commissioned officer.

"What is it I need?" he asked, moving around the desk. "Well, for starters, I could use some answers."

He leaned down, putting one hand on the desk and one on the back of my chair and lowered his smirking face to look me in the eye.

"You see, I've been here in this bloody building all bloody day, asking the same questions I've been asking for three days and waiting for someone from the American Army, the one what is called the greatest Army on earth, to tell me what the bloody hell happened to the two British journalists, what was last seen in your care."

I realized then where I had seen him before. He'd been in a shouting match with someone about the missing reporters. Three days ago, I wouldn't have been able to help him. Today, I knew about Delray's pictures. I smiled back at him and stood up. It forced him to take a step back, but he didn't go far. I craned my head back to look up at him. He obviously meant to intimidate me. Instead he'd only sparked my interest. He cocked an eyebrow and grinned wider. We stared each other down, smiling. The crow's feet around his green eyes were prominent, giving away his mirth.

"I'm sorry you haven't had satisfactory answers to your questions, Sergeant Major." I could have read the name on his uniform, but I didn't want to look away.

"The name is Fogg, mum," he said quietly. "Spelled the British way with two Gs it is; Sergeant Major Harold Fogg, at your service. My friends call me Harry, but since you and I have not yet established whether or not we will be friends, you had better just stick to Sergeant Fogg, if it's not too much of a bother."

I chuckled, enjoying the glint in his eye, and decided I would like to be one of his friends. Stepping back, I stuck out my hand.

"Master Sergeant Lauren Harper," I said. "You could keep calling me luv, if you like … it's kind of a novelty. But it probably wouldn't go over too well."

"Ah. More's the pity," he said.

My hand disappeared in his meaty paw, the shake gentler than I expected. After a long beat, I released his hand and I leaned on the side of my desk, crossing my arms.

I glanced around him and noticed two more British soldiers hidden by Fogg's bulky form. They were younger enlisteds, one with English pale skin, white hair to match and round wire-rimmed glasses. The other soldier, dark haired and pudgy, with a face that hadn't recovered well from teenage acne. They stood back grinning, watching the show.

"The sprogs over there are having a bit of fun, but let me make myself very clear, Master Sergeant Harper, this is not a laughing matter."

Fogg shot a warning look at the two soldiers, who quickly stopped laughing and stood to attention, snapping their left knee up waist high then down and shouting, "Sir!" as their feet hit the ground.

Sergeant Major Fogg nodded his head in satisfaction and turned back to me. He swung his large arms behind himself and clasped his hands there. He puffed out his chest and began to rock back and forth from his heels to his toes.

"As I was saying, I have been given the task of assisting the Americans in locating these missing journalists from the BBC, said network by the by, has been constantly updating British citizens of their disappearance in every broadcast, on every hour, of every day, since they bloody disappeared."

His voice rang forceful and serious. Others working in the TOC found excuses to leave the area. Fogg wasn't smiling anymore, but the light danced in his eyes when he looked at me. I got the impression the joke, if there was one, was just between us and I liked that. At first glance, he seemed like a big scary guy in both size and voice. When he trained those green eyes on me, I found his gruff barking utterly appealing.

M. L. Doyle

"And since you are the soldier on this camp who has the responsibility for the care and keeping of reporters in this area," he went on, "it is to you, your colleagues have finally directed me. Therefore, I am here to inform you that Her Majesty's Army is now here to assist you, in any way that you require." He paused for a moment, stepped closer and narrowed his eyes at me, trying to look wicked. "Have I made myself clear?"

"Oh, perfectly clear, Sergeant Major Fogg," I said, grinning back.

"Good," he said, still standing closer than was proper, his intense gaze roaming my face. The way he stared at me combined with his proximity, affected me to the core, as if our atoms were shifting and aligning, creating the gentle pull of a magnet about to grab hold. After a lingering look, he stepped back again and the tug of attraction diminished. He cocked his head to the side, "This could be interesting."

"That's putting it mildly," I said, more to myself than to Fogg and wondered where the hell he had come from. It didn't matter. I needed something to take my mind off how awful most of my day had been. Sergeant Major Fogg presented a rather large and intriguing distraction.

He shook his head as if to clear his thoughts. "I suggest, Master Sergeant Harper, that we begin with you telling me everything you know about the last where 'bouts of Ian Tooley and Franklyn Hannerty."

"Of course, Sergeant Major Fogg," I said. "I do have a bit of information you might be interested in."

He raised his long bushy eyebrow.

"But first, would you like a cup of tea?"

His mouth dropped open in surprise. He snapped his arm in front of his face, checking his watch, and must have realized it was teatime. He relaxed.

"I would love a brew, now that you mention it, but not any of that Lipton rot," he said. "If the Boston tea party was called to throw that rot overboard then the British should have just let them have their bash and job done." Fogg grabbed a folding chair from another desk and plopped it down near mine. He lowered his hulk into it, and I worried for a moment that the flimsy metal would fail to support him. Fogg draped one leg over the other and crossed his wrists over his knee to wait.

I opened a lower drawer of my desk and took out my electric water pot. I busied myself pouring bottled water into the pot and plugging it in to warm. I pulled out several selections of teas and watched Fogg's reaction as he realized I wasn't messing around.

Teatime isn't just a British custom. Over the years, I've learned that offering tea to journalists from around the world, be they British, Indian, Asian, African or Arabic, relaxed people and changed their regard of you from that of an uncouth American. I kept good loose leaf and bagged tea and an assortment of cookies or biscuits as the British call them, on hand just for that purpose. I pulled out a small pile of napkins, a large tin of Scottish short bread, powdered cream, a box of sugar cubes and several good large tea mugs—teacups were for old ladies—and watched their magic work on Sergeant Fogg.

I offered him the tin of short bread.

"Lovely," he said, picking up a napkin and taking three cookies, laying them one by one, neatly in the massive palm of his hand.

"What kind of tea would you like?" I asked him.

"I like my Earl Grey NATO, Sergeant."

"NATO?"

"Ah, sorry. Normal Army Tea Order. Means white with two sugars. If you don't mind."

I'd never heard the expression before but there seemed to be a lot that came out of Fogg's mouth that I hadn't heard before. His unpredictable speech combined with his accent captured my attention so completely, I found myself smiling and feeling lighter than I had since before I found Delray.

I opened two Earl Grey tea bags and dropped them into our mugs. The water hadn't boiled yet, so I took a couple of napkins, the mugs and the tin of cookies to a nearby desk and put them there, indicating the two young soldiers should help themselves.

They both looked at Fogg for permission. He gave them a curt nod and they elbowed each other with smiles, moving to take up chairs there.

By this time, the water bubbled rapidly and the pot light clicked off indicating its readiness. I poured the boiled water into our mugs and brought the hotpot and tea tin over to the soldiers.

Sergeant Major Fogg dumped a scoop of powered cream and two heaping spoonful's of sugar into his mug then dragged the plastic spoon around and around while watching me. I sat down opposite him and as we waited for the tea to steep, we looked at each other. His frank gaze felt comfortable, curious and safe, as if I'd known him for years. We simply stared at each other, considering the possibilities. I found myself, not only willing, but anxious to tell him everything.

"You've seen the press release, about the dead soldier?" I asked, indicating the release on my desk.

"Of course," he said, a question in his voice wondering what the dead soldier had to do with the BBC reporters.

"She was my soldier. And my roommate."

"Ruddy hell," he said. "That's bleeding awful, pardon my French. I am very sorry for your loss, sergeant. How did she die?"

"She was strangled. Murdered."

His hand froze mid-stir, but he didn't ask the question on his lips. He studied me for a minute, the wheels turning in his big head. "Are you saying her death had something to do with the disappearance of those reporters?"

"She was a print and photo journalist. She was out on a story with an engineer crew assigned to rebuild a road in downtown Brcko. Later that evening we received the first report that the two journalists hadn't reported into their station. That same evening, she asked me if she could go out with the engineers again. She said there was more she wanted to do on the story. I agreed. Delray often needed more than one day to get a story done."

I could have elaborated, talked about her failings, her inability to capture all of the information she needed to get a story done, but I couldn't. Just thinking about her lack of training made me want to cringe and hide in shame. Fogg waited patiently. My shame in front the senior NCO felt worse, in that I knew by looking at him, he would go to any length to ensure the soldiers under his charge would never fail.

"You alright?" he asked, a look of concern on his face.

I nodded, cleared my throat and forged on. "The following day, yesterday, I left early in the morning to go out on a story with an EOD team. She was supposed to go out with the engineers as planned, but when I came back that afternoon, I found her dead in our trailer. At some point, she managed to slip her computer card where she knew I would find it. The only pictures on the card that seemed to have any significance were pictures of Ian Tooley and Franklyn Hannerty going into ... a building in Brcko. The place is reportedly a whorehouse called the Weeping Rose."

Sergeant Fogg sat silently staring at me as he listened to every word. The other two soldiers leaned in and listened, their mouths hanging open in concentration. Fogg took a long slow drink of his tea, set it down and uncrossed his legs.

"Right. So we've got a bloody mystery to solve, haven't we," he said. "The Weeping Rose is not unfamiliar to me."

He turned slowly and shot a look at the soldiers. As soon as his eyes were on them, they straightened up again and tried to appear as if they hadn't been listening.

"It's also familiar to this lot. Isn't it boys?" He poked his head in their direction. "These two can tell us a little bit about the bloody Weeping Rose, can't they? As the Regimental Sergeant Major, it is up to me to ensure good order and discipline amongst the ranks. The sprogs...or excuse me, the privates here, are in the shit for going into that dodgy place, and now, they are tied to me like children to my bloody apron strings."

"But I thought the British were allowed to, ah, mix with the locals," I said.

Fogg was shaking his head. "This is another misconception you Americans have about we British. Unlike the American soldiers, we are permitted to go to dinner, to shop and to socialize with the locals. But paid shagging is illegal in England and it is illegal here," he said, turning to his soldiers again. "And we do not engage in illegal activity, do we boys?"

"No, Sergeant," they responded.

"But they've been in there? In the Weeping Rose?" I asked hopefully, looking at the two. They seemed embarrassed at the attention and kept their eyes on their boots, the acne-scared soldier blushing brightly. Fogg stared at them, eyebrow raised.

They looked at each other, silently negotiating which one of them would talk. In a timid voice that cracked, the pale one answered, "Yes, mum. We've been in there."

Fogg turned around and looked at me, an eyebrow raised. "Well, there you are then."

He stood up and motioned for the two to come closer. "All right you lot. Come over here and tell us what you know."

General Order (GO) One lives on, and troops supporting Operation Joint Guard must follow the restrictions. These restrictions help maintain the security, health and welfare of U.S. forces. They prevent conduct prejudicial to good order and discipline, or of a nature to bring discredit upon the U.S. forces. They also improve relations with local nationals and friendly forces.

Printed in *Info Briefs*, Talon magazine, June 20, 1997

Sixteen

The soldiers brought their chairs closer to my desk. I scanned the room, wishing we could go somewhere more private. A few people worked nearby, some looked bored sitting behind computers, and others talked on phones. The presence of the large British NCO and his soldiers drew attention. People around the room glanced at us surreptitiously, curious.

In a far corner of the room, Major Townson stood up and stared at me, eyes narrowed, lips pressed together. What I'd heard about his manipulation of the interpreters changed his appearance from one of just curiosity, to something more sinister. Falsifying ID cards is a serious violation of operational security, not to mention illegal. Would he murder to protect his activities? And why do it anyway? It couldn't be that hard to find qualified interpreters. There had to be something about his scheme that brought him benefits. It didn't make sense.

"Sergeant Fogg," I leaned in whispering. "Let's not forget that someone was murdered and it might have been because she knew something that made her a target. It might not have anything to do with the Weeping Rose..." I shrugged letting the sentence hang.

"You're saying a bit of discretion would be a right smart thing to consider and I agree. You lot," and he turned to his young soldiers, "will not repeat this conversation to anyone. Have I made myself clear?"

They both nodded their heads, their eyes big as saucers.

"And you will discretely tell us everything you know beginning now and no blaggin' about. Give it to us straight."

"Well, Sergeant Major," the pale one said. "I'm not sure what you want to know."

"Why don't you start by telling me your names," I said, trying to quiet their discomfort. My job as a journalist put me in the position of questioning people almost every day. Most started by thinking they didn't have anything of interest to tell you, until you probed, asked the right questions, managed to get them to reveal the thing they didn't realize would be of interest to anyone else.

"I'm Terry," and he shot a look at his Sergeant, then nervously cleared his throat, his pimply cheeks bright pink from embarrassment. "I'm Private Terry Oxley, mum," and he elbowed his friend.

"Private Jonathan Stewart, mum. They call me Johnny."

Private Stewart had a thick Scottish accent and charming dimples he flashed at me with a wide smile. I suspected it was the charming blond, mischievous Stewart who egged nervous and timid Oxley into trouble.

"Alright Private Oxley, tell me about this place. How did you first hear about it?"

"We heard about it....ah, around like. People said...well, that the girls mostly spoke English and it was clean and where everybody went."

Fogg raised an eyebrow at that and I was glad when he kept silent.

"What's the place like?" I asked.

Private Stewart leaned closer. "Well, when you walk in the first door, there's another door, one with a little window in it like. You knock on this little window and someone opens it and looks out at you. This bloke, he doesn't say anything to us, he just sort of looks at us like. Then he closes the little window and we wait a few seconds there, not really knowing what to do."

Stewart pointed his thumb at Oxley. "This one, he wanted to leg it, he was that scared."

"And leave you both should have, shouldn't ya?" piped in

Fogg.

I shot Fogg a look. They were just starting to open up and I didn't want him making them so nervous that they clammed up again. Fogg realized what he had done.

"Go ahead, lads. The deed is already done, isn't it? You may as well put your knowledge to good use." He sat back in his chair to let them speak.

Oxley took up the story again. "So after a while, the door opens and the guy there, he asked to see our ID cards."

"What?" I asked. "Do you mean he asked for your papers?"

"No, he goes 'NATO card,' like that," said Stewart.

Interesting. Why would a brothel be concerned about NATO ID cards? I wondered what would have happened if they hadn't had them.

"So did you show them?" I asked.

The soldiers exchanged looks a little nervous now. "We didn't want to," said Oxley. "We weren't supposed to be there, you see. We just wanted to be regular customers, but when we said no, no NATO cards, the bloke wouldn't let us in. He just started to close the door."

"But you wanted to go in?"

Stewart spoke up then. "What could be the problem, I was wondering? It wasn't like he was going to take them or anything. He just wanted to see them. So, we showed them to him."

"And then he let you in?"

"Yeah, naturally," he said with a cocky smile. When Sergeant Fogg cleared his throat, Stewart added, "mum."

They described walking into the main room and feeling shocked at the modern furniture and the dimly lit opulence of the place after so many months away from the comforts of home. They said there were women everywhere in various forms of dress, mostly lingerie and "pretty under things," as Oxley called them. A man came out, one they described as being "mean lookin', and right dangerous." The man instructed in broken English that, "there would be no messin' about in his place," and the soldiers had taken the man at his word.

"Did he give you his name?" I asked.

"No, mum. Just said he was the one what was in charge and that we was to follow his rules or suffer the consequences," Stewart said.

The man told them they could just sit and drink with the women if they wanted or they could take one or more to a private room. If they drank with the women they paid for all the drinks, what the women drank and what they drank. I thought the price they quoted for the drinks reasonable for such a place, equivalent to about three British pounds.

"That's rich for this town," Fogg added. I raised an eyebrow at him. "Most bars, a pint is less than half a pound. They're asking six times what a normal drink costs in this town. I would guess there are few locals who can afford those prices."

"And who else was in there besides you two?" I asked.

Oxley turned bright red and began to fidget. Stewart locked his gaze onto his boots, refusing to say anything further.

"I asked them the same question when their escapade came to my attention," said Fogg. "They stayed mum then. This is different boys." Fogg leaned in and put a hand on Stewart's shoulder. "Come on, lads," he said in a quiet voice. "A girl has been murdered. This isn't about breaking regulations anymore. Out with it now."

His gentle manner surprised me. He kept his hand on Stewart's shoulder, and gave him a friendly shake to encourage him.

"Everyone in there was NATO," Stewart said. "Germans, Italians, Turks...." he shrugged. "Most of 'em was Rodneys and Ruperts.

I raised an eyebrow at Fogg, not understanding.

"Officers," he translated.

"Ah," I said, as Oxley continued.

"There was Paks, Polish, Danish and the Australians, yeah, there was a group a them as well. Some of them was minging, drunk off their asses, stumbling about."

I sat back in my chair. A brothel that charged prices no Bosnian could afford, that catered only to the NATO troops, right in the middle of our peacekeeping mission. Griffin, Tooley and Hannerty, all seen there, and Delray's last mission involved pictures of the joint. Activities around the Weeping Rose smacked more and more significant.

Fogg leaned further into the circle, elbows on his knees, speaking to them like someone trying to coax a frightened animal out of hiding.

"Come on, lads. Tell us all of it. Were there other British?"

Stewart and Oxley exchanged looks and nodded their heads, too nervous to look up from the floor.

"Americans?" I asked.

"Sure, yeah. They were there, too," Oxley said.

I wondered how American soldiers did it, how they were able to get away with it without people knowing. Then I thought, maybe everyone knew. Maybe it was one of those things people accepted and didn't consider wrong. Most soldiers on the camp didn't even have civilian clothes to walk around in. We were either in uniform all the time or in our PT sweat pants and nothing in between. Not to mention that, because of force protection rules, to travel off the camp we had to be in a four-vehicle convoy. American customers in the Weeping Rose must have enlisted the support of others in order to pull it off. I sat stunned by it all.

Oxley and Stewart had sat in the bar with a couple of women, girls really, they said, maybe eighteen or nineteen years old according to Oxley. They bought the girls drinks and talked, the girls surprisingly spoke English well. Eventually they each took a girl upstairs. Oxley turned bright red at this point in his story and his hands started shaking, embarrassed to talk about the evening.

Stewart forged ahead with his story about the small, dark room, a curtain for a door, the thin walls and squeaky bed. The place smelled heavily of floor cleaner and flowers.

"Reminded me a bit of my grandmother. The lavender, she wore all the time. Not the kind of memory you want to have when you've got your grollies 'round your ankles with a woman in the room, yeah?"

He laughed and elbowed Oxley, but none of us laughed with him. He sobered, realizing the weight of his information.

"I heard one girl crying some, and this man talking to her, but I didn't understand the language."

After a short time in the room with the girl, he said, someone knocked telling him his time had run out. He met up with Oxley downstairs again.

"Did you boys at least use protection?" Fogg asked.

I wondered the same thing myself. It couldn't have been a very healthy place if the management didn't care enough about their girls to enforce such a policy. From the further redness of Private Oxley and Stewart's continued attention to his boots, I guessed the health of the work force wasn't a concern to those running the joint.

Fogg gave them both a glare that would have had me trembling with fear if he'd directed it at me. He mumbled his distaste under his breath. "Couple of nits muckin' about not knowin's ones arse from the other one's elbow the stupid bleedin' pair a ya."

The men exchanged embarrassed looks again. Fogg took a deep breath and cleared his throat, and attempted to egg them on. "At what point did you pay?" he asked.

They paid for the drinks and for the services they wanted before they went upstairs they said. But when they came back down, the same guy tried to get more money from them.

"He said we was longer in the rooms than we paid for," said Stewart, angry again at the memory of the shake down they had received.

"We had a packet, what with no place to spend our beer tokens, but I told him no, we wasn't going to pay another copper, he threatened to turn us in, but I knew better. They wasn't going to have much luck with NATO soldiers if they went around reporting on them, now were they?" He seemed proud that he had seen through the extortion.

"So he didn't squeeze you for more?" Fogg asked.

"No. I guess he just took us for a couple of pansies ripe for a scam and was going to take advantage of the opportunity, but I set him straight."

"I know this will sound like a stupid question," I said. "But did the other girls seem….happy? Like they were there willingly?"

Oxley shrugged his shoulders. "I don't know. The ones that were speaking English, they seemed okay. But there was that Russian one I guess, I don't know what language she was speaking…"

"Wait a minute," I interrupted. "Weren't all the women Bosnian?"

Oxley and Stewart were shaking their heads no.

"No, mum," said Oxley. "They was Romanian, one of them said, and Russian."

Stewart chimed in, "One kept saying she was Serb from Serbia and she was very proud of that, and some of them looked like you, mum, like they was African. Real pretty."

I sat back in my chair in shock. They were shipping girls here to service the soldiers. I wondered if *any* of the girls in that brothel were local. Maybe they moved them around so they were away from familiar territory. It would be another way to keep them in line and desperate enough about their situation.

I glanced at Fogg. I could see by the wrinkle in his forehead and the press of his lips that he agreed with my distaste of the situation. The Weeping Rose sat in the middle of the town we were supposed to be protecting. The restoration of law and order played a large part in the long recovery from war. A whorehouse in the middle of town is one thing. A place where they shipped foreign women in to perform services meant something else entirely. It smacked of human trafficking, possibly even slavery, mob-like activity conducted by serious criminals. This blatant illegal activity—activity everyone seemed to know about and accept—flew in the face of our efforts here. Prostitution set up specifically to cater to NATO soldiers.

"Well, that's it then. Do you have any idea what this could have to do with your soldier?" Fogg asked.

"Not the slightest idea," I said. "But it must be connected to her murder somehow. What could she possibly have known about that place that put her in danger?"

"Whatever it was," Fogg said, "it got her killed."

Seventeen

"Alright lads, that will be all. Wait for me at the Wolf, yeah?"

Oxley and Stewart gave each other furtive glances then stood to leave. Before they could do as ordered, their Sergeant had one more word of advice for them. He gave them each a hard stare. "You will both remember that this entire conversation is of the utmost secrecy. We did not have this discussion. I may ask you for specifics later, but for now, you are both sworn to secrecy. Have I made myself perfectly clear?"

"Yes, Sergeant Major," they said in unison.

Oxley picked up his beret and turned to leave, but Stewart seemed reluctant to go. He snapped to attention.

"Request permission to speak, sergeant major!" he said.

"Let's not make a world-wide announcement, Stewart," Fogg said, glancing around the room.

I scanned the TOC and noticed several people look away quickly, pretending they hadn't been watching. Major Townson, still at the front of the room, openly stared, and I have to admit, it made me nervous to know that he had witnessed the conversation. His attention intensified my belief that he had things to hide.

Stewart leaned down, and spoke in a quiet voice.

"You can trust me to keep this quiet, sergeant major," he said. "And I'm known there now, aren't I? I could go back in there, safe as houses, take a decko at the place and find out what you like."

"All right, Private, I hear you. But the good Sergeant and I have a few things to discuss," Fogg said. "You did a right fine job of it, telling us all you know." Fogg looked over at Oxley who waited anxiously.

"You both did, but we have a few details to discuss. So move along now, lads. I'll be with you presently."

Private Stewart still looked dejected as he and Oxley left.

When they were gone, Fogg turned to me, and visibly deflated. He uncrossed his legs and leaned an elbow on the corner of my desk.

"A right bloody mess, this is, isn't it?" he said. He ran his hand through his crew cut and met my eyes.

"More tea?" I asked him, already collecting the pot from the other desk and plugging it back in to reheat.

"A snog of whisky might be more appropriate," he said.

"Yes, it would. Wish I had some to offer."

He shrugged his acceptance. "No worries. It's Harry by the way," he said as he tossed back the last of his cold tea.

"Ah, so I'm to be considered a friend now."

He smiled "After what we just heard, I'd say it is inevitable."

"It's Lauren, Harry. You can call me Lauren."

"Ah," he said, revealing the full extent of his broken front teeth. "Lauren. While I am shocked at what we've just learned, I'm not sure what any of it has to do with my missing reporters, other than it was the last place they were seen."

"Or what it has to do with my murdered soldier, but they're connected somehow. I'm sure of it."

Harry watched as I started with the water routine again.

"Right, so what do we do now?" he asked.

To say that his question surprised me is an understatement. After all my years in the military, I could count on one hand the number of times a male senior ranking soldier, officer or enlisted, had deferred to me for what to do next. I peered at him from the corner of my eye as I poured freshly boiled water into his cup containing a new packet of Earl Grey.

"There is something about those pictures...the ones with

Tooley and Hannerty going into the brothel...something that, well that I haven't told you yet," I hoped he wouldn't be angry at me for withholding the information until now.

He dunked his tea a few times without saying anything, looking up at me in an expectant way. I marshaled on.

"The pictures showed Hannerty and Tooley going into the brothel. What I didn't tell you is that my commanding general's aide, Captain Griffin, held the door open for them."

He continued to dunk his tea into his cup, but with a decidedly more rapid flick of his wrist. After a long pause he said, "So what you are saying is that the General of the American peacekeeping effort here in Brcko is connected with a bloody prostitution ring and possibly the trafficking of humans?"

His jade eyes met mine with a fierce look of disbelief and fury. His eyebrows pulled down to match the direction of his widow's peak. He held that look for several seconds and for some reason, perhaps because he splashed tea all over the desk, or perhaps because of how unbelievable the situation seemed, Harry put his elbow on his knee, pinched his eyebrows together with two fingers and tried not to laugh.

His response shocked me at first. How could he laugh?

But watching him lose his struggle to swallow his laughter drew me to see how ridiculous the whole situation appeared. NATO soldiers frequenting brothels so often, it seemed, the brothels trucked women in from across the border to accommodate them. If cross-border prostitution wasn't enough, two high-profile journalists had disappeared, coming even closer to causing an international scandal. Top it off with my own commanding officer, a brigadier general in the U.S. Army, implicated in the whole affair. You had to laugh or go insane.

Fogg struggled to keep his laughter in check. When I began to chuckle along with him, the infection spread to bursting. Soon we were crying, laughing and crying, holding our bellies, which hurt even more since we knew people were watching.

"They asked for a NATO ID card," said Harry with a dead on imitation of Stewart's Scottish cockiness. "An ID card. To go whoring."

We doubled over with that one.

"Some of them prostitutes kind of looked like you," I said, trying my own attempt at Stewart's thickly accented speech.

"A bloody General! A bloody American General," Fogg said in a harsh whisper.

There were a few more moments of mirth, but as the laughter died down, the seriousness of the situation settled around us. We couldn't deny how serious—and when you thought about what happened to Delray—how dangerous the situation appeared.

We may have realized the lethality of the state of affairs at the same time since we both grew quiet as we contemplated what might come next.

"The picture showed Captain Griffin in the brothel, but the General wasn't in the shots," I said. "Either the General was there and he didn't get into camera range or Griffin was alone."

Harry bounced his foot over his knee and scanned the room. After a time, he took a deep breath. "What was she like, your soldier?"

I wished I had a simple answer. Was she as annoying, undisciplined and naive as I thought of her, or had I been too wrapped up in my own stuff to notice who she really was?

"To be honest, since I found her yesterday, I keep learning how much I didn't know about her. Evidently, she went to church often, liked to sing and was good at it, and she had a boyfriend. A great big, handsome, black man. I'm fairly certain she kept that relationship secret because she didn't think I'd approve of their mixed relationship." I pressed my lips together, struggling to control the sudden flood of emotion that threatened to overspill.

"Nonsense," he said, leaning in, forcing me to meet his green eyes. "People don't worry about that sort of thing these days, do they? The interracial thing, I mean?" He leaned back in his chair, grinning. "You remind me of this girl I loved in primary school. Cordelia was her name. I liked to sit behind her so I could clock her every movement without her knowing. I'd go to bed at night, dreaming about how her thick, curly hair would look when it wasn't in a tight braid. What her caramel colored skin would feel like, if she would only let me touch her."

A girl he'd loved. What could I say to that? He had more on his mind.

"Course, those days, white lads couldn't be seen with girls like Cordelia. It simply wasn't done. Besides she came from a posh family. She didn't have time for the likes of me. That didn't stop me from thinking about her, wishing I could say something."

The heat in my face made me want to look away from him, but I couldn't. His confession brought color to his own cheeks, a warm blush that made him look young and vulnerable. The urge to run my hand over his closely cropped hair seemed an inappropriate gesture, considering I'd only known him for about an hour. Besides, my palms were embarrassingly damp. I rubbed them on my thighs, then retreated, grabbing my mug and taking a long sip of tea.

"Point is, there are any number of reasons why your soldier could have kept her relationship secret. No need to speculate that it had anything to do with you."

I smiled at him, appreciating his attempt to make me feel better.

He nodded, then took a long, noisy sip of tea. Neither of us said anything for a while, but the silence felt comfortable. After a while, he fixed me with his green-eyed gaze the warmth in his voice felt like a caress.

"Don't misunderstand. The seriousness of this situation is not lost on me," he said. "But you're a rare bird. I can see that already. I always regretted never saying anything to Cordelia. Just like you regret not getting to know your soldier. I for one, don't want to live with that kind of regret. Not again. Which is why I'd like to have all of your particulars, now, this very minute, so that I can keep in touch when all of this other business is settled."

"You don't mince words, do you, Harry?"

"I'm a soldier, Lauren. One cannot afford to let a moment slip past. Not in our profession." He let his words linger for a moment, waiting.

I pulled open my desk drawer to retrieve one of my business cards. I could have just given it to him as it was, but that felt too official. I turned it over and wrote on the back.

"This is my personal handi number and email address and I'll add the number for reaching me at this desk. The front has all of my contact information back in Heidelberg."

He smiled, reached into a back pocket and pulled out his own card, scribbling several numbers on the back in strong but neat block letters and numbers. When he gave me the card, he locked eyes with mine. "I expect we'll be memorizing these numbers in time, but until then, don't lose it, yeah?"

My heart tripped faster at his mention of a future. Somehow, after only just meeting him, I knew we would have one—a future. "I won't lose it, Harry." His name already felt familiar on my lips.

The moment felt charged with possibility but as military professionals, we both knew a TOC was not the place and the middle of a mission that had cost people their lives was not the time. Harry grinned and rapped his knuckles on the desk to mark a change in topic.

"Right, well, on this other business. What do you suggest?"

He was right to bring us back on topic, but I felt as if someone had snapped the lid closed on the candy box before I was done. I looked down, took a deep breath to try to slow down my rapidly beating heart.

"Well, if the pictures tell us anything, it's that Hannerty and Tooley were last seen going into that place. It may very well be that Captain Griffin was one of the last people to see them before they disappeared. It's probably unwise to speculate on the General. He wasn't in the pictures and I have a hard time believing that he would arrange to meet reporters inside a brothel."

"So, you think the meeting between this Captain and the reporters was arranged?"

"Hannerty was obviously waiting outside the building. When the door opened they both moved to the door as if they had been expected."

"Right, well I suppose someone has to go in there and check the place out then."

I smiled, letting him know I agreed with the decision. He'd be going into the same place he had forbidden his soldiers to enter, but his cause was just.

"Will it be any problem for you?" I asked. "I mean, you do have freedom of movement around town."

"Oh yes, not like you American chaps with your convoys and helmets and body army. You know, the locals call you turtles, the way you hide behind your hard shells. We move about as we need to. Of course, I might just take young Stewart along, seeing as how he's already reconnoitered the place."

Abruptly, we both jumped when three piercing, rapid bleeps from the TOC radio interrupted our conversation. The startling noise meant there was an emergency in the field. Every person in the area froze, attention riveted to the message that would follow. The radio crackled loudly and an urgent voice used the day's two-word code combination to authenticate the message.

"Flash, Flash. Sniper fire, Sniper fire! One down, repeat, one down. Life and limb injury. We need MEDEVAC. Break. Sniper fire from multi-story apartment building vicinity crossroads Utah, Michigan. Squad moving to contact. Break. Request immediate security back up, vicinity crossroads Utah, Michigan. Break. MEDEVAC now! Over."

Goose bumps danced across my skin. Harry and I stared at each other and I thought about his words. One cannot afford to let a moment slip past. Not in our profession.

Eighteen

The room erupted in movement. Someone got on the radio and ordered the QRF to respond to the call. Someone else launched the MEDEVAC helicopter to the area. Others went to the map, looking for the intersection where the squad reported the sniper fire.

"Who's out there?"

"A ten man patrol from Bravo two-six. Lieutenant DeBarto in charge. There hasn't been any hostile contact in that area for months."

After a few minutes, Captain Griffin and Colonel Raybourn walked briskly out of the General's office toward the radio set, asking questions.

"Harry, that's Griffin," I said. "The general's aide."

"Kind of a little guy, ain't he? Who's the other bloke?"

"Raybourn, the executive officer. General Paterson must not be around or he'd be out here. Raybourn takes over when Paterson isn't here. But if Paterson isn't here, why is Griffin here? Doesn't make sense. Paterson and Griffin are usually chained together. "

The radios crackled in a constant flow of information and reports coming from the security support squad and the QRF on their progress getting to the area. Reports from the airfield as the medical helicopter prepared to take off, then a message to change mission and prepare to fly directly to Tuzla with the wounded. The patrol decided they were close enough that, by the time they could establish a landing zone at the site and wait for the chopper to arrive, they could be back at camp. The voices of the men sounded urgent. Their commands and reports professionally calm but clearly, things were critical.

Then I heard something that sent chills down my spine. Through the squelch of the radio, the soldier was breathing heavily.

"Medic's got pressure on the wound, but she's bleeding bad, over."

"She," I said, not realizing I said it out loud.

"What'd you say, luv?"

"They said, she. Bravo two-six is an infantry patrol. No women in the unit, but the wounded person is female. There could have been a female combat camera along, but it seems more likely that the female would be an interpreter."

My thoughts immediately went to Mishka. The girl had seemed panicked, frightened. There were scores of female interpreters, though, so I knew chances were slim it was the girl I had recently met. Still, I couldn't help but worry about the little blonde who had tried to tell me something.

I turned from the activity, intending to tell Harry what I knew about the interpreters, and saw McCallen. He stood behind us, dark circles of fatigue under his eyes, his arms crossed over his chest and his helmet on as if preparing to leave the TOC. He nodded to me, but kept his attention focused on the activity in the front of the room.

I directed Harry's attention to McCallen and made quiet introductions, not wanting to disturb the activity around us.

"Sergeant Major Fogg, this is Colonel Neil McCallen, the task force Public Affairs Officer."

Harry, snapped to attention, said, "Sir," and rendered a British style salute, his right elbow straight out to the side, his hand snapping, palm outward, squarely at his forehead. Neil returned a very relaxed salute and then stuck his hand out for a shake. They looked each other in the eye, sizing each other up.

"McCallen, sir? Like that fine Scots whiskey?"

"Yes," Neil chuckled, "but no relation."

"Pity," said Harry.

"Tell me about it. You'd think a case a year for Christmas wouldn't be too much to ask..."

"Bloody right," Harry responded easily.

"I've been talking to Sergeant Fogg about the missing BBC reporters," I said.

Neil nodded his head and raised an eyebrow. That worried me. The eyebrow usually meant he wasn't happy.

"We've had a fruitful exchange of information," I forged on. "Maybe we should go somewhere so I can tell you what I've learned."

Neil scanned the room, scowling. I tried to gauge what put that look on his face. Ramsey's interrogation could be the cause. Since I'd been through the experience a couple of times myself, I knew the interview could have a very negative effect on his mood. I wondered what Ramsey had asked him. More importantly, I wondered what Neil told him.

McCallen's furrowed brow and inability to look at me broadcasted that he wasn't happy with me. We still needed to talk, despite his anger, and the middle of the TOC wasn't the place for it.

"My quarters then," Neil said, and turned to leave the room.

I glanced at Harry, wondering if he read the sour mood. The slight lift in his eyebrow told me that he did. My new friend appeared to be very observant.

I put on my helmet and flak vest, and slung my weapon over my back.

"There she goes. Putting on her shell," he said with a chuckle as he settled his brown beret on his head. When I'd finished my preparations I glanced up at him and paused, my mouth open at how utterly handsome he looked in the headgear. He gazed down at me, a glint in his eye and his full lips stretched into a smile as if acknowledging complete awareness of his effect on me. Standing so close to him, the way he gazed down at me, I felt like a swooning teenager with no control over my emotions. He winked, then gestured for me to precede him. I took a shaky breath and started walking. With his hands casually clasped behind his back we strolled out of the TOC where activity had reached a frantic pace.

As soon as we stepped outside, I could hear the MEDEVAC helicopter cycling up its rotors for departure. Oxley and Stewart sprawled casually around a British Land Rover and scrambled to attention as soon as they saw Fogg. As we crossed the road toward Harry's men, two soldiers ran to the gates, flung up the large bar locking them in place and pulled them open. Neil, Harry and I moved quickly to the side of the road, just as a single humvee drove speeding into the camp. They careened toward the landing zone.

I turned to McCallen and said, "I'll meet you at Disneyland. I need to see who that is, sir." Neil turned and opened his mouth as if to object, but I took off running.

The landing zone sat behind the trailer park, not far from Disneyland. I ran on the walkway, my boots making a racket, and people moved out of my way without much notice.

By the time I arrived at the landing zone, the medics already had the wounded person on a stretcher and were running toward the helicopter. The side door of the chopper stood open and waiting, the bright white box with the red medical cross emblazoned on the side announcing that the Blackhawk was for medical evacuation. The medical team ran alongside the stretcher holding up IV bags and other equipment, the patient covered with a blanket.

Just as they lifted the stretcher to load it into the chopper, a corner of the blanket blew away from the patient's face. I stood there panting, a wave of disbelief washing over me. A thick smear of blood marred her bleached, white hair, her red bandana almost black with blood. Her arm, with the huge cuff at the bottom of the sleeve, hung off the side of the stretcher. One of the medics lifted it and strapped it to her chest, securing her in place.

It was Mishka.

She had been asking questions about her sister. She had been crying and upset and made herself known as someone who wanted some answers. Maybe she asked the wrong questions. Maybe she got some people nervous. Or maybe she was just in the wrong place on a patrol when a sniper's bullet found its target.

It just seemed too convenient to me, too much of a coincidence. Some very serious illegal things were going on here, false documents, interpreters and reporters that disappeared, prostitution, maybe even slavery, and of course, murder. One couldn't forget that.

The chopper lifted off, kicking up grass and dirt as it rose into the air. I tried to send positive vibes that the girl inside would come out of this all right. I turned away from the wash of the rotor blades, shielding myself from the flying debris and felt the walkway bounce with the running of feet. Sergeant Steele ran at a dead sprint, that huge SAW bouncing against his thighs. He saw the chopper lifting off and then cursed that he hadn't made it in time. He glistened in sweat. With his hands on his hips, he paced in frustration. When his gaze landed on me, he cursed again and spun on his heel to leave.

"Wait, Sergeant Steel. Wait a second."

He stopped abruptly with his back toward me. He wanted to ignore me, but the soldier in him wouldn't allow him to disregard a senior NCO. After a second or two, he turned and went into parade rest, but his nostrils flared, and the glare in his eyes warned he didn't want to talk to me.

I walked toward him not wanting to give him the news.

"It was Mishka." I said.

The look of anger in his eyes suddenly changed to pain and then disbelief. He threw his head back and bellowed "NO!"

He paced back and forth for a while, cursing under his breath, his fists clenched, the massive weapon bouncing around in front of him as if it were weightless. A crowd had gathered to watch the MEDEVAC but now they watched this painful show. I let him continue for a GFwhile until he began to tire. He shook his head. "No, no, no. It was my fault," he said to himself. "All my fault."

I said his name, but he refused to hear me. I kept repeating it, "Sergeant Steele, Sergeant Steele."

He finally stopped in front of me, his head down, refusing to look at me, his chest rising and falling.

"You and I need to talk. I know you've been asking questions. So have I. Mishka told me that she knew Virginia and I'm beginning to think that Virginia learned something or saw something that put her in danger." He glared down at me, but I could see that some of it was getting through.

"I think we both have information that could be helpful to each other. It doesn't make any sense for us to be going at this from opposite sides," I told him.

His wheels were turning. He wanted to say something to me, but hesitated.

"She said.....she said you thought she was stupid. That you didn't respect her." His voice was a low rumble that matched his size, a strong southern lilt to his speech. The words were harsh, a challenge. He demanded an explanation.

I had thought that Virginia Delray was a shallow, empty-headed girl with little awareness of the world and little desire to improve herself. She'd caused me hours of headaches as I re-wrote most of her work, struggled to find pictures she'd taken that weren't out of focus and attempted to keep her wandering mind centered on the tasks at hand. My frustration with her work blinded me to her qualities as a human. The reality of my disregard for her shamed me.

"I know. I was wrong about her. I'm....well I can't tell you how sorry I am."

I turned away from him. My chest felt tight and then my chin trembled and the tears spilled over beyond my control. I cursed at their unexpected arrival. This wouldn't do. I took a deep breath and spent a few seconds staring down at my boots. When I finally gained some control, I turned back to him.

"There was obviously more to Virginia than I was willing to see. I'm sorry," I said again.

He stood there looking at me, not saying anything. It was hard to tell what he was thinking.

"Look," I said. "I've got to go meet with my boss, but we need to talk. I've learned some things that could be helpful, but I'm not sure how all of it comes together. What I do know is there are some serious things going on around here and people are dying because of it. Just give me a chance to explain."

He thought about it, his eyes scanning the area. I knew he didn't like me and probably never would, but I hoped he cared enough about finding Virginia's killer to overlook his dislike.

He finally met my eyes for a second and silently nodded his agreement.

"Meet me in the motor pool at fifteen hundred," I said.

He narrowed his eyes at me. "That was you, wasn't it? In that truck this morning."

My first instinct was to lie. Admitting that I had eavesdropped on his conversation with Mishka wasn't a good way to gain his trust, but lying wouldn't help the trust factor either.

"Yeah, that was me. I just happened to be there and I heard the two of you. It was purely an accident."

"That's how you know about Mishka. About her being afraid," he said.

"Yes. I heard some of what she told you. And last night she tried to talk to me, but the other interpreters wouldn't let her. One of them slapped her. Mishka seemed petrified."

Steele stared down at me, deciding. He glanced at his watch then took a deep breath, the tension seeping out of him.

"Okay, at fifteen hundred."

His agreement to meet with me made me smile. I didn't expect the smile to be returned and it wasn't. Steele turned and left, his slow steady gate away from me broadcast a man with a lot on his mind.

I made my way to Disneyland. Colonel McCallen and Sergeant Fogg were strong personalities probably in the process of sizing each other up and marking their territory. It could prove to be an interesting meeting, putting them together in a room. On the other hand, it could be a disaster. The way my luck was running, I should have known which one to expect.

Nineteen

Oxley and Stewart had followed their Sergeant into Disneyland but stood outside the trailer leaning on opposite sides of a light pole. Oxley chattered away. Stewart, looking dejected, stared off, ignoring Oxley's banter. They stood at attention when they saw me approach.

I told them to be at ease, climbed the steps and knocked quickly on McCallen's door.

McCallen, his lips pressed into a thin line, opened the door and motioned for me to come in. He was still pissed off about something.

A series of muddy boot tracks from one end of the trailer to the other already marred the previously clean carpet. I regretted adding more to the mix but it couldn't be helped.

McCallen cleared his throat and stepped behind his desk, avoiding my gaze. The tension in the air felt as thick as the Bosnian humidity.

"Your colonel has given me a quick tour of your VIP area," said Harry. "Impressive. Had the chaps outside green with envy, it did."

"Yes, well, we don't all have the privilege of living in such luxury," I said.

McCallen shot me an angry look. I mentally prepared myself for a bumpy interview, and filled the silence that settled around us by removing my helmet and propping my weapon by the door. I took off my flak vest and tossed it on the sofa then settled myself there next to it. McCallen took his seat behind the desk, leaning back in the squeaky chair, a thumb hooked into his shoulder holster. Harry took a place in a chair near the desk.

The silence felt prickly. I didn't know where to begin. I leaned forward, my elbows resting on my knees. Forging ahead seemed the best idea.

"Sir, I've just had a very interesting conversation with Sergeant Fogg and his soldiers," I said. "Sergeant Major, maybe you should tell Colonel McCallen what we talked about."

"Oh, right," said Harry. He stood with his hands behind his back and started pacing. "Sir, as you know, two journalists from the BBC have been missing for several days. Sergeant Harper told me there is evidence that they entered the Weeping Rose on the day they went missing. Now it just so happens that the two young lads outside have been in that brothel, against orders I should add..." But McCallen interrupted him.

"Wait, wait, wait a minute," said McCallen rising slowly from behind his desk. "What is this, Sergeant Harper?" he said. He leaned on the desk, his fisted hands supporting his weight, his raised eyebrows displaying a mild state of shock.

His interruption surprised me. The man I knew to be a good listener, was acting out of character.

Since everyone else was standing, I stood, wondering what to say to get him to listen before he jumped to any conclusions. "Sir, if you would just allow the Sergeant Major to finish..."

He put his hand up, palm to me as a clear sign to stop talking. "I *thought* we were going to discuss the disappearance of the reporters," McCallen said.

"We are, Sir. If you would let Sergeant Major Fogg ...,"

"First of all, I want to hear this from you. What are you doing discussing that establishment with a soldier from a coalition army?"

He glared at me from across the room, a deep crease in his forehead and his head cocked to the side as if I had done something inexplicable. Harry, thankfully, kept quiet, and stood rooted to the floor. I hoped I could keep my voice calm.

"Sir, Sergeant Major Fogg came to me with questions about the missing journalists. After a lengthy discussion...'

"And a fine cup of tea," Harry interjected in a vain attempt to lighten the mood. I smiled at him in gratitude, but I knew it wasn't going to do the trick.

"And after a cup of tea." I went on, "I discovered that he had information about the Weeping Rose. The same place we saw in the pictures..."

"Wait, wait, Sergeant Harper," McCallen said, his palm to me again as he stepped around his desk. "You will stop now. I cannot allow you to continue with this." He stalked past Harry and stopped when he was inches from me, and glared down. I glanced at Harry, who frowned at McCallen's back.

"Sir?"

"I need to speak to you, alone. Right now." He turned to Fogg. "Excuse us, but my sergeant and I have something urgent to discuss. Please, wait outside."

It sounded like a request but it wasn't. Fogg opened his mouth to say something, his eyes narrowed, but decided against it. "Sir," he said and rendered a salute, executed a perfect left face and marched toward the door. Just before he opened the door, he glanced at me, tilting his head up quickly. *Chin up*, he was saying. *Don't let it get to you.*

In the one small gesture, he exuded encouragement. When he shut the door behind him with a final sounding click, it felt like half the light in the room had left with him.

I turned back to McCallen, my hands going to my hips, my head cocked to the side, my frustration, I'm sure, clearly written on my face. We listened to the air conditioner running for several seconds, the silence stretching uncomfortably. I had expected him to listen to the whole story, the way he had so often listened to reason and explanations in the past. At the very least, I had hoped he would trust my judgment enough to hear me out.

I stared into the grey eyes I had stared into so many times in the past, but knew they belonged to a different man. A different man than the one I had kissed only a few hours before.

Here we were again, alone in his trailer, the mood far different from the last time we stood here.

"Lauren, tell me you didn't...." He stopped, took a deep breath, but it didn't seem to help much. "Tell me what in the hell you are doing?"

He enunciated the words, glaring at me.

"I am trying to find out what happened to Specialist Delray, sir. The same thing I was doing the last time we talked." I looked at my watch, "which was only about an hour ago."

"Sergeant Harper, how much did you tell him?" The familiar crimson blush washed up from his neck to his face, his eyes narrowed at me in an angry glare.

My hands still on my hips, I stood my ground and two things went rolling around in my head that I didn't like having in there. First, he'd thrown my rank at me. The hierarchy of command hadn't played a major role in our relationship for some time. I respected him as my commanding officer, respected his work and his judgment, but he had never really pulled rank on me before. That had changed. If he wanted me to explain why I had confided in Harry, all he had to do was ask.

The other thought in my head that I didn't like, the one that disturbed me even more, had to do with that damn kiss. Our brief show of affection, that one moment of weakness that had happened only a few hours ago, but now seemed more like weeks, may have cost me a friend that I sorely needed.

That damn kiss. That kiss, and our embarrassment of it, had betrayed our feelings to Ramsey. That kiss made me the focus of a murder investigation. That kiss and McCallen's guilt over it had landed him in an interrogation room. I could understand his frustration at being implicated in Ramsey's investigation, his fear of what those implications meant for his career, his marriage and his family. All because of that damn kiss.

I should have left when I'd had the chance, but he'd begged me not to. We'd done a very stupid thing. His new show of authority wouldn't help the situation.

"I pretty much told him what I knew, *sir*."

"Sergeant Harper, tell me that you did not speculate with a coalition soldier about General Paterson and his aide. Just tell me you didn't do that."

His voice was getting increasingly louder as his anger got the best of him.

"Sir, if you would allow us to tell you the entire story, I'm sure you'll understand why I felt it necessary to share that information."

"You felt it necessary. Did you think for a moment that perhaps you should have cleared that action with someone first?"

"No, sir," I said, clenching my fists. "I didn't think clearing it with anyone was necessary, but obviously you feel that was a mistake."

"You are not Nancy Drew and this is not some childhood game you can play without consequences. A murder investigation is underway in the middle of a NATO-lead peacekeeping mission. The eyes of the world are on this place and you will not just willy nillie..."

"Willy nillie?" I said. "Maybe you've forgotten that we're talking about the murder of one of your soldiers. Maybe you've forgotten that I am the focus of the investigation, not to mention that I'm supposed to be someone you might want to help."

"I *am* trying to help you, Sergeant Harper," he said, biting my rank out pointedly between clenched teeth. "You have no idea what those pictures really showed. You are purely speculating about what they mean and I am telling you right now that you cannot and will not volunteer information about the General's aide to someone in a foreign army."

During the pregnant pause that followed, we both realized, almost simultaneously, that we were practically nose-to-nose. The furious expressions on our faces might have been comical if we both hadn't been deadly serious. I took a step back and took a deep breath, but my fury wouldn't abate.

"Well, sorry, sir," I said sarcastically. "That order has already been violated. I've already told Fogg about the pictures, and if you would simply listen to what he has to say about it, you would understand why."

"You've made a very grave error, Sergeant Harper." His voice sounded calmer but his eyes still pierced me through hooded lids. He shook his head at me as if I were a poorly-behaved child. "Obviously your judgment has been compromised by the shock of finding Specialist Delray."

"My judgment has been compromised? What the hell does that mean? Are you going to report me or something?"

"I may have to," he said in a voice that sounded whiney to my ears as he tried to get me to see things his way. "Those pictures, as you described them to me, cannot stand on their own. They call for an explanation. What if your Sergeant Fogg gives that information to British authorities and they demand Brigadier General Paterson and his aide explain themselves? How do you think that will play to the international community? How do you think that will play when the world turns their eyes on this camp when Vice President Gore steps off his plane here?"

"Aren't you leaving out how it might impact your career?"

'Damn it, Lauren!" he said, towering over me again.

His outburst and his body language made me flinch and take a step back as if I were afraid. He stood stunned and either embarrassed or ashamed by my reaction. Did I really think he would hit me? It didn't matter what I thought. My instincts had taken over. He paused, coiled, stiff with anger, and then his shoulders slumped. He turned and walked behind his desk and sat down heavily.

"I just spent more than an hour being grilled by that CID team. Ramsey asked me if we were sleeping together. He asked me if my wife knows how I feel about you. He read me passages from your diary, for Christ sake!"

Good lord, I thought. I wanted to crawl under a rock and die. Were there any more humiliations I could suffer over this stupid crush?

"Forgive me if I consider my career and my family here," he went on. "But the reality is, even if....even when you are found innocent of these suspicions, the speculation about an affair isn't going away. It will never go away."

"You're worried about being accused of having an affair. I agree, it's not something that will be good for your career. But Delray is dead. And God damn it, I could use some help here!"

He sat there for a moment staring at me, the color drained from his face. With a sigh, he put his face in his hands. Seeing him like that gave me an ache in the middle of my chest. I hated to be the cause of so much distress. His desire to protect those closest to him drove his actions, but I hadn't gotten into this mess alone. He'd refused my transfer. He'd begged me not to leave the trailer. He'd begged me for that kiss. He'd played a part in the danger to his own career. The blame didn't belong solely to me.

When he lifted his face to me, his eyes were cold. He stood up slowly and walked around his desk again.

"I want to help you Lauren. I really do. I understand the position you're in, but I have two priorities here. The first is to my family, my children. The second is to this peacekeeping mission."

He took a deep breath as if steeling himself in preparation for what he would say next. "You were unauthorized to share sensitive information with a foreign military. You stepped way over your authority here."

"How long have you known me? How many times have you questioned my actions like this?"

"These are extreme circumstances and you are under severe pressure here, Harper. I would expect that you might make decisions that aren't based on sound judgment. It's completely understandable. You put your trust in someone you barely know...."

He went on like that for a while, making excuses for me. He said I shouldn't have trusted Harry since I hardly knew him. That Harry could have been manipulating me to get the information he wanted. He said I might be panicking, and even that I should trust the military legal system to sort it all out in the end.

"Ramsey knows what he's doing. The forensic evidence will eventually prove you innocent. You've got to let this investigation run its course and stop digging around where you don't belong."

If I hadn't stopped him, stopped what had happened only a few hours earlier, he would have done much more than just kiss me. Now he looked at me as if I were confused and pathetic. An attitude from him I had never seen in the years I'd known him and never wanted to see again.

He was right about one thing. The pressure I felt seemed insurmountable. I couldn't handle it alone. What I really needed was someone to go to bat for me, but I wasn't going to find that pinch hitter here. McCallen continued to talk. I'd heard enough.

"There's no need to lecture me," I said. "It's perfectly clear to me where you're coming from."

If I allowed myself to reach back, to the far reaches of my mind, I knew what McCallen said made sense. The whole international coalition thing and pouring all of that information out to Harry probably hadn't been the diplomatically correct thing to do. But I would never admit that to the cold, hard officer facing me now. The McCallen I knew before this morning didn't exist anymore. My friend and ally disappeared with an interrogation and a threat to his career.

"What am I supposed to do about this now, Harper?"

"You have plenty of options I should think, Sir. You could report what I've told Sergeant Fogg to Chief Ramsey. You could have me confined to quarters."

"Be reasonable, Sergeant Harper."

We stared at each other for a moment. It made me sad, this impasse. Sad and very tired.

"Imagine me saluting smartly and following orders, sir."

I picked up my flak vest and let the weight settle onto my shoulders, wishing the heavy thing could protect me from the danger I felt pursuing me.

"I'll have a press release ready for your approval on today's sniper shooting by the end of the day."

"That's a good idea. Get some work done. It might take your mind off all of this. Help you to see things a little more clearly. Why don't we set two hours for a deadline? We've probably been getting calls in the TOC already. "

"Yes, sir, in two hours then. I'll leave the release in the TOC for you to approve. Tuzla has probably updated information on Delray's release as well. I responded to a few queries this morning, but there are probably more."

"Under the circumstances, I think I'd better handle any queries we have on that case now. I had a query earlier today from AP trying to confirm that an American soldier was the main suspect in the case."

If the *Associated Press* were asking, that meant the rumor mill had already kicked into gear. My name wouldn't be released to the press unless Ramsey charged me with something, but that didn't mean people wouldn't talk. I thought about calling Loretta and telling her before she heard something from somewhere else. She had lived on military posts with me enough years to have her own network of informants. If I didn't tell her what was going on, she'd be worried sick. I thought about all my friends in the States and in Germany who would hear the stories, and thought it would be nice to have just one of them here to stand by me.

When I glanced at McCallen he turned away from me. I felt the rejection like a stab to my chest. If he couldn't look me in the eye anymore, something fundamental had permanently changed. A change that meant the loss of a friendship I had valued over many years.

I put my helmet on and slung my weapon over my back. Before I went out the door, I turned and stared at him. It seemed like a replay of earlier today but it didn't feel at all the same. Us standing there looking at each other across the room, both knowing a huge change in our relationship had just taken place. When I left this morning with the feel of his lips lingering on mine, I felt fearful, on edge. I had no idea what would happen next or how I would take hold of the feelings I had. Now, I felt clear understanding and a certainty. Neil had been truthful to Ramsey. There was nothing going on between us. After this discussion, I would have little trouble finally accepting what would never be and move on. As hurtful as this scene had been, I felt the morass of feelings for him clear like a sticky fog. I wanted suddenly, to smile, but I wouldn't do it here.

"I'd like you to ask Sergeant Fogg to step inside, please."

"Sir, he's not going to…"

"Tell him to come in please." It was an order.

I opened the door and all three of them, Stewart, Oxley and Fogg tried to pretend they hadn't been listening through the thin walls of the trailer. I figured they must have heard most of the conversation.

"The colonel wants to see you," I said. Harry exaggeratedly pointed at himself and rolled his eyes and I had to stop myself from smiling. He quickly and expertly whipped the smirk from his face as he stepped smartly into the trailer and rendered a salute, "Sir!"

Colonel McCallen started pacing, his hands behind his back trying to convey the importance of what he was about to say. To me, he looked rather silly.

"I'm sure you can understand the gravity of what Master Sergeant Harper has told you about those pictures."

"Sir!"

"What is in those pictures is part of a murder investigation, and an investigation into the disappearance of two reporters and potentially could impact the career of the commander of this U.S. Army camp."

"Sir!"

Fogg stood at attention, his eyes directed straight ahead. I stood next to him, my hands on my hips, staring at my boots and biting my tongue, hoping I could get out of there without losing my temper.

"I would ask that you refrain from discussing those pictures with anyone."

"Sir?"

This time it was a question. There was no way Harry could withhold what he knew from his superiors. McCallen forged ahead.

"We can't afford to let that information out, Sergeant Fogg."

"Begging the Colonel's pardon, but that information is already out, Sir. I am obligated to let my superiors know that the two reporters were spotted near that brothel, sir!'

I chimed in. "I'm sure Sergeant Major Fogg can be convinced to keep Captain Griffin's name out of his report for the time being, Colonel McCallen. However, as I'm sure you would agree, since Sergeant Fogg is assisting in the British investigation to locate the journalists, he has to report that they were seen going into the Weeping Rose."

"Of course," said Harry. "One American soldier looks like another to me. All I was told was that there was a picture with someone in an American Army uniform and two British journalists...if someone was to ask me, sir."

"Good" said Neil. "Very good."

"However, sir, I will need assurances that the officer in the pictures will be questioned and that any information you discover is passed on to me. If not, then I will have no choice but to relay this information to my superiors, sir."

"Yes, of course. I will personally let the CID team know your interest in the matter. When they do question the officer, I'll ask that they share any pertinent information with you."

"Excuse me sir, but I would request that you share *any* information you get from this officer. It should be up to the British forces to determine pertinence," and after a beat Harry added, "Sir!"

McCallen stopped pacing and peered at Harry. The colonel was making a new assessment of the stocky soldier. "Agreed," McCallen said. "I appreciate that you understand the delicacy of the situation."

Harry slowly relaxed himself from his rigid stand of attention until he was staring directly at McCallen, openly challenging him. He slowly turned and met my eyes, his eyebrow raised. With his eyes on me he said, "Oh, I think I appreciate the delicacy of the situation, sir." He turned toward McCallen again and with a much different tone of voice. "I think I understand completely, sir!"

I could see the street brawler in Harry then, and before Neil could say another word, Harry snapped to attention again, rendered a salute, turned smartly and left the trailer.

In the moments of silence that followed, Neil stood staring at me. I was trying mightily not to, but I couldn't help but smile a little. I may have lost one friend, but I had clearly gained a new one in Sergeant Major Harry Fogg.

"I believe he was being insubordinate just then," McCallen said.

"Ah, yeah. I think so too. Is there anything else, sir?"

He walked over to the window and looked out at the men waiting for me.

"You're going to continue this investigation of yours, aren't you, even if I order you to stop?"

He could have me confined to quarters. He could tell Ramsey what I was doing. He could order me to stop and then charge me with disobeying those orders. In any other circumstance, I never would have thought McCallen would consider any of those options, but the day had already been full of surprises. I left the question unanswered.

"I assumed as much," he said. After a moment he added, "just....just try to be careful, Sergeant Harper. And remember where you are."

"Roger, sir."

"Carry on." He dismissed me.

I left the trailer, closing the door behind me, slipped my helmet on my head and made my way slowly to stand before Harry. I gazed up at him. He grinned, then turned and started us walking away from the trailer. We walked side by side in a calm stroll, Oxley and Stewart following silently behind. I breathed in deeply and chuckled.

"Well, that didn't go quite the way I'd planned."

He smiled, flashing his white broken grin. "No. Don't suppose it did. Anything I can do to make it right, luv?"

"To make it right between my colonel and me? No. That dog has walked."

Saying it made me grin wider. I felt lighter. Every step I made away from the trailer and McCallen pushed the destructive sentiments I held for my boss further away, down the well of emotions where they could no longer control me. I hoped I could make them stay there.

"There are two things you can do for me though," I said.

"What? Only two?"

"I'd like you to talk to the CID investigator. To Chief Ramsey. I'd like you to tell him what we've talked about. He won't listen to me, but I bet he'll listen to you."

"Of course. It was already on the top of my list of things to do."

"But first, there's one more person I think you need to meet." I glanced at my watch. Steele might already be at the motor pool, waiting.

"Master Sergeant Harper," Harry said. "So far, my time with you has been, shall we say, very intriguing. If there is another person you want me to see, I wouldn't miss it for the world. Please, lead on."

Twenty

The motor pool was on the opposite side of the camp, about a half a mile away from Disneyland. We took our time, strolling along, Harry and his soldiers checking out portions of the American camp they may not have seen before.

After a time, we walked into the motor pool, stepping off the wooden walkway, our boots crunching on the loose gravel and sloshing through mud. We walked the rows of neatly parked vehicles searching for some sign of the large African-American soldier, Sergeant Marcus Steele, who evidently, had become the paramour of my soldier, Specialist Delray.

I finally spotted him, towering over the top of a humvee. We made our way over to him, but waited to interrupt him as he seemed fully engrossed in PMCSing his vehicle. The preventive maintenance checks and services on the fat tired, wide-bodied truck, is a daily requirement before leaving on a mission.

Steele's assistant driver, a slight pale kid with no stripes on his uniform signaling he was a buck private, stood next to the vehicle with the front grill pulled down and the huge hood propped open. He held the vehicle manual, flipping through pages and looking confused.

Steele made a tsking noise and stood with his hands on his hips. "Bliven, how many times you got to look at the dad gum book to do the same dad gum thing we do every dang day?"

Bliven craned his head back to gaze up at his sergeant from under his helmet. Then he spotted us approaching. When he saw

Fogg, he snapped to attention and saluted him. Steele made that tsking sound again and took the book from the young private, saying under his breath, "He's not an officer, knucklehead."

Sergeant Fogg gave Bliven a friendly nod, saying "Carry on, lad. Don't want to interrupt."

Steele checked us out one by one, his gaze gliding over the group. He'd been expecting to talk to me, but probably wondered why everyone else had come along. His forehead wrinkled, he glared at me. Bliven ignored the tension radiating from his NCO.

"I just want to make sure I don't forget anything this time," Bliven said. "Every time we do this, you tell me I forgot something. So I decided to go strictly by the checklist. That way I don't forget anything."

He sounded eager to please. Steele gave him back the book then stood with his hands casually draped over the back of the weapon strapped across his chest.

"All right then. What's the first thing you're going to do?"

"Check the oil?" asked Bliven.

"Is that what it says there on the list?" asked Steele.

"Yes," said Bliven consulting the list once again before responding.

"Then check the oil, Private Bliven." It sounded like a conversation they had often; Bliven trying to please his intimidating sergeant and his sergeant trying to have patience with Bliven's insecurities.

His patience served to remind me of how little I had shown toward my own soldier. Maybe if I had been as good of an NCO as Steele, Delray would still be alive. I shook my head to try to clear it of my self-recrimination.

"Sergeant Steele," I said, "I think Privates Oxley and Stewart might appreciate a chance to see how we conduct vehicle PMCS."

Steele shot an angry look at me, and held my gaze for a long moment. Eventually he shrugged.

"Sure," he said, shaking his huge head. He motioned for Oxley and Stewart to come over as Bliven searched inside the engine for the dipstick. Oxley and Stewart stuck their heads in there too.

Bliven reached in and pulled the dipstick out, so long it seemed to never end. He wiped it clean, replaced it in the tube, and pulled it out one more time. The three of them put their heads together to check the level. Oxley and Stewart made several comments in the process, but Bliven was having trouble understanding them—Oxley's thick British and Stewart's heavy Scottish brogue too foreign to Bliven's ear. 'Huh?' he kept asking.

Steele watched the interchange, his arms crossed, shaking his head.

"The blind leading the bloody blind that lot is," said Harry with a sigh. "Right, so Sergeant Harper, care to explain what I'm doing here?"

I took a few steps away from the vehicle to give us some privacy. The men followed me as we moved down a row of humvees. I stopped after a time and turned to them.

"Staff Sergeant Steele, this is Sergeant Major Fogg with the British Army here."

Harry stuck his hand out to Steele. They shook. Somehow their combined bulk made both men seem like a matched pair. Harry didn't say anything, just shook the man's hand, but his gaze made Steele relax noticeably. Then Harry looked at me, an eyebrow raised.

"Staff Sergeant Steele was my soldier's boyfriend. He can tell you about some strange things going on around here that I thought you should know." Then I turned to Steele.

"Sergeant Major Fogg is looking for two British journalists that disappeared. The same journalists that were in pictures Virginia took on her last assignment in Brcko. Did you know about those pictures?"

Steele consulted his boots for a long moment then nodded his head.

"You're talking about the ones she took on her day out with the engineers?"

"Yes. Did she tell you about them?"

"No. They made her nervous though. She seemed very nervous when she came back that day. I tried to talk to her about it, but she wouldn't tell me anything."

"It's understandable that she was nervous. Her pictures could get an officer in a lot of trouble."

I told him how I had found them and that I thought she must have felt she was in danger when she dropped the memory card into my backpack. Steele clenched his teeth at the thought that she had been frightened.

"It was Captain Griffin, plain as day," I said. "But that's not all. We found out some things about the place where she took the pictures. About the Weeping Rose. If Griffin is associated with it, it could only mean he's involved in some serious stuff."

Fogg told Steele about Oxley and Stewart going into the brothel, about the security at the door, all the different women in there. When he got to the part about where all the women came from, Steele got very still and I could tell his interest had piqued but he stayed quiet and let Fogg finish.

Fogg went on to tell him about Tooley and Hannerty going missing, about how his government had ordered him to find out what we knew and that others in the government were putting all kinds of pressure on anyone, anywhere to figure out what had happened to them.

"My commander is upset with me," I said. "He thinks I shouldn't have told the British that Captain Griffin is even remotely connected to the disappearance of the reporters."

"He may not have wanted you to tell me," Harry said. "But he seemed overly pigheaded about listening to reason. More going on there than it appears I would wager." He looked down his nose at me, his lips pursed.

"There is," I said. "But I'd rather not go into it."

"No need. I wasn't born yesterday."

The heat rushed to my face. Between strangers reading my diary, to this man I'd just met seeing though the emotionally fraught relationship I had with my boss, there seemed no end to the humiliating trials of the day. Harry's knowing eyes made me cringe. I swallowed down my hurt pride and marshaled on.

"The part you don't know about, Sergeant Major, is about the interpreters. Something really strange is going on there."

I told them about the night in the shower trailer and how Mishka was crying and that she tried to tell me something before the other interpreters stopped her.

"When I overheard you talking to her this morning, Sergeant Steele, it confirmed for me that she was frightened too. I just don't know about what."

Then I told them about the conversation I had with the scout platoon, and what they had told me about their interpreter. That the person had changed but her name and papers hadn't and then I told Sergeant Fogg that Mishka had been the victim in the sniper shooting he'd heard about in the TOC and the one MEDEVAC'd out.

"You're not suggesting that she was targeted on purpose, are you?" Harry asked.

"She was wearing a red bandana around her neck, and her sleeves and pants legs were rolled up into huge cuffs. Like every interpreter out there, she made sure she couldn't be mistaken for a soldier," I said.

"But still, snipers miss, don't they?" Harry said. "It could have been a mistake."

"No," Steele said definitively and he went on in his slow southern drawl. "I started sniper training, but I washed out. My eyesight just ain't that good. We used to study the Bosnian and Serb snipers in class. They were used a lot in this war and no, snipers don't miss. Now he could have been making a point. Don't work with the Americans or something, but if he hit Mishka, you can bet he meant to hit her."

It was the most I'd ever heard him say. He stood there, looking at his boots. "I wonder if she's okay," he said.

"As soon as I get back to the TOC I'll be able to check on her condition. But in the meantime, do you have anything to add to all of this?"

"I don't know," he said. I had a feeling Steele kept most of what he thought to himself, speaking only rarely. "I can tell you Virginia was scared. When she came back from Brcko that day with the engineers, she was scared." We waited for him to go on, and when he didn't Fogg prompted him.

"Scared of what, mate?"

He shrugged. "At first she said it was nothing, that she probably didn't have any reason to be worried, but as the night wore on, the more she got scared. She said she saw something that she shouldn't have."

"But she didn't tell you what that was?" I asked.

"No," he hesitated. "But I think it had to do with Mishka's sister and that her sister wanted to go the states. Mishka said her sister would do anything to go to the U.S. And I know there's supposed to be someone on the camp who will help the girls do that."

"Someone on camp?"

"That's what Mishka said. She told Virginia about it when they were out the other day. She said there was a guy who would do it, if you paid, of course."

"So is there a chance that Mishka's sister just went to the U.S.? Could she be there now?"

Steele shook his head. "Virginia didn't think so. She thought the girls were being tricked. I don't know why she thought that, but that's what she said."

Harry stared down at his feet, arms crossed over his chest, his chin cupped in one hand. He'd kept quiet the whole time, listening, but he finally shook his head, and looked up at us.

"Sorry, luv, but I don't see a connection. All we know is that the BBC chaps went into this Weeping Rose. What has that to do with interpreters or generals or murdered girls? It just doesn't seem connected."

After laying it all out, I had to agree with him. So the reporters went into the Weeping Rose. They were investigative reporters, paid to dig into places like that. If their disappearance had anything to do with the brothel, the chance a connection existed between it and Virginia and Bosnian interpreters seemed remote.

"Captain Griffin is in the picture," I said. "They are doing a story on brothels so they go to a brothel, but Captain Griffin is there. Why?"

Steele shuffled around, adjusted the weapon over his shoulders. He opened his mouth to speak then shook his head.

"Out with it then," demanded Fogg.

"There's a back door...to the Weeping Rose. There's a back door and that's the way the General was going in, at least until he got the apartment. That's what the guys told me anyway."

Fogg and I stared at Steele. I'm sure my mouth hung open.

"You're talking about our Brigadier General Paterson? Would go in the back door?"

Steele nodded his head. "Yep. That's what the guys told me."

Twenty-one

W hen Sergeant Tucker went on emergency leave, I replaced him in the General's PSD," Steele said, continuing his story. "Paterson picked me himself. Said he liked my size." His nostrils flared and he seemed to hunch down into his shoulders, as if uncomfortable with the attention his bulk drew.

The shock of his revelation still tingled down my spine. No more speculation about it. The connection between Griffin, the Weeping Rose and Paterson existed.

The General's PSD or personal security detachment is the team of soldiers who serve as his bodyguards, charged with keeping the General safe. Anytime he travels off base, they go with him. They are trained to form a protective perimeter around him to watch everyone while everyone is looking at the general. Since they rarely leave his side, they also, like it or not, keep the General's secrets.

Sergeant Steele's revelation went against the unspoken rules of security detachments; to keep the confidence of the person you protect. One doesn't blab about what you see. Your proximity to someone of power does not give you permission to gossip about what that person does in his or her spare time.

Steele's desire to find Virginia's killer overrode his fidelity to the PSD protocols. If anyone knew he had spoken with us about things he learned while on that detachment, his career could suffer, not in any official capacity, but soldiers talk to soldiers. The story, that Steele couldn't be trusted, would spread.

"He visited this woman in an apartment," Steele went on. "Some Bulgarian woman. It ain't no big deal for an officer to have a girlfriend, right? Happens all the time."

During the two weeks he served with the PSD, Steele traveled everywhere with the General, including frequent trips with Paterson to the apartment building.

"It's just down the street from that Rose place. It doesn't look like much from the outside, but for around here, it's pretty nice. At least that's what I heard. I never went up in there. I can tell you one thing though. At night, you see a lot of activity around that place."

The General would arrive bearing gifts he had ordered from online stores. While waiting for hours with the rest of the PSD outside the apartment building, the other soldiers, bored and with nothing to do, told Steele that the general had met the girl during a visit to the Weeping Rose.

The General had used the back door of the Rose one night. The next night, they were told to go to the apartment building.

"And that's where they always met up, I guess, after that. We'd be hanging out there, in the parking lot, waiting for him for hours and we'd see other security detachments from all over. Germany, Turkey, Australia, you name it. They was all going up in there."

How very comfy and convenient, I thought.

"Griffin must have leaked it to those reporters," I said. "He might be kind of a weasel, but I can't see him going along with an arrangement like that."

Still, the revelation astounded me. The shock of the announcement must have addled my brain, because when Harry spoke next, my surprise left me feeling foolish yet again.

"Right. The Weeping Rose it is then. I'd better get back to base and report what I've learned. Hopefully, we can get some chaps over there tonight to investigate."

He prepared to leave, sticking out his hand for Steele to shake.

"Thanks for your help, Sergeant Steele. I'll not forget it," he said.

Steele nodded, but kept quiet.

"You're leaving." The sound of surprise and worry in my voice humiliated me further. Of course he had to leave. I fought against the urge to beg him not to.

"Must, I'm afraid. I will stop by your headquarters again. Speak to that investigator for you, but the hour marches forward. I've got to get cracking on."

"Of course."

"Can't say that it helps find your soldier's killer. She was poking around in places where serious criminal activity was going on. Poking at a hornets' nest sounds like. Dangerous stuff that. Not sure what that Captain was up to."

"I have a feeling our Captain Griffin is none too fond of the General," I said. "I wouldn't be surprised if Griffin approached Tooley and Hannerty to expose what Paterson was doing."

If Paterson regularly abused Griffin physically the way I had witnessed, it seemed plenty of motivation for Griffin to expose his commander's actions. Why would he go to the press without consulting with his public affairs officer? I had asked the question when I saw those pictures. The answer was that he didn't want anyone to know that he had served up his commander in a career-ending scandal. He'd made a smart move, leaking the story to the BBC and not an American media outlet. It served as good misdirection and might help keep some of the suspicion off those closest to the General, at least for a time.

How could he have known that Delray took those pictures? When she heard that knock on her trailer door, was she hiding the pictures from Captain Griffin? He hadn't even looked in her direction in the shot.

"Some of the last pictures Delray took were of that brothel. That had to figure in her death somehow. I just feel it," I said.

"How do you know the pictures you saw were her last ones?" Steele stared down at me, a hard look in his face.

"The memory card has pictures on it that are date stamped the day before she died. They had to be the last ones," I said. "Her camera is missing. Chief Ramsey seems to think that whoever killed her has the camera."

"Well, he'd be wrong about that then," said Steele and he glanced down at me, a kind of challenge in his eyes. I kept staring at him and finally, when I raised my eyebrows in question, he nodded his head slowly.

"Yeah, I have her camera."

"Holy shit!" I whispered in amazement. I sputtered a question, "What .... how .... why?"

He just shrugged. "She came back from the field. It was late. She was nervous and jittery. We had dinner together in the chow hall and after dinner we .... well, we came out here to get some .... you know, private time. She left her bag in my humvee."

He walked toward his vehicle, Harry and I following. He circled around to the back of the vehicle, lifted up the canvas flap that covered the hold of the truck, and pulled out her camera bag. I moved quickly toward him, motioning for him to put it back, put it away before anyone saw. He seemed surprised.

"If someone killed her for what was on that camera, we don't want anyone to know you have it, right?" I asked him.

"Yeah, you're probably right."

"Didn't Ramsey ask you about the camera?"

"No, he mostly asked me about you and how you got along with Virginia, and if I ever saw you two fight or anything. I figured he already pretty much decided who did it, he was just looking for..." and he shrugged.

Looking for enough evidence to arrest me. I cussed in frustration. How can you prove that you didn't do something?

"I don't think you did it," Steele said. "You wouldn't be going through all this if you had."

I thought him a bit naive. If I had murdered her, I'd probably still run around trying to find ways to point the finger at others. I could tell Ramsey that Virginia's lover had the missing camera knowing that Ramsey wanted it. Pointing the finger at someone else would relieve some of the pressure I felt, but I wouldn't do that. Not to Steele. Eventually, I hoped, the forensics would prove me innocent. In the meantime, I was glad to have Steele on my side.

He looked at the bag sitting in the back of his truck. Mud and dust covered the black canvas. A sloppy camera bag for the girl I always thought of as a sloppy soldier. Steele just stared at it. When he looked down at me, his eyes glistened.

"She said she was scared, but she hid it pretty well. When she was with me, she seemed like she was happy. She made me feel ... lighter, like I could take anything, do anything. I could talk to her." He turned his back to me, pinching his nose between his eyes.

I rubbed my hand back and forth on his broad back, feeling his body quake with his silent sobs. Harry stepped away to the front of the vehicle, giving the soldier some privacy.

He'd been walking around all day, holding his grief in, trying to hide how much her passing had affected him. Did anyone really know how much he had cared about her? I felt a stab of shame again, at my ignorance. They'd obviously spent a lot of time together, and I had been totally unaware.

Finally, he took a deep breath and straightened to his full height. He apologized, sniffling away the last of the evidence.

"Have you looked to see if there's another memory card in the camera?" I asked him.

"Yes. There's one in there. I tried to look at the pictures, but the batteries are dead and I don't have a computer."

"I'd love to know what's there, but you have to take it to Ramsey. If he finds out you've had it and didn't say anything, he'll suspect you."

"But he never asked me about it. How would I know it's important?"

Taking it to Ramsey right away was the right thing to do, but also frustrating. We would be giving up the chance of ever knowing what her last pictures revealed. Ramsey would never tell us. He could also turn his attention to Steele, becoming suspicious of him just because he had her camera in the first place.

"I could try to take the memory card to the TOC and look at it there," I said.

Steele shook his head. "If he catches you with it, he'll arrest you for sure," Steele said. "He's only looking for an excuse now. You get caught with evidence and that's all she wrote."

"There are three batteries sitting on a charger in my trailer. If I could get in there…"

"But you can't," he said. "Don't even think about it. I'll take it to Ramsey myself before you do anything like that."

He tried to brush some of the dirt off the bag, his huge hand rubbing the canvas. It didn't do much good. He grabbed a handful of the cloth and clutched it in his fist.

"I could give it to him, but I don't want to. Not yet. I'll just hang onto it for a while longer." He glanced down at me. "You won't tell anyone?"

"Me? Who would I tell?" I said smiling.

He nodded. We wandered around to the front of the humvee. Bliven, Oxley, and Stewart were finished with their safety checks and Stewart was busy telling Harry why the humvee was a superior vehicle to the British Land Rover. Harry indulged his young soldier by allowing him to ramble on at great length.

When Harry noticed us, he motioned Steele to step away from the group. I couldn't hear what Harry said to him, but it looked as if he thanked Steele for his help, shaking his hand. Then, from the way he stood there holding the grip, laying a hand on Steele's shoulder, I thought he might have been giving him a word of sympathy for his loss. Whatever he said next made Steele throw his head back and belch out a huge belly laugh. It seemed such on emotional swing from the crying man I'd seen moments before. Hearing that deep rumble of amusement made me smile. My admiration for Harry rose yet again. He'd found the right thing to say to bring some humor to the grieving soldier. They shook hands warmly and ambled back in our direction, Steele still chuckling from whatever Harry had said.

"Right then, lads. We're off! Care to escort us back to our seemingly inferior vehicle, Sergeant Harper?"

"Of course," I said. I turned to Steele. "The Chaplain told me you're going to sing at her memorial service."

"Yeah, haven't decided what yet." He shook his head, gritting his teeth. "It's a damn shame."

"She'll appreciate it, whatever you sing," I said. I understood Specialist Delray's attraction to him. My estimation of her improved by the quality of man she had chosen.

On the walk back to the TOC, a new realization settled around me like slow moving fog. I might not ever see Harry again.

It happened so often in my life. A soldier walks in, stays a few hours, maybe I'm writing a story about him or her, maybe we're working together on a project and then they're gone. In a place like Bosnia, it happened almost every week, and I hated to see that happen with Harry. I'd only known him a couple of hours, but I knew I wanted to know more about him. I watched him out of the corner of my eye, his casual stride, sure and confident. His head swiveled slowly as if inspecting everything he saw.

"Harry, I know you said you didn't think the murder has anything to do with your journalists, but don't you think it's tied to that brothel somehow? I mean, she was taking pictures of the place." I talked quietly as we walked, not wanting a casual listener to hear what I said. Harry leaned down to listen. Oxley and Stewart walked behind us, engaged in their own conversation.

"It rings true that she might have been on to something in that place, but I don't see it having anything to do with the BBC boys. Not with their disappearance. Her murderer had to be someone who could get on base here. How could someone associated with the Weeping Rose come here to do her in?"

He must have seen the disappointment on my face.

"My responsibilities are narrowed to finding those two and finding them as quickly as possible. You understand, don't you?"

"Of course," I said. I wanted to say more but he interrupted me.

"Not sure the chap will want to listen to anything I have to say, but I'll go talk to that Ramsey fellow. I'll tell him about the general and the apartment, the women, even the interpreters. The whole lot. He may just think I'm daft, but I'll give it a go."

"Thank you," I said. "That means a lot."

He instructed Oxley and Stewart to stay by the Land Rover, then strode into the TOC, as good as his word. The one person I had thought I could count on was Neil, but he concerned himself more with his own reputation. I couldn't blame him for that. With Harry going off on his quest, aside from Sergeant Steele, there wasn't anyone left to help me.

Somehow, Sergeant Major Harry Fogg with two Gs had made me feel like this whole nightmare wasn't quite as bad as I thought. The instant he left my side, the feeling of confidence, that all would eventually work itself out, left with him.

It started to rain again and I found that to be very fitting weather for my mood. I checked my watch and realized I only had about 40 minutes to get the promised press release done. I headed into the TOC. The last thing I wanted to do was give McCallen another excuse to be angry with me.

Twenty-two

I entered the emergency operations cell in the TOC with the objective of speaking with the people who operated the radios and received all the messages from the field. Sergeant First Class Jackson had manned the radios during the first twelve-hour shift of the day in the EOC. He flipped through his messages and answered all of my questions easily.

"Her name was what again?" I asked.

He spelled it for me in the military alphabet so I wouldn't be mistaken.

"First name, Delta, Alpha, Delta, Alpha. Last name, Alpha, Bravo, Delta, India, Charlie. Dada Abdic. That's the name I have here."

"Do you have any idea how long she's been an interpreter with us?" I asked.

He shook his head. "Negative. You'd have to check with Major Townson for that information."

Major Townson would probably tell me that Dada Abdic had been working with the American soldiers in Bosnia since the beginning of this mission, at least two years. It was Dada Abdic listed as shot and in critical condition in a hospital in Sarajevo because that's the name that had been on the ID card when Mishka took the job and the name she assumed when she started working here. I wondered how Major Townson would continue his practice of falsifying ID cards now that one of his interpreters lay wounded in a hospital.

The press release wouldn't reveal her name anyway. The standard line of—names are withheld until the family is notified—would go in the press release for now. Eventually I would have to confront Major Townson about what I knew. Mishka and Dada Abdic would be as good a place as any to start.

"And progress on finding the sniper? Did they arrest anyone?" I asked.

"Negative," said Jackson. "Major Purser put Captain Kazalski in charge of handling the investigation."

Jackson pointed to a corner where several soldiers gathered, looking at pictures tacked to a wall. I thanked him and headed in the direction of the Military Police.

Major Purser towered over the rest of the soldiers in the group, but he seemed to be taking a backseat to the discussion going on, letting his Captain take charge. I had seen Kazalski during morning BUBs but never actually met him. I recognized one of the MPs in the group as the same soldier who had escorted me to my interrogation sessions with Ramsey.

Approaching a group of police as a suspect in a murder investigation felt awkward to say the least. Confirmation of the awkwardness came when they all turned and gave me the cop stare as I approached. After a long pause, they ignored me and turned back to what they were doing. I moved around their perimeter, trying to get a look at the pictures they studied.

They stood in front of a board with about thirty, eight-by-ten photographs tacked on the wall, some of the pictures still a little damp, as if recently spit out from an inkjet printer. The street scenes showed soldiers on patrol; Mishka walked alongside the platoon. She stuck close to the lieutenant in charge. He seemed to look at her often, smiling. It appeared to me as if they flirted with each other. Then a few pictures with them talking to a shopkeeper, his white apron tied over an ample belly. Mishka appeared to be translating for the lieutenant.

"Did they have a combat camera soldier with them?" I asked.

Captain Kazalski turned and looked down at me, making a pointed assessment cops do in an instant. Apparently, his was that

I didn't have any business asking him any questions. He turned his back on me and continued looking at the pictures. Unnecessarily rude, but nothing I hadn't faced before.

"I'm Master Sergeant Harper, Captain. Public Affairs. I'm writing the press release on the incident and I'd like to know…"

Without turning around he interrupted me. "I know who you are," he said.

Fame is not always a good thing.

"You can tell them our investigation is ongoing, Sergeant." It was a dismissal.

"That's pretty obvious, Captain, since you're standing there studying those pictures and not interrogating a suspect, but you see, if I make the press release extremely vague, the more questions you're going to have to answer later on."

Kazalski glanced at Purser, who shrugged. The Captain was on his own evidently. Kazalski put his hands on his hips and stared down his nose at me.

"Why would I have to answer any questions? You're the public affairs officer. That's your job."

Cute. His snide remark got his men chuckling but Purser crossed his ample arms over his chest and rolled his eyes to the ceiling. Kazalski didn't notice.

"I may be the one standing in front of the press, but you'll be the one responsible if they get angry and decide to make this an ugly story, Captain. Bosnian contract worker gets shot in the street and the Americans aren't doing anything to catch the killer. Or how 'bout this? American soldiers stand by while unarmed interpreter is shot." I shrugged. "If you stonewall, you give them no choice but to speculate and make stuff up. On the other hand, all you have to do is get me up to date on what's going on and I'll be more than happy to do my job the way it should be done."

His face tightened and gave me that cop stare again. He didn't want to share. It wasn't in his nature. What I wouldn't tell him is that my desire for knowledge had little to do with the press and more for my own purposes.

"This is an ongoing investigation. The last thing we need is the press running around knowing about our leads."

"My job is to assess how to tell them what we can tell them without hurting your investigation. I can't do my job unless I know what you've got."

He still wasn't convinced. The other MPs were giving me the same look as if I were a waste of their time, an unwanted complication in their day.

"I'm on your side, Captain. I knew the girl that was hit." That stopped him for a minute. He exchanged looks with Purser again, looking for approval, but Purser remained the silent observer. I forged ahead.

"It looks like you had some luck today. If combat camera went along on the patrol, that's a great break for your investigation, right?"

Combat camera, soldiers whose job it is to document for training and historical purposes what soldiers do every day on the job. Sometimes they shoot video of an entire patrol's activity, interviewing the soldiers before, during and after to get an accurate record of the mission for the day. Sometimes they shoot still-photos, capturing the moment-to-moment events that happen in the field. Having a combat documentation soldier along on a patrol hit by a sniper was a stroke of luck.

I shouldered my way in closer to the board, hoping Kazalski would relent and let me in on what they knew. I glanced up at him over my shoulder with an expectant smile and it seemed to work.

"It's a stroke of luck but it raises questions too," he said.

"What questions?"

Purser cleared his throat and took up the story.

"We've had patrol after patrol in that area for weeks. Rarely has combat camera been along for the ride. Why would they choose the one patrol in the sector with combat camera to target? It doesn't make much sense."

The hair on the back of my neck stood up. The sniper chose that patrol, despite knowing every step of the way would be captured in pictures, because Mishka served as interpreter on it.

They didn't want to miss their opportunity to kill her. I shuddered and wrapped my arms around myself. That poor, frightened girl.

"Sergeant Harper? You alright?" Kazalski put his hand on my arm and I'm sure, could feel me tremble.

"I'm fine. Just, ah, tell me what you know so far."

He stared at me for a long moment then turned his attention back to the pictures. "This is the victim, the interpreter," he said, pointing at Mishka.

They had been patrolling down a quiet downtown street. Soldiers of the squad deployed along the street on opposite sidewalks, walking in a staggered formation, their weapons casually slung in front of themselves, covering multiple directions. Cars parked on both sides of the road, multi-storied buildings along the street. Kids rode by on old bicycles, dogging the patrols, smiling at the soldiers and the camera.

Kazalski pointed to one of the photos where a pickup truck sat parked near a grassy area.

"Looks like two people inside the truck. In this picture, it looks like one of them is looking through binoculars and the other one is on a cell phone."

"You think they were spotters for the sniper?"

"Yes. The sniper could be anywhere, in any of those buildings. And in this picture here, she's down."

Mishka looked dead. Blood already pooling around her, her eyes staring up, her hand pressed to her neck and covered in blood. The lieutenant, who had been smiling and flirting with her, now had blood splattered on his face. He kneeled over her, pointing at a building, his mouth open, giving orders. The shopkeeper they had been talking to had turned toward his shop and was in mid-stride as he ran away, his mouth open, eyes wide in fear. The rest of the squad in the frame had either gone to a knee with their weapon at the ready in a firing position, or were prone on the ground, all of them scanning the area to see where the shot had come from. It was a powerful photograph. Looking at her lying there in a pool of blood and the intensity on the lieutenant's blood-splattered face made gooseflesh rise on my arms.

"Is there any chance, in your opinion, that the sniper was targeting the lieutenant or do you think the interpreter was purposely targeted?"

They all looked at each other, shrugging. "It's too hard to tell at this point," Kazalski said. "If I had to make a guess, I'd say, especially with the spotters and the guy on the cell phone, they were aiming for the girl."

The white pickup drew my gaze back to the picture. The wide shot of the street with the lieutenant, Mishka and the shopkeeper in the center of the photograph, showed the front of the truck just barely in the frame. Clearly, two people sat in the cab, but only as silhouettes. A slight reflective flash from one lens and the way the elbows flared out gave the impression of someone looking through binoculars. The one on the cell phone was a big guy, his head turned away, not looking at the soldiers, his face unrecognizable.

"Combat camera says they can increase the size of this, enhance it some. We might get some more information from the pictures." He shrugged, much more relaxed now that he had decided to talk to me.

"Great, well now I can say that it appears to have been a coordinated attack, that good progress has been made and we will continue our vigorous investigation."

The captain nodded his head and, trying not to smile, said, "Just make sure the bastards spell my name right, would ya?"

I thanked the captain, shouldered my way out of the cluster of police and started on my way to my desk, until a commotion drew my attention. Clayton Hawes, standing at the very back of the TOC, had slammed a phone down, obviously angry.

"God damn it," he said through clenched teeth. His face red and his white-knuckled fist still clutching the receiver, he swayed slightly, his face glistening and I realized he'd been drinking. From the looks of it, he'd been drinking quite a lot. He glanced around the room, but his eyes didn't seem to focus on anything. Finally, he turned and stumbled toward the door of the TOC, his drunkenness more apparent as he attempted to walk.

Suddenly Hawes stopped as if startled, afraid. I shifted my gaze in the direction he stared and saw Dr. Cosic, the Bosnian kitchen worker, standing near the door. Cosic wore his white coat, the red bandana around his neck and his hands shoved deep into his pants pockets. He simply stood there, staring at Hawes. I doubted Cosic had the credentials necessary to gain entry to the TOC and I wondered how he had been allowed into the headquarters tent. Not a place one would normally expect to see a kitchen worker. Cosic merely stood there, but evidently, his presence was enough to leave Hawes frozen in indecision.

The big Texan finally mustered up his courage and strode out of the tent, past Cosic, shoving the smaller man away. Cosic stumbled slightly, but recovered, then casually strolled after Hawes.

It was the second time I had witnessed Hawes appear intimidated by his employees. First, Chicago and now Dr. Cosic. Cosic hadn't appeared angry or threatening in any way, but his mere presence had sent the drunken Hawes into fits. What was the big man doing getting drunk? Rules against drinking held true for soldiers and civilians alike. His drunkenness could cost him his job. Obviously, something had upset the contractor.

I didn't have time to contemplate what that could be. I had a deadline looming. Colonel McCallen expected to see a finished release in only a few minutes, so I pushed the scene between Hawes and Cosic to the back of my mind. I had other priorities.

Twenty-three

I headed straight to my desk and tried to shut out all the noise and commotion going on around me as I punched out a quick press release on the sniper shooting. Wounded and in critical condition. I wanted more information to pass on to Sergeant Steele, but the vague details were enough to put in a press release. As soon as I had a moment, I planned to call down to the hospital to see if I could get additional information on Mishka's situation.

When I glanced up, Harry stood in front of my desk, his forehead pulled down into a frown.

"Bloody stubborn bastard that one is."

He didn't have to tell me who he meant.

"Ramsey wouldn't listen to you?"

"Oh, he listened alright. He just didn't bloody care. Not about the interpreters, not about the Weeping bloody Rose, none of it. Sure, it's all speculation, but you'd think a bloke wouldn't chuck it all out with the fish scraps to the bins."

I stood and walked around my desk. I wanted to hug him, but not in front of everyone.

"Thanks for trying. It was a long shot. I didn't think he'd listen."

Harry smiled and stuck out his hand. "I'm sorry I couldn't be of more help, Master Sergeant Harper"

I smiled. I liked the way my name sounded coming from his lips. We shook hands, then he covered mine with his other beefy paw.

"I'll keep you posted on what I learn. Keep your chin up. Don't let that blond bugger get the best of you. Do you hear?"

"Thanks, Harry. I appreciate that you tried."

"Cheers. I hope to see you again. I really do. It's been a right pleasure."

He smiled his wicked smile, then turned and strode away. I watched him leave, people stepping aside as his bulky form approached. He nearly bumped into Colonel McCallen on his way out. Harry turned and glared at McCallen's back as the man stalked by him without acknowledging his presence.

McCallen ignored Harry and moved with a purpose directly up to my desk. He hadn't even seen the press release yet and he already looked wound up. I braced myself to hear angry words from him and wasn't surprised when I heard the command that came out of his mouth.

"Sergeant Harper, come with me immediately please."

"Yes, sir."

It didn't sound good, but he didn't leave any room for me to ask questions, so I followed him. He led me to the front of the command briefing room where a group of officers, including Captain Griffin and Colonel Raybourn, gathered around a table looking down at something. They all turned to watch Colonel McCallen and me as we approached the table. Colonel Raybourn pointed to the thing that had captured all of their attention. It was a videotape lying on top of a large brown envelope.

"Do you have anything that can play that?" he asked.

I nodded, "Of course, sir. It's a professional grade beta tape. I've got a deck in the trailer that can play it."

"Let's go then," he said.

I cautioned them. "I'd suggest clearing that with Chief Ramsey first, sir. The trailer is still blocked off as a crime scene."

Raybourn wouldn't be deterred. "Later. Right now we need to know what's on that tape."

Everyone scattered to grab their gear before leaving. Raybourn slipped his helmet on then tugged on the shoulder holster that held his weapon. Colonel McCallen picked up the tape by grabbing the sides of the envelope it laid on, attempting to avoid touching it. I turned and led them out of the TOC and toward my trailer. "Where did it come from?" I asked the crowd.

"A kid handed it to some soldiers on patrol and ran away," Colonel McCallen explained. "The squad brought it back here unopened. Unfortunately the kid disappeared in the crowd."

We got to the trailer and the yellow police tape and the do-not-enter sign still draped the doorway. McCallen stepped forward, yanked the flimsy barriers down and opened the door. He stopped in the doorway and looked back at me.

"I suggest we attempt to avoid touching anything as much as possible," he cautioned.

"The monitor is right there," I said. "You might be able to watch it from the doorway without coming inside."

"All right, do it," Raybourn ordered.

I climbed the stairs and stepped into the trailer, turned on the deck and monitor, and tilted the monitor so it would be visible from the door. I inserted the tape, listened to it load and hit play. At first, noisy snow filled the screen, then a gloved hand fumbled in front of the lens of the camera. When the hand moved away, the whole scene became clear.

"Who are they?" someone asked and was quickly shushed.

"The BBC journalists," Colonel McCallen answered in a whisper.

Ian Tooley and Frank Hannerty, blindfolded, sat next to each other, their arms drawn behind their backs. They both looked a little roughed up, black and blue marks on their foreheads and around their mouths, a trickle of blood down Hannerty's chin. They sat before an old and distressed looking, clapboard wall. Someone had pinned the front page of a local newspaper to Hannerty's shirt.

"Can you see the date on the paper?" Raybourn asked.

"No, sir. I'd have to enhance the shot to be sure."

We could hear some shuffling, but the image remained the same. In a thick Bosnian accent came a voice from someone probably speaking directly into the camera shotgun microphone.

"Five million British pounds or they die. Wait for instructions."

Then a slow zoom into their faces, first one then the other. They appeared calm but weary, their heads turning that way people do when they can't see but want to. Then the tape went back to snowy hiss. The images chilled me to the bone.

Twenty-four

P lay it again," Raybourn ordered.
I shuttled the tape back to the beginning and played it again. When it was over, everyone just stood there, Colonel McCallen, Captain Griffin, Colonel Raybourn and a couple of other officers, contemplating what they had seen.

"Contact the British. Tell them what we've got," ordered Raybourn.

"Sergeant Major Fogg just left, sir," I said. "He was here earlier asking questions about the reporters."

"Fine. Tell him he needs to get back here." One of the officers took off for the TOC. I had the completely inappropriate feeling that I looked forward to having Harry around again.

"Go back to the beginning, but play it slower," Raybourn ordered.

I rewound to the beginning and this time used the shuttle wheel to turn through the tape, frame by frame. We got a good look at the gloved hand. The glove was black and had small holes in it.

"A driving glove," McCallen suggested.

We all agreed. When the tape got to a clear frame showing Tooley and Hannerty, I stopped it to try to see if we could get a good look at the newspaper.

"Today's," McCallen confirmed. "I recognize the front page picture from the Brcko paper."

Everyone stared silently as we watched each frame. I broke the silence.

"From the quality of the tape and image, I'd say they shot the video with Tooley's own camera. Notice how the image has a blue tint to it? Whoever set this up didn't white balance...professional beta cameras, you have to tell the camera what color white is so it understands the rest of the color spectrum. These shots weren't white balanced, so the colors are off...a little blue. It could have been on the wrong filter...anyway, the shooter didn't know how to operate this camera, other than to push the record button."

They took that information in for a minute. I shuttled through the rest of the hostage scene but didn't learn anything new. No mysterious shadows or other movement, no extraneous sounds that might give away location, no way to tell how many people had been in the room.

"Why would they give the tape to American soldiers and ask for British pounds?" someone asked.

"The soldiers were probably just convenient messengers," Griffin said. "Their camera says BBC on the side. The kidnappers couldn't have been mistaken that they were British."

I wasn't sure if anyone else noticed his slip, but I had. How would Griffin know what markings their camera had unless he had met the reporter and his photographer before? He was right. Their camera did have BBC on the side. I knew it because I saw Delray's pictures; the pictures that showed Griffin meeting the hostages on the sly, and now here they were, kidnapped and obviously beaten, and Griffin tried to pretend he didn't know them. I glanced at McCallen to see if he heard the slip up and he had. He narrowed his eyes at me, and if I read him correctly, he wanted me to stay quiet.

"All right," Raybourn said. "Keep the tape here and don't remove it from the machine. We don't want any more fingerprints on it than absolutely necessary. We'll let the British get what they can from it and hand it over to them. Understood?" he asked.

"Hooah, sir."

Raybourn abruptly turned and walked away, the others following him.

I was relieved when McCallen stepped into the trailer and closed the door behind him.

"What do you make of that?" I asked him.

"Are you sure it was Griffin in those pictures?" he asked.

"There was no mistaking him, sir. He was standing..."

I stopped because I heard something coming from the tape. I turned and saw that I had left the tape playing after the last run through. The tape had run past the point of the kidnap video and the noisy snow and now showed images recorded previously.

"It's the street. The street in front of the brothel," I told him breathlessly.

The kidnappers must have rewound the tape they found in the camera and recorded over it. Tooley must have shot these images on the day they disappeared.

There was the road repair operation, a few expertly shot sequences of soldiers doing their work. Then Specialist Delray, smiling and pointing her camera at Tooley. Against regulations, she had taken off her flak vest and helmet. She wore her soft-cap but she had that on backwards, so the bill of the cap hung down the back of her neck. Wisps of her white blond hair stuck out unruly from the sides and front of her cap. Her face gleamed in sweat from a day out shooting. Dried mud covered the knees of her uniform. She wore her weapon slung over her back and the camera bag, which Steele now had in the back of his humvee, drooped heavily from her shoulder.

She took a few pictures of Tooley, the same pictures we had seen on her disk. Then she struck a pose, one hand on her hip, the other behind her head in a mock centerfold pose. She laughed, waved and spoke in her thick southern accent. "Hi, Momma! Hi y'all back in Thelma, Mississippi!"

She laughed again in that annoying high-pitched, uninhibited giggle she used to punctuate every conversation. I'd heard it a million times and a million times it had rankled my nerves.

I stood there looking at that footage, her laughter echoing in my head. Since I had found her body, I had learned how deeply she felt about people she barely knew, how she must have known her life was in danger and yet still could think clearly enough to pass on evidence of her killers. I learned about her relationship with Steele, a good man who remained strong and forthright in his devotion to her, even after her death. I had learned far more about her after she died than I had ever known about her while she lived.

Shame settled over me. I felt ashamed of my assumptions about her and sorry for my loss of ever knowing the real Virginia. Before I could stop myself, the tears were flowing down my face. I slammed my hand on the stop button and pulled my helmet off my head, dropping it on the floor. I sobbed and hiccupped, my emotions out of control, my face in my hands.

"Oh, Lauren," Neil whispered.

At first he ran his hand back and forth across my shoulders to comfort me, but when that had little effect he gathered me up in his arms, pressed my head to his chest, telling me everything would be all right, everything would be okay. He crushed me in his embrace and rocked me gently. Virginia, being a suspect, the drama with Neil – not to mention that I'd cried more than I had in years. Crying was not something I did, ever. The excess emotion contributed to my humiliation and shame. Finally, I managed to control myself.

I stepped out of his arms, turning my back to him, looking away and wiping my face. I didn't want to see the pity in his eyes.

When he spoke to me, his voice sounded husky.

"You have to make a copy of the tape, Lauren. We can't just hand it off to the British now. We need to know what else is on there."

I nodded, but I didn't want to speak. When I finally glanced back at him, his eyes were shining and a red flush rose up from his neck. I could see his chest rising and falling. He backed away toward the door to put some distance between us, but he didn't take his eyes off me. I thought I would see pity in his eyes. Instead they burned with desire.

The shock of his heated stare forced me to move. I peeked into the deck where the original tape played.

"It's a thirty-minute tape."

I would need a full thirty minutes to ensure I got everything recorded on it.

I cranked the shuttle all the way to the left and let the original tape fly back to its start point.

"Hand me one of those tapes there, in the black case."

He moved to the stack of tapes on the other side of the edit desk and handed me a blank. I punched up the proper machine on the router, shoved the tape into the second machine, and hit play and record on the deck at the same time. I watched the meters to make sure I had sound going into the machine. When it was rolling without a problem, I didn't know where to look.

I heard and felt Neil move back to the door. When I finally glanced at him, he simply stood there watching me, his face still flushed. He put his hand on the doorknob as if ready to leave, but he didn't go. He looked down, having an internal conversation with himself. I didn't know what to say to him. He finally turned his gaze to me, his eyes searching my face.

"I'm a fool, Lauren. You were right to ask for a transfer. And I'm sorry. For all of this."

He opened the door, went down the steps, and closed the door behind him. I heard him on the wooden walkway as he left. He took a couple of steps and stopped for a few moments, and then I heard his slow and steady progress away.

Twenty-five

I collapsed into the nearest chair. Breaking down in front of Neil left me feeling embarrassed, but also proud of myself that I hadn't indulged in an emotional replay of the earlier scene with him. *I will get over this infatuation,* I thought to myself, watching the tape again as it recorded. I could easily have cried some more, but I didn't have time to fall apart. I kept my eyes on the tape to see if anything new presented itself.

The street scenes continued after Delray's happy wave to family and friends, then after a few more sequences, color bars appeared. I feared there wouldn't be anything else to see. Then over the color bars, I could hear talking and the familiar sounds of pinning a microphone on someone.

"Hang on. Let me get this on here properly," a voice mumbled with a heavy British accent.

The color bars disappeared to reveal a young woman sitting on a stool in front of a window. She looked uncomfortable and wide-eyed, watching everything going on around her. Tooley walked to the windows behind her and opened the blinds so that meager light streamed in. He then set up a light directly behind her, on the floor and shining on her back. The result left her image in total silhouette, a darkened form sitting in front of a bright light.

In the brief time that her face appeared, she looked to be in her early twenties, maybe not even that old. Her well-made-up face, with dark lipstick and perfectly arched eyebrows, seemed an attempt to make herself look older, but it didn't quite work. She wore a tight top with a plunging neckline, her obvious assets well displayed. Her dark brown hair and petite frame left the impression of a beautiful, young and frightened woman.

Tooley, after setting up the light, went back to look through the viewfinder.

"Yeah, perfect. I promise you. No one will be able to see your face at all. And when I edit this, we'll alter your voice so that no one can recognize it."

I heard another voice from off camera. I couldn't be sure, but it sounded like Captain Griffin.

"Let me see," the voice said. "He's right, Ritza. No one could recognize you from this. I promise."

Then Hannerty's voice piped in to take control of the situation. "Right, so we don't have much time. Let's just get to it shall we?"

The young woman nodded her head.

"I won't ask you your name. I don't even want to know it."

"Okay," she said in a very small, frightened voice.

"Where are you from?"

"Plavdiv, I am from Plavdiv, Bulgaria."

"Bulgaria?"

"Yes."

"How did you come to be here?"

She shifted around in her seat, nervous and probably searching for the right words in English.

"A man, a man tell me he will help me to ... ah, to leave Bulgaria. My mother, she want me to marry a man I no want to marry. I want very much to leave. So I go to this man and he say he help me to go."

"And did he? Did he help you to leave Plavdiv?"

She shook her head, and she chuckled.

"He help me to leave but I no go to Germany like I ask. I go here."

"To Bosnia?"

"Yes, Bosnia."

"You didn't know you were coming here?"

She let out a loud guffaw. "No, of course not. Why would I

want to come to this place?" She laughed a nervous, girlish laugh.

"So what happened when you found yourself here in Bosnia and not in Germany like you thought?"

"I say this not right. This not Germany. And man say I have no choice. He have my papers ... my ..."

"He had your passport?"

"Yes, passport. And I owe him money and I must pay." She looked down and she was quiet for a bit.

"At first, he is nice. He say they make mistake, but I know. I know this is what it is. There are other girls, they all say the same, that he take passport and they must work." She shook her head and shrugged her shoulders.

"So you worked here?"

"Yes, for many weeks. I must go with the men or I don't eat, I can't go out, I am prisoner."

"Did they give you any money?"

She laughed at this idea. "Ha, no, no money. But when I meet Paterson he give me things sometimes, he buy me things. Some I keep, sometimes I sell to get money." She shrugged her shoulders.

"Paterson....?" He began to ask, but the voice off-camera stepped in.

"No, no names."

"I'm just trying to clarify..."

"I said no names, and I mean it. And you won't use the line where she says his name either."

"Well, it's a little late for that, mate."

"All right, we stop right now."

The young woman listened to them argue, her head turning back and forth, growing more and more nervous as the exchange became more heated. Then someone in a camouflage uniform walked in front of the camera, blocking the view and he's angry now.

"I told you before we got here that no names...."

Tooley must have wanted to preserve tape because he stopped recording. About ten minutes of tape remained, but the rest of the tape was empty.

I stopped the tapes and rewound them both, thinking about what I had just seen. Ritza had to be the woman Paterson kept in the apartment just the way Steele said. Captain Griffin wanted to help her. His voice, telling her the promise that she wouldn't be recognized, had been gentle and reassuring. I could only assume he really cared about her to do what he had done. He didn't want names used, but that wouldn't really matter. If the press had proof that American soldiers were involved in prostitution, in giving gifts to women who were being held against their will, that would be more than enough to launch an investigation; an investigation that would eventually reveal the truth. I had to admire the Captain for his guts. What he had done presented more than enough proof to ruin his career and Paterson's.

I rewound both tapes, ejected the copy and took my time writing out a label. Ramsey and Santos would want to be able to watch the video at their leisure, so I started a VHS copy for them. When the new copy was rolling, I settled back, and scanned the trailer, glancing over to Delray's cot. Purple finger print dust touched every surface. Fresh muddy boot prints combined with a thick layer of dust to litter the floor. Delray's things still sat folded in her little closet. I needed to pack them up and ship them to her family.

I wanted to ship her things home along with some concrete information about what had happened to their daughter. There were too many pieces, too many different angles going on to understand what any of it had to do with Delray. Delray gets herself killed after taking pictures of Griffin and the reporters. The reporters interview Ritza, a young woman who is a prisoner in some kind of human trafficking mess. The reporters are kidnapped and held for ransom. An interpreter, poor Mishka, is shot in a sniper attack. None of it made sense. None of it seemed connected.

Then I looked at my things. I had only spent one night away from my hooch, but it felt as if weeks had gone by. So much had happened. Thinking about it exhausted me.

Just as the VHS copy of the tape ended, I heard boot steps

outside the trailer. A long line of people who wanted to see the video came and asked me to play it for them. Major Purser, Captain Kazalski, and a few of his MPs were among the first viewers. For them I only played it through the hostage demand and stopped the tape immediately after. I wasn't sure why, but I figured the rest of what was on the tape probably shouldn't be widely known.

After a while, Chiefs Ramsey and Santos showed up.

"I guess police tape doesn't mean much around here," Ramsey said. He and Santos stood in the doorway of the trailer, Santos with a blank look on his face, but Ramsey's clenched jaw and furrowed brow broadcast exactly how he felt.

"I didn't have much choice, Chief," I said. "It was the only place we could play the tape the kidnappers sent."

I played it for him. He stood with his arms crossed and all those dimples etched in his face. When the hostage demand ended, he ordered me to play it again.

"Chief there's something else on here you should see. Remember the pictures we saw from Delray's memory card? Here's what Tooley shot while Delray took those pictures of him."

I played the street scenes, Delray's giggle, her silly pose. The investigators saw their first images of her alive. I hoped it would give them more motivation to solve the case.

"Now here is what they did when they went inside the Weeping Rose."

Ramsey and Santos looked equally shocked but stayed quiet throughout the interview scene with Ritza. When they got to the part where Griffin stops the interview, Ramsey looked at me.

"We've been trying to get together with Captain Griffin and the general all day, but Paterson flew down to Tuzla this afternoon and won't be back until tomorrow. I asked Griffin why the general didn't take his aide along and Griffin said the general had ordered him to stay here for some reason. He wouldn't elaborate."

"Why haven't you just asked Griffin about the pictures? He's the one in them." Ramsey and Santos exchanged a look that I didn't understand.

"Look," I said. "There's no way Paterson knew Griffin was meeting with those reporters, not when the purpose was to expose the general's sex slave. When Delray took that picture, she had Griffin's entire career in her hands. He might have found out that she had them."

When they didn't respond, I pressed on. "Well, isn't that motivation to kill someone?"

"Griffin didn't kill her," Ramsey said simply.

"Just like that...he didn't kill her. Why is that so easy for you to believe?"

"Because saving his career wasn't a motivator for him, that's why. He put in a request for separation from service two weeks ago. He wanted out of the Army, Sergeant."

"But he's a general's aide."

"A move that might indicate he wanted to make the Army a career, but maybe it convinced him that he wasn't cut out for service."

"Or, something else was driving him out?"

"Again, you're grasping at straws. In any case, furthering his career was not on Griffin's mind. He must have already decided to expose Paterson, in which case, killing Delray wouldn't have benefited him."

Ramsey let the information hang in the air and the implications settle around my shoulders. It felt an impossible weight to hold without my knees buckling.

"So, as I'm sure you've figured out by now," he continued, "while that doesn't remove him from our list of suspects, it definitely moves him down in the priorities. He doesn't have a motive. Care to guess who is at the top of the list?"

"What about the General? You just saw that Griffin was exposing the General's affair with a woman who was prostituting herself against her will..."

"If that were the motivator, then Griffin would be dead and not your soldier. No, the General didn't have anything to do with Specialist Delray's death. He may be in serious trouble, but he didn't kill your soldier. You're still number one on the list,

Harper."

"Why? Why am I at the top of the list? Because I had an argument with her once or twice? Because I lived with her?"

Ramsey crossed his arms over his chest and smiled. "I've told you all the reasons before, but let's review. You're at the top of our list because you are known to have an explosive temper. You swore in front of witnesses that you would kill her. The murder weapon belonged to you. You admit that you didn't like her, that she got on your nerves and oh by the way, you're having an affair with a married officer. Your journal has been very interesting reading, I might add. I haven't finished reading all of it, but you can't deny that your relationship with your commander is corrupt."

"Having a crush on your boss isn't a crime, last time I checked. Just because I fantasized about it in a personal diary, doesn't mean I acted on it!" I was shouting, my temper getting the best of me, but my freedom, my everything lay in the balance.

"Even if Delray did know how I felt, it would be embarrassing at most," I said. "But it's not motivation to kill her over it."

Ramsey ignored that rationalization as if I hadn't spoken. He casually leaned against the trailer door.

"You can pretend nothing happened, but my belief is that your roommate knew about your affair. She may have even threatened to ruin your career and McCallen's for that matter."

My desperation meant nothing to him. He seemed to enjoy my discomfort. I still couldn't stop myself from arguing my case.

"You are ignoring serious criminal behavior to focus on a scandal you've made up in your head, Chief. Human trafficking, a general officer involved in keeping a sex slave, not to mention an officer leaking the information to the international media. How could you possibly ignore all of that to center your investigation on me?"

"Explain to me how any of that has anything to do with your soldier's death. Sure, we'll investigate that activity. General Paterson's career is over, but I see all of that as a separate case. Not anything to do with your specialist."

"You're wrong, Chief. I am not having an affair with Colonel McCallen and I didn't kill Delray. And if you keep looking at me for this murder, you're going to let the guy who really did it get away."

"DNA results should be back soon. Did I tell you that your blood type matches the blood found under her fingernails?" He said it with a satisfied grin and it made me shudder.

"The blood may match but the DNA won't. I don't have any of the defensive wounds you said the killer would have."

"We'll see. In any case, with the blood and a DNA match, I'd say we're going to have a pretty airtight case. If we weren't on a secure base camp, you would be in custody. As it is, custody isn't really necessary." He stuck his hands deep into the cargo pocket of his pants, pulling out a set of rubber gloves. "I need to get finger prints from that tape."

I hit the eject button and Ramsey pulled the tape out with his gloved hands. Santos stepped forward with the finger print kit and they did what they needed to do. I moved out of the way, trying to come to grips with the idea that, no matter what I did or said, Ramsey seemed determined to charge me with murder. The overwhelming need to call my sister engulfed me. *Oh, Loretta. What are you going to think when I tell you I'm facing murder charges.*

"You might as well enjoy being around your things for a while. We may have the DNA results as soon as Monday or Tuesday. Once they come in, I'm sure we'll be making an arrest."

"Are you saying I can move back into the trailer?"

"Might as well. Everything in here has been compromised now. Enjoy it while you can." He dropped the tape into a large evidence bag, sealing it shut. When he and Santos left, Ramsey turned back for one last look at me, that knowing smirk on his face.

When the trailer door slammed closed behind them, I flopped into a chair and buried my face in my hands. I can admit now that I was damn scared. The idea of going to jail, of even being charged with murder, made my blood run cold. I knew Ramsey didn't have a thread of evidence to prove that Colonel McCallen and I were actually having an affair, but the stuff I'd written in my journal and the open accusation would be enough to make life very difficult for the Colonel and his family. I hated to see that happen.

Those dark thoughts whirled around my head when the trailer door flew open and in stepped Sergeant Major Harry Fogg.

"Hello, Master Sergeant Harper. Did you miss me, then?" he said with a cocky grin.

The effects of Ramsey's accusation couldn't be washed away even by Harry's arrival. I wanted to tell him that I had missed him terribly, but I kept it to myself. He hadn't come alone and I didn't want to embarrass him by being unprofessional. I stood up, gave him a formal but warm handshake, and tried to smile. It came out as more of a grimace.

McCallen led the group of officers, both British and American. He briefed them about how the tape came into our possession and what steps had been taken so far. McCallen kept shifting his gaze to me but I avoided making eye contact.

"The investigators took the original tape," I told the group, "but I made a copy for you."

Over the next hour or so, I played the recording for them repeatedly. The British officers called back to their base camp to see if they had "the proper machine" to play the professional beta tape. When they confirmed that they didn't have one, I offered to make a VHS copy for them.

I felt and moved like a zombie through most of it. Harry didn't know what had me so out of sorts, but he tried nonetheless to lighten my mood. He whispered funny comments in my ear and generally tried to alter my attitude, but I couldn't get my mind off my imminent confinement. He knew something weighed on me.

I copied only the hostage portion of the tape on VHS and made a label for them. When they had everything they needed from me, the group left abruptly without much thanks, Colonel McCallen giving me a brief smile as he left, escorting them away.

When they were all out of the trailer, Harry closed the door and turned to me.

"You look completely knackered, luv. Is there anything I can do?"

"Oh, I'm all right, Harry," I lied.

"Wish I had the time for a brew. Put some shine back into those eyes of yours." He stepped close and cupped my chin in his hand, staring down at me. His gaze roamed my face, his green eyes full of concern. When he bent down slowly, I couldn't hide my surprise. He gave me a lingering kiss on each cheek, pressing his stubble-covered face to mine. He started to move away then thought better of it. "Chuck it," he said and kissed me full on the lips, his eyes closed to slits, but still watching, smiling. He kissed me twice more, light but prolonged kisses, soft and growing slightly more urgent and familiar with each repeat. After the third one, I wanted to taste his tongue and lose myself in his kiss, but he was having none of that. He peered at me with a mischievous grin, handsome wrinkles at the corners of his eyes.

"Yes, and there, there's that nice shine back in those eyes." He brushed my face with the back of his fingers. I grinned at him feeling soft as putty. He winked and then left, taking everything bright with him.

I let out a noisy sigh. "Cheeky bastard," I said.

Twenty-six

amsey had given me permission but I couldn't spend the night in that trailer. I just couldn't do it. I grabbed one of my duffle bags and loaded it up with uniforms, the book I had been reading, my PT clothes, and some odds and ends. I moved it all into the female tent knowing I would never live in that trailer again. Just before I left, I grabbed one of Delray's camera batteries. I wanted to have a look at the pictures she left in her camera. Steele's patrol shift had already started for the night so I'd have to wait until the morning.

Harry had been right about one thing. I felt completely knackered, a perfect word to describe my drained and lifeless mood, but I still had some work to do before I could turn in for the night.

I went back to the TOC to send off the sniper press release, all the while thinking about Harry kissing me, that wicked look in his eye and the delight the kiss promised. It was a fantastic diversion from all the other darkness going on around me. I savored it and enjoyed the warmth the memory left me.

As soon as I sent the release out over fax and email, the phone started ringing. I responded to questions, returned phone and email messages, made changes to the PowerPoint slides for the BUB in the morning and left a note for McCallen that I was calling it a night.

By the time I finished, I had missed the dinner meal again. I didn't feel much like eating anyway. I went to my tent, changed into PT clothes and headed to the gym. After forty-five minutes on the treadmill punching up the speed and the incline the whole time, I was drenched in sweat and panting. All of that and I still couldn't outrun the demons that chased me.

Ramsey was right. If Griffin planned to end his military career, he didn't have a motive for killing Delray. If Griffin hadn't killed her, who did? What did she see that got her killed? Hopefully, I would understand it all as soon as I saw the pictures on her camera.

I went to the mess tent to get something to eat before bed. The tent was almost empty, only a few stragglers hanging out. Dr. Cosic in his white coat, ascot and pink rubber gloves mopped the floors and whistled a tune I didn't recognize.

"You sound awfully cheerful tonight, Professor," I said to him.

"Ha, Professor. No one has called me that for a long time," he said, but seemed pleased to hear the title again.

"Do you think you will ever go back to teaching?"

He stopped mopping and shook his head. "Oh no," he answered smiling. "That is all finished. Many things have changed for me. And for you, I think. This murdered girl, she lived with you, yes?" He didn't wait for me to answer. "Is all so very sad. And now this other girl, today shot," he shook his head and tsked loudly as he returned to mopping the floors. "You women, you want to work and wear a uniform like a man but it is a very dangerous world out there, very dangerous."

I ignored his sexist comment. "You seem happy though, despite the changes in your life."

"One must be...what is the word? Adaptable. I am very adaptable, Master Sergeant Harper. It is a good quality to have when your country goes to war."

I moved toward the soup bar and Cosic followed me, mopping along the way. He stayed nearby as I poured my soup and grabbed a handful of crackers.

"I saw you today," I said. "In headquarters, when Hawes was in there." I glanced at him to see his reaction. He nodded his head and grinned.

"Yes. Disgraceful way to act, Mr. Hawes."

"So he was drunk."

Cosic made a few long strokes with his mop and glanced up at me. "Mr. Hawes. He is not so adaptable, you see."

When a group of soldiers barreled into the tent, loud and laughing, Cosic focused his attention on them as they tracked mud over his freshly mopped floor. He mumbled something in Serbo-Croatian. Then he stuck his mop in the bucket and dragged them both toward the door. He took up his whistling tune again as he restarted his task of cleaning the floor from the beginning. Adaptable.

= = = = = = = = = =

I didn't sleep well. I kept turning on my book light and reading for a while. As soon as I got drowsy enough, I turned the light off and rolled over, but sleep continued to allude me. I must have finally slept for a few hours. I opened my eyes at the sounds of the other women in the tent rising and preparing for the day. They pretty much ignored me. I would normally expect some small talk, some gossip maybe, but they gave me a wide berth. It was okay by me. I didn't feel like talking anyway.

I went to the morning BUB and stood in the back of the room as all the departments presented the current situation. General Paterson was still in Tuzla and would be for several more days. Colonel Raybourn ran the meeting. McCallen would brief our slide, so I stood back and observed. I noticed Captain Griffin was missing. So were Ramsey and Santos. I wondered if they were all in a room together somewhere, having a conversation about BBC journalists and prostitution.

McCallen briefed details about the Vice Presidential visit explaining how the event would flow from start to finish. He answered all the questions, standing on the platform referring now and then to the slides. At the end of his briefing about the visit, he said a word or two about how we should respond if we received any queries about the kidnapping.

"Everything should be referred to the British camp. Even though the tape came here, this is their show," he said. Colonel Raybourn agreed.

Major Purser briefed about the kidnapping.

"CID didn't find any useable fingerprints on the tape. So far, no one has heard anything further."

"What about the kid who passed the package to the patrol?" Raybourn asked.

"We've asked the original patrol to keep an eye out for the boy. They've seen the kid around before so it's just a matter of time before they find him," Purser said. "All patrols have been briefed to be prepared should any further packages be passed on to them."

"Okay, noted. Next."

Townson took his place on the briefing platform and I was relieved to hear that Mishka was in "stable but guarded condition."

"Sir, some of the interpreters have voiced concern about being sniper targets. Some have threatened to quit," Townson said.

"We issue helmets and flak vests for a reason, Major," said Colonel Raybourn. "This is an inherently dangerous job. They knew that's what they signed up for."

"Hooah, sir," Townson responded.

Finally, the Chaplain gave a reminder to attend the memorial service for Delray tomorrow morning in the chapel. Then the meeting was over and Raybourn dismissed us.

I went looking for Sergeant Steele. The desk sergeant at his company headquarters told me he was sleeping. They had just returned from an overnight patrol. "Probably won't be up until late this afternoon, Sergeant. Is it an emergency? I can get him up." I told him no, but to let Sergeant Steele know that I wanted to see him as soon as he was available.

While there, I talked to the first sergeant who had ridden with Delray on her day out with the company as they repaired the roads. First Sergeant Adam Bennell could have retired from the Army years ago, but he loved the Army, loved his men, and loved this deployment to Bosnia. On many occasions, he had told me that building roads, repairing the schools, and clearing the landmines scattered all over the country was exactly the kind of legacy he wanted to leave. "We're doing good things here," was what he told his troops every day, and he meant it.

We stood outside his headquarters tent so he could smoke the filter-less Camel cigarettes that were a fixture in his hand. No matter where you saw Bennell, in the mess hall, in a meeting or out on a road mission, he always had a cigarette between his fingers. Most of the time, they were unlit.

"I finally had to order Delray to stay within eye sight," he told me. "She kept wandering off and disappearing on me. I'd turn around and she'd be gone."

"Where was she going?" I asked him.

He shrugged his shoulders and blew out a cloud of smoke between his teeth. "I asked her the same thing. Where the hell were you? I asked her. She just giggled and said she was taking pictures. That girl giggled all the damn time." He shook his head and stuck the tiny remains of his cigarette butt in a sand-filled coffee can where it joined many others that looked similar. "It's a damn shame," he said. "A goddamn shame.'

I spent some time with the Chaplain making the final arrangements for the memorial service scheduled for the next day. When I told the Chaplain that I might need some help writing my eulogy, he grew uncomfortable.

"I didn't realize that you were still planning to give a eulogy," he said.

"Of course I am. I thought you wanted me to."

"Well, that would be appropriate normally, yes .... but I only learned recently that you were a suspect in her murder."

My anger rose quickly. I tried to keep it in check, but I'm sure my face turned red. "Chaplain Hirsch, I didn't kill her."

He sputtered and grew agitated. "Of course not," he said, patting my hand in a patronizing way. "I know you didn't do it, but many people on the camp know that you are a suspect. It's just," and he looked down, unable for the first time since I'd known him to look me in the eye. "This is supposed to be a solemn time to remember Specialist Delray. I don't want people to get … well some might show up just to see what you're going to say. You see what I mean, don't you?"

He didn't want it to turn into a spectacle about me. I could see his point. I had already received requests from four different media outlets who wanted to cover the service, one of them CNN. McCallen hadn't decided whether or not to allow them to come but if they did, the cameras and the murder suspect could turn the whole memorial into a circus.

"I understand, sir. I was having trouble figuring out what to say anyway."

He went on about who would talk when, and what songs would be in the program, when the setup would happen and how long the service would last. I tuned much of it out. I should have been spending my time thinking about Delray and the service we were about to have for her. Instead, I worried that Ramsey could decide at anytime to take me into custody.

Later that morning, McCallen and I joined the tour given to the team of Secret Service agents in preparation for Vice President Gore's visit on Monday. The visit was supposed to be secret and unannounced, but we had known about it for weeks. The White House staff had given us a long list of tasks to complete prior to his arrival.

The vice president would be staying for two nights and spending one full day at the camp. His entourage included a full press corps. The press would stay on cots in a tent set aside just for them. It would give them a chance to see how soldiers lived every day, and there simply wasn't any place else to put them.

A large security detail would also need a tent, but we didn't know how many of them there would be and no one was going to tell us. McCallen would lose his coveted trailer for the length of the VPs stay. All of the trailers in Disney Land were reserved for people much more important than a public affairs colonel.

On the itinerary was a luncheon so that a select group of soldiers could have some face time with the Vice President. The

White House suggested we find soldiers from all 50 states to attend the meal, but we were falling short. Rhode Island, Maine, Alaska, and New Mexico were proving difficult.

I was glad to have the visit to keep my mind off things. I stayed busy planning the press accommodations, setting up a place for them to get interviews with a nice background that would indicate clearly that we were at Camp McGovern in Bosnia.

I sat in while the operations officer briefed the Secret Service team on the kidnapping situation. Everyone seemed on edge, expecting to get another message with the kidnapping demands but nothing had come yet. No one knew if the British were planning to pay the ransom. They, like the U.S., always said they didn't negotiate with terrorists. No one knew if the kidnappers were terrorists or just plain old criminals, but I was certain the non-negotiate rule would apply either way.

Through much of the day I had avoided being near McCallen without others around. While conducting the tour with the secret service, we had walked along side each other, consulted over details and things to do, but an icy barrier separated us from the old high-speed public affairs team we used to be. I'm sure no one else noticed anything different, but I did. I knew we'd never get back to how it had been before that stupid kiss. The permanent change to our relationship made me sad, but also seemed a relief. As Loretta would say, I was a big girl and I'd get over it.

As soon as I had a minute, I went to the Morale, Welfare tent and called my sister. Telling her about McCallen was the hardest thing I'd done in a long time.

"A married man, Lauren? Why haven't you ever told me about this?"

"Because he's a married man! And because I'm embarrassed. I'm ashamed of this stupid, stupid, impossible crush I've had. God, what a mess."

"You should be thanking God you never acted on it, and that Momma's not alive to hear about it. Lord, she'd be marchin' you into Reverend Thomas's office so fast, it'd make your head spin."

I groaned at the thought of what my mother would have done

had she known her daughter had even dreamed about having anything to do with a married man.

"If Momma were alive," I said, "I'd be far more afraid of her than anything this Ramsey dude could do to me."

"That's for sure," Loretta said. "But that Ramsey sounds like a damn idiot."

"That's the problem. He's not stupid at all. It feels like no matter what I say or do, I've got a target on my back."

I heard the quiver in my voice and hated it.

"Hush, now. I refuse to believe the truth won't come out before anything truly bad happens. The DNA will prove you're innocent. You've got to believe that."

I hoped she was right. Her encouragement helped, but I couldn't stop feeling the weight of impending doom on my shoulders. Loretta interrupted my dark thoughts.

"Now enough of all that. Tell me something good."

I chuckled. Our mother's view had been that no matter how bad things got, there was always something good to report. She demanded it.

"Well, there's this British soldier," I said.

"Ooh girl. I love that accent. Tell me about him."

Ten minutes later, after having told Loretta just enough about Harry to have her asking a million and one questions, I had to end the conversation and get back to work. We promised to talk again soon.

Conversations with Loretta were like medicine for my soul. A spoonful of her voice had left me feeling more positive about the potential outcome of my situation. I returned to work determined to believe everything would shake out in the best way possible.

All of that positivity withered like a burst balloon when I stepped into the TOC and saw the look on McCallen's face as he strode up to me, his face flushed and agitated. He grabbed my arm, towering over me.

"I have to talk to you."

His eyes wide with shock, he realized that he had grabbed me, glancing down at his hand. He let go, mumbling an apology, his face ashen.

"Sir, what is it?"

"I just got a Red Cross call. It's Michelle."

There weren't many reasons a soldier would ever be pulled from a deployment. A Red Cross call was one of them, and no one wanted one of those. It usually meant a death in the family or, in this case, a grave medical emergency. Michelle and the baby must be in serious trouble.

Twenty-seven

E arly labor. Some other complications," he mumbled.

The point being, his wife and child needed him. He had to get back to Germany. First he'd have to get to Tuzla. The two options were either a two-hour drive over the pothole riddled road or a much shorter helicopter flight. No matter when he left, it would take at least a day of travel to get him back to Germany.

"The Vice President," he said and he started to list all of the things we still needed to do.

"Don't worry about any of that, Neil. It's just another VIP visit. Go pack your things and I'll try to arrange a flight for you."

His clenched jaw and the severe crease down the middle of his forehead told me he had more to say but fought against it.

"Call down to Tuzla. Tell Mason to get up here right away," he ordered. He stepped closer, took a deep breath scanning the room, and turned his gaze back to me.

"I hate to leave you like this, with so much on your plate."

There were a dozen different ways I could take that simple statement. His proximity made me uncomfortable.

"Get going, Colonel. The sooner you get started, the sooner you'll be there."

He gathered up his helmet, adjusted his shoulder holster and, without another look, moved out with a purpose.

I headed straight to flight operations to see when the next flight was scheduled. All I had to say to the Warrant Officer on duty was that the Colonel had received a Red Cross message and he immediately got on the radios and started making arrangements. I called down to Tuzla to let the Press Information Office know what was going on.

"Yeah, we heard," said Major Jeff Mason, the second in command down there. "The Red Cross called here first and we directed them up to your camp. We already planned to send a team up for the big visitor you've got coming. I was trying to see if I could get someone up there by this evening, but that's not going to happen. And we're working on finding someone to take over the print mission for Delray. I haven't had any volunteers yet. Seems everyone is a little intimidated by you, Master Sergeant Harper."

I liked Major Mason. He was a straight talker and I knew he could be trusted.

"Well, it might help if you tell them I didn't kill her."

He laughed and said, "Why? Some of these guys, it might help if they think their NCO is a killer. Keep 'em in line, ya know?"

"No, Mark, I really didn't kill her," I insisted. I thought the joking might be cover up for what he really thought. I needed to be sure.

"Of course you didn't," he said and I believed him. "Look, I know this can't be easy for you, but trust me. We've got your six. We'll put a team together. I'll be there no later than tomorrow, early afternoon. Just keep it together for a few more hours, okay? The cavalry is coming."

"It would be nice if you guys could get here before the memorial service tomorrow morning. The Colonel was going to give a eulogy, and for obvious reasons the Chaplain has asked me not to speak. It would be nice if someone could...."

"Got it. I'll take care of it. It's the least we can do for Delray."

We discussed a few more details about Neil's emergency leave orders, where the team would stay when they arrived and what additional equipment needs we might have with the added bodies in my little press area. By the time we settled all of those details, the aviation chief was standing at my desk saying Neil's name made it onto the manifest for the next flight going out. If we could get his orders in time, he could be on his way to Germany by 1800 hours.

"Thanks, Chief. I know you had to pull some strings to make that happen," I told him.

He shrugged. "I just bumped a young Lieutenant from the flight. Rank does have its privileges."

When Neil came back into the TOC, he had his rucksack and laptop in hand. I told him about the flight plans and the arrangements. He listened intently. A vein pulsed at his temple, his jaw clenched. Despite the worry for his wife and new baby, he contained it, doing what needed doing. I left him at my desk and waited by the fax machine for his orders to arrive, watching him from across the room as he made phone calls and talked to people, trying in vain to tie up all the loose ends.

Finally, the fax machine kicked into action and his orders spewed out. I made several copies and brought them to the desk where he stood pacing nervously.

"You've got about fifteen minutes before the chopper leaves," I said, handing him the documents.

He took the copies of the orders with obvious relief and shoved them into his laptop bag.

"I better get to the airfield then," he said, looking at me. He must have realized in that second what his departure really meant. Anything could happen in the next few days. I might be arrested. He probably wouldn't return to Bosnia. There was a strong possibility that we might not see each other for a very long time. I struggled with emotions I didn't understand. We stood there like that, staring at each other, searching for something appropriate to say.

"Such a short stay in Disneyland," I finally said. "Wasn't exactly the Magic Kingdom, was it?"

It was hard to believe he had only arrived two days ago. So much had happened.

"No, no Magic Kingdom," he said, shaking his head. He inhaled a deep breath and took a step closer, lowering his voice.

"I know you're afraid, Lauren, but Ramsey's not a fool.

Eventually the DNA evidence will clear you."

I wasn't so sure about that, but I nodded my head, afraid to say anything.

"Well, Sergeant Harper," he said, sticking out his hand for a shake, "I guess I'll see you when I see you."

"Yes, sir, and please give my best to Michelle."

He stopped shaking my hand and just held it for a second, giving it a gentle squeeze, his gaze scanning my face. When he let go, the warmth of his fingers lingered on my hand as he turned and marched out to catch his flight.

Twenty-eight

I thought about going to the airfield with McCallen but knew the gesture would only make us both uncomfortable. Instead, I stood behind my desk, shuffling papers around from one corner to the next. I grit my teeth and sucked in deep breaths, mumbling to myself. "You will not cry, damn it. You will not cry."

When I finally had my emotions in check, I sat down and stared at my computer screen, replaying every moment that had happened since McCallen stepped off that chopper two days ago. The relief I felt at seeing him. The passion I felt at wanting him. The anger I felt when his guilt prompted him to pull rank on me, and now the emptiness I felt at his absence. I worried about Michelle and the baby. He would be devastated if anything bad happened to either of them.

I was running through all of this in my head when I realized someone was saying my name.

"Master Sergeant Harper?"

Sergeant Steele stood near my desk staring down at me from his great height, a worried frown on his face.

"Hey, Sergeant Steele, how are you?" I asked, rustling up a fake smile, trying to sound natural, but not doing a very good job of it.

"I heard you were looking for me."

I indicated a chair and he gently lowered his towering bulk into it.

"I have a battery for Delray's camera. I thought we could go look at those pictures now."

Steele shook his head. "That Bliven. The commander's vehicle is red lined. They had to take mine for their trip down to Tuzla. They left a couple hours ago. Bliven was driving for the Captain, but he didn't tell me. If I'd known, I could have taken the camera out of the truck. Now, they won't be back till sometime tomorrow." Steele shrugged his big shoulders. "That boy ain't got no sense."

"It's all right, Sergeant Steele. It doesn't matter."

My pathetic attempts at investigation seemed hopeless anyway. The original pictures hadn't proven anything to Ramsey other than that Captain Griffin was trying to help a poor girl who had been forced into prostitution. I felt like the chances were slim to none that anything on the camera would help me if Chief Ramsey decided to charge me with murder.

I told Steele that Miska was reportedly doing fine and recovering well. I filled him in about Colonel's Red Cross message and that he had already left. We chatted about the memorial service and how the program would run. I told him the chaplain asked me not to speak and he nodded his head at that.

"I know you didn't have nothin' to do with Virginia's death, Sergeant Harper, but other people think you did. Not much we can do about that, is there?"

I didn't realize how much I hoped he believed in my innocence until he said it. After a few more minutes of chatting, he left saying he'd see me in the chapel in the morning.

Steele's brief visit had accomplished one thing. It had taken my mind off Neil and his departure. I made myself a cup of tea and dug into the work that needed to be done in preparation for the Vice Presidential visit. There was plenty to keep me occupied. I wrote emails, returned phone calls, talked to people, and gathered information. I skipped lunch and before I knew it I had missed dinner as well.

By the time I finally realized how late it was the cavalry had arrived.

"Hey, Harper, how's it going?" Major Mason said from behind

me.

I jumped at his voice, not expecting to see him so soon.

"I thought you guys weren't arriving until tomorrow."

He made a pointed show of looking at his watch, "I told you we'd get here as soon as we could. You want us to go back and..."

"Oh, no you don't," I said, jumping up and shaking his hand, smiling. "I can't tell you how glad I am to see you."

Major Jeffrey Mason was the first-born son of West African immigrants. Upon meeting him, most people expected him to have some kind of an African accent and were usually surprised to hear the Midwestern lilt to his speech. He was half a foot shorter than me, and about as dark as a person's skin can get without being blue. He had a generally happy and positive disposition, one I wished I could emulate but never quite achieved.

He stood there rubbing his hands together, smiling at the challenge in front of him.

"I didn't think I was going to get the chance to see the Vice President, but like, here I am. Cool huh? Bad luck for Colonel McCallen, though."

"How did you get up here so soon?" I asked.

"We tagged onto a convoy that was headed this way. I've got Specialist Baker and Sergeant Cody with me. Cody has agreed to stay up here as your new print journalist. According to him he wants to get away from Tuzla and that headquarters mentality anyway. He says there's more real soldiering going on up here," Mason said, using air quotes around the words.

I didn't blame Cody his desire to get away from Tuzla. The headquarters camp had permanent buildings, paved roads, flush toilets, and real showers. Some soldiers even had real beds with sheets and blankets. They had a movie theatre, an ice cream stand, and other permanent vendors where soldiers could shop. They even had a Burger King. Coming up here meant leaving a lot of luxury behind, but it also meant being away from all the brass associated with working near a headquarters. Here, it would just be Sergeant Cody and me. He would be trading luxury for more freedom and a lot more responsibility. I knew Cody and liked him. He was a great writer and didn't shy from hard work. As a young sergeant, the new duty assignment would benefit his career.

By the time I finished the rundown of duties and a brief tour of the camp, it was after nine o'clock. I showed Major Mason and the rest of the team to their quarters. They would all be staying in the same tent, at least until after the Vice Presidential visit. I planned to offer Cody the trailer if he wanted it. I'd never sleep in there again.

By the time I finally went to bed that night, I felt good about our preparations for the visit and about having Cody with me for the rest of the deployment. Mason had kept me laughing. Cody displayed excitement about his new assignment. Their positive attitude infected me. I lay wrapped in my sleeping bag that night, allowing positivity to seep into my thoughts. Hope invaded my imaginings. There was no way I would actually be charged with murder. No way. The DNA would prove me innocent. Ramsey would figure out that I couldn't have killed Virginia. Somehow, he would find the true murderer and I would be exonerated. I just knew things would work out for the best.

I had no idea just how much worse they would get.

Twenty-nine

Sunlight and a rare, cool breeze wafted through the large tent door. A muted brightness seeped into mesh windows along the sides of the tent, illuminating the gathering, lending a false cheerfulness to the somber occasion.

I stood in the back of the chapel tent and watched soldiers arriving. They walked down the center aisle and stopped in front of the traditional military memorial used to honor the fallen, and on this day, to represent my soldier, Specialist Virginia Delray.

On a platform, in the center of the room, stood a pair of gleaming combat boots. Sergeant Steele had polished Virginia's boots for the occasion and they were perfect. Behind the boots stood an M16 rifle propped rigidly with the barrel pointed straight down and the rifle stock up. A Kevlar helmet sat atop the rifle butt, "DELRAY" written in large block letters on the helmet band. Her dog tags hung from the rifle's trigger grip; the small silver rectangular plates made a tinkling sound as they bounced against the rifle. Small homemade floral arrangements were on either side of the rifle memorial. I wondered where they had come from.

Every time I saw the boot, helmet, and rifle display at a memorial service I felt the eerie chill that the fallen soldier was there watching what we did. It was no different this time, and even more so, since I knew the dead soldier personally. I wondered how Virginia would feel about what we were going to do here today.

I had given the chaplain several pictures of her to use for the memorial. An enlarged version of one of them stared back at me, printed on the front of the program, an official looking photo of Virginia with a wide grin wearing her dress green uniform and the American flag behind her as a backdrop. Enlarged and propped on an easel sat another picture of her. In this one, she wore a broad smile, her hand in a wave, striking a silly pose. It reminded me of the tape Tooley had shot of her.

I tried to be inconspicuous and stayed in the back of the room. A few soldiers stopped to say hello to me and offer their condolences. Others avoided me, speculating about what I might have done. Sergeant Steele sat at the front of the chapel and a steady stream of folks went directly to him to shake his hand and offer words of support.

A soldier with a video camera stood off to the side recording the service. Delray's family would receive a copy of the tape so they could witness how her Army family had said their farewells. Since McCallen had left the decision to Mason, I had encouraged him to refuse the press permission to attend the service. Mason had cheerfully denied CNN and the rest of the media outlets access to the service. I felt grateful for that at least.

Virginia's body already waited in Germany for her final transport home. The thought of her lying in a morgue made me flash back to how she looked lying in her cot, that horrible yellow strap around her neck.

Chaplain Hirsh asked everyone to take a seat, shaking me out of that awful mental picture. He announced that to open the service, we would sing *Amazing Grace*, the words printed inside the program. A soldier played an introduction on a small electronic organ and we started the slow, off-keyed singing. The tent was full, every seat taken and many soldiers stood lining the walls. Captain Griffin stood near the back, alone, General Paterson reportedly still in Tuzla. Major Townson sat in the middle of a row surrounded by soldiers. First Sergeant Bennell and all the soldiers from the Engineer Company Delray had last worked with took up several rows of seats. I thought that was a nice gesture on their part.

After the song, the Chaplain said a prayer, then talked for a while about the precious moments of life and how something unexpected could quickly snatch those moments away. I wanted to know who the bastard was that had snatched Virginia's moments away.

Major Mason stood up and talked about Virginia the soldier, where she was from, about her simple beginnings, and her desire to serve.

"Virginia told me once that her mother had been furious when she learned that her daughter had joined the Army. Good girls don't wear combat boots, her mother had said. But Virginia said," and he imitated her southern drawl, 'No Momma, only the best girls wear combat boots and I'm one of them!'"

He got a polite chuckle from the crowd and I could picture Delray doing and saying exactly that. Sergeant Cody stood and read a poem Virginia had written that had been published in the Army Times. I remember how excited she had been when she learned they were going to publish her work. She sent a stack of copies home to her mother when the paper came out.

I wasn't much into poetry, but it was a nice enough poem about soldiers and freedom and the desire to make a difference. It was sentimental and simple, very much like Virginia.

Sergeant Steele stood next and moved slowly to the podium. His shoulders hunched around his ears, he looked down as if in the middle of a silent prayer. When he brought his head up, he threw his shoulders back, stood to his full height and belted out the first notes of an old spiritual.

Precious Lord, take my hand
Lead me on, let me stand
I'm tired, I'm weak, I'm alone
Through the storm, through the night
Lead me on to the light
Take my hand precious Lord, lead me home

An impossibly deep and soulful sound resonated from him. He closed his eyes as he filled his lungs repeatedly and crooned the song to the heavens. Goose bumps dotted my skin and unchecked tears overflowed from my eyes. It seemed miraculous to me, the sounds he made. I wondered how he had the strength to sing that sweetness without crying, but somehow he did, the depth of his grieving so raw and clear in the plea of each refrain. When the song ended it felt as if the air had been sucked out of the room. We all sat there breathless at the beauty of what we had heard.

Then it was time for the roll call. I hated this part of memorial ceremonies because it always made me cry, but Army tradition was Army tradition. The roll call represented the final formation the soldier would miss. I had argued with the Chaplain that I should at least participate in this section of the service, but he had been adamant that I stay away. The more I thought about it, the more it seemed to me that I was admitting guilt by not playing my role as her sergeant. I hadn't killed her and, as her sergeant, this was my small part to play in the service. I was determined to play it.

I marched up the center aisle. Before Sergeant Cody stood up, I put a firm hand on his shoulder to let him know I intended to take over. He nodded his agreement and motioned me to the front of the chapel. Chaplain Hirsh shook his head at me, unhappy, but I didn't care. This was my job. It was the least I could do for Virginia.

I arrived at the front of the chapel, stepped to the right side of the memorial stand, executed an about face and stood at attention.

"Roll call," I announced in my command voice. "Private Anderson," I began.

A soldier in the back of the chapel stood to attention and gave the reply, "Here sergeant."

"Private Baker," I called.

"Here, sergeant."

"Sergeant Cody," and the replay from the soldier who would be my new journalist rang loud and clear as he stood to attention.

"Here, sergeant."

"Specialist Delray," I called, knowing there would be no response from her. After a moment, I called again.

"Specialist Delray." Even though you knew there would be no response, the silence seemed filled with anticipation. I had to call her name one more time.

"Specialist Virginia Delray."

After another moment of silence, when the last echo of her name faded, the bugler played the first note of taps from the back of the chapel. He stood outside, framed in the tied back tent door, in full view of the congregation. He stood at attention alone in the center of the opening, the slow and mournful song reverberating through the room.

I was still standing at the front of the chapel listening to the final notes of Taps and what should have been the end of the service when another sound came rushing up from the back of the chapel. It was the unmistakable moan of bagpipes getting their wind up.

The bugler executed a right face, marched away and was replaced by Private Stewart dressed in full kilt, a green and blue tartan fabric with a furry sporran hanging in front. He played a Scottish dirge I didn't recognize, but he played it well, the slow melodic skirl of the pipes flooding the chapel. Sergeant Steele twisted in his seat looking back at Stewart as he played. Then Steele turned to me smiling as big fat tears slowly rolled down his face.

Just as the song was over, Sergeant Fogg marched into the chapel, holding a floral arrangement in his left hand, his right arm swinging widely, his boot heels muffled on the plastic tent floor. He marched up directly in front of the memorial, executed a snappy salute then slowly laid the flowers at the foot of the memorial. It was a purely classy and thoughtful act on Harry's part. I smiled at him.

He glanced over at me, winked, giving me his broken-toothed grin, then executed an about face, British style, and marched out.

I thanked the crowd for coming and as each Army ceremony

requires, I said, "This concludes our ceremony."

Sergeant Steele sat in the front row grinning at me. I stepped off the podium and he drew me into a crushing hug.

"Oh wee!" he said, his shoulders rocking in a silent sob. "Oh wee, Sergeant Harper." He had trouble speaking between his tears and his laughter, a jumble of mixed emotions tumbling from him. "She would have loved that. She would have laughed and laughed. Oh wee! I can almost hear her now."

He shook his head and held me at arm's length. We smiled at each other. Then he dragged me into a hug again.

"Lord, lord. She would have loved it."

"I had no idea you could sing like that," I said to him, my face buried in his chest.

"Me? You should have heard Virginia. That girl could sing, now. Yeah man," he said proudly.

He finally released me and stood smiling down at me. Then someone stepped in front of me, anxious for a chance to pass on their condolences to him. I stepped away, watching as the big man stood there, with the grin on his face and the tears flowing down thanking everyone who approached him.

I headed to the back of the chapel to see if Harry was still around, and wasn't disappointed.

"Well, aren't you full of surprises," I said when I located him.

"That's me, Lauren. Harry full-of-surprises Fogg at your service. And what pray tell, do you make of our Private Stewart, here? Looking rather lovely he is, in his little skirt."

"Yes, very lovely Private Stewart. Thank you so much."

Stewart nodded his head, his face bright red but his shy grin displayed that he was pleased at the compliment.

"It really was a classy gesture, Harry. You didn't even know Virginia."

"No, but I know you, and I know that big Sergeant in there, don't I? And you can't bloody well have a funeral without bleedin' bagpipes, now can ya?"

"Can you stay for a cup of tea?" I asked him hopefully. He shook his head no.

"Sorry Lauren, but we've got to be off. They've got us on a short leash, what with the hostage situation and all. Everybody's holding their breath, waiting for the next contact, but it hasn't come yet. Bloody well want it over with, me, one way or the other." After a brief pause he put a hand to my cheek and gave me that cocky grin. "But you look like you're holding up alright, luv. You be sure to let Harry know if you was to need anything, hear?"

I nodded yes, then grabbed his big face and gave him lingering kisses on both cheeks, feeling like I was about to shed more tears. His face turned a bright crimson. "Well, that's bloody alright isn't it?" He murmured under his breath looking me in the eye for a few seconds longer than was proper. Then motioning for Stewart, they were off. "Come along, Stewart, no time for standing around gawking. We've got the Queen's business to attend to."

With a wave at me, they headed to their Land Rover.

I glanced in the chapel. Steele stood calmly accepting condolences and people lingered, talking about the service. The whole thing had left me feeling exhausted but happy; pleased that it had gone so well.

I decided my fatigue required something stronger then tea. I headed to the mess tent knowing there would be coffee there.

The tent stood almost deserted for a change, a lull in the need for food between the breakfast and lunch service. Most people on the camp were at the chapel. I hadn't passed anyone on my way. The entire camp seemed unusually quiet.

I poured coffee into a paper cup and turned to leave when I spotted Dr. Cosic standing in the storage area of the mess kitchens. He fumbled in his pockets for something, a broom propped in the crook of his shoulder and his forehead wrinkled in concentration.

"Good morning, Professor," I said.

He turned to me and smiled, surprised. "Hello, Sergeant Harper. The funeral is over already?"

"Oh, you know about that, do you?"

"Oh yes," he said finally locating what he looked for, his cigarette pack crushed and mostly empty. "I know just about

227

everything that goes on around this place."

"Do you?" I said, chuckling at his bragging. I wondered why I hadn't thought of asking him before.

"Well, since you know so much, can I ask you something?"

"Of course," he said, bending his head down to put the cigarette to a lighted match.

"I've heard that there is someone on the camp that offers to help interpreters go to America if they want to. Is that true?" I blew on my coffee, taking a tentative sip.

He took a slow drag of his cigarette, pinching it between his thumb and forefinger and blowing the smoke out slowly. He scrunched his eyes against the smoke and peered at me.

"You Americans," he said, shaking his head. "You always assume people want to go to America, but these girls, they don't always want to go there. Germany, Switzerland, England. There are many places a girl dreams about. It doesn't have to be America."

His dark gaze bore into me. The intensity I saw there made me feel uncomfortable. His tone of voice rang different than I had ever heard from him. I narrowed my eyes at him. I remembered that Ritza had said she wanted to go to Germany and she ended up a prisoner in a brothel here in Bosnia.

Cosic removed the bandana he always wore from around his neck and wiped sweat from his forehead. My gaze landed on his neck. The bandana had covered them, but now the deep red scratches down his neck stood out starkly against his olive-colored skin. He grinned, and brought the cigarette pinched between his fingers slowly to his lips. He didn't seem to care that the sleeves of his white coat slipped down to reveal more scratches on his wrists, deep, red and angry. When my eyes met his again, I couldn't hide the fact that I knew what he had done. I was in serious trouble.

Thirty

The world seemed to stop rotating. I held my breath as Cosic's dark gaze locked on me. Options flashed through my head. Run. Hit him. Scream. I tossed my coffee in his face, then stepped back, grabbed the butt of the weapon strapped to my back, intending to use it as a club, first to his gut, then to his head, but he was quicker. He'd ducked most of the coffee, or he didn't care that it was scalding. In any case, it had little effect on him.

He slammed his fist into my stomach, then grabbed my shoulder and rammed his fist home again. I doubled over, my breath completely gone. The next blow connected under my chin. My head snapped back and rattled around inside my helmet as I went down on my knees seeing stars. I intended to punch him in the groin, but missed, hitting him in the top of the thigh. He batted my hand away, then grabbed me by the back of my coat collar and dragged me further back into the storage area, calling someone's name. I struggled for traction and tried to scream, but the front of my coat was under my chin, choking me. I felt close to passing out. He dropped the collar of my coat and ripped the helmet off my head. My head bounced off the floor with a shattering whack. I fought to stay conscious, my weapon digging into my back. I thrashed around, trying to roll over and stand up, taking in a deep breath to scream. He kicked me in the side so hard it lifted me off the ground. A high-pitched whine gushed out of me, along with the very last drop of breath from my lungs.

Then he straddled me and leaned down, slamming his fist into the side of my head. I struggled to breathe, while battering him, punching, scratching, biting when I could but he didn't seem to feel anything. I realized Virginia had fought like this and lost. His fist connected repeatedly with the side of my head, over and over.

Eventually, I passed out.

= = = = = = = = = =

I came to, in fits and starts. My arms felt painfully numb, my hands useless blocks of throbbing flesh. I lay in a storage locker surrounded by shelves of food. They had tied my hands behind my back, and tied my arms again at the elbows, pulling my back into an agonizing arch. Cord held my legs together at my ankles and knees. I felt thoroughly trussed up. The gag in my mouth made breathing difficult since my nose was bloody and wet.

Cosic and Clayton Hawes came into the room. Clayton took one look at me and cursed.

"Are you crazy? She's a soldier! They won't ever stop looking for her," he hissed between his teeth.

Cosic shrugged calmly. "They will look for her yes. But they will think she ran away. She is a murder suspect. They will never connect her to us."

He was right, but I wasn't going to think about that. I had to concentrate on how to get out of there. My weapon, flak vest, and helmet were gone. I usually wore a Swiss army knife on my belt but my belt and the knife were gone too.

They saw me looking at them. Cosic slowly walked toward me. I watched him draw his foot back but couldn't do anything to stop him. He kicked me in the side of the head and I was out again.

= = = = = = = = = =

The next time I came to, pain shot up my arm to my shoulder as my body slammed onto the floor of a truck. They had thrown a blanket or something over my head. When I hit the bed of the truck, I landed on my shoulder and felt something in my arm rip painfully. Hands grabbed my shoulders and dragged me further. I tried to lift my body off my sore shoulder but someone put a foot on my chest slamming me back onto the floor.

Then I felt a sharp prick in my shoulder and Cosic's voice, "Sleep now."

A few seconds later, I was out again.

= = = = = = = = = =

The next time I woke up, it took a while for my situation to grow clear enough for me to understand how much worse it was. The first thing I noticed was that I was cold. Very cold. I shuddered with it. Then I realized I didn't have any clothes on. I felt sick to my stomach, my head hurt, my shoulder throbbed, but cold seemed the predominant feeling. My nakedness pissed me off. Cosic, the little prick, would pay. Damn right, he would pay for this.

"Get it together, Harper," I said to myself through gritted teeth. I didn't like how small my voice sounded to my own ears. I lay on hay. The distinct smell of animals, horses if I had to guess, filled my nostrils. My hands, numb and useless, remained tied behind my back. They had removed the tie at my elbows and my legs were free. I wasn't wearing the gag anymore or a blindfold. Those were the only positives to my state of affairs. It took time for my eyes to grow accustomed to the darkness. I wondered how long I had been out. Long enough for my skin to crawl with scratchiness from the hay.

Since I didn't have the gag, I figured they must have me somewhere far from people. Calling out wouldn't help, but I had to try.

"Hello?" I yelled.

"No, don't call them," someone said in a harsh whisper. It was a man's voice and if I wasn't mistaken, he had a British accent. I heard more whispering, at least two voices from a short distance away, coming from the other side of a wall. I struggled to stand up. This took a while. I ached everywhere. Every movement brought fresh pain to my shoulder. My hands felt as if they would never function normally again. I crawled to a wall, then used it for leverage to get my legs underneath me. Once standing, I shuffled toward the voices. As my eyes adjusted to the darkness, I realized I was in an animal stall in a barn.

"Let me guess, one of you is Ian Tooley and the other is Frank Hannerty?" I whispered through the wall.

I could hear them discussing it between themselves, surprised that I knew who they were.

"I'm an American soldier; Master Sergeant Lauren Harper. A lot of people are looking for you two."

"Bloody right they should be," one of them said.

"Do you have any idea what time it is or what day?" I asked them.

"It's about eight. They brought you in several hours ago. We didn't know it was a person. We just heard a loud thud when you hit the floor. You all right then?"

Am I all right? I chuckled, not sure how to answer that and feeling like I had to laugh or I'd cry, and I was determined not to cry. "Well, I'm bruised, my lip feels like it's twice its normal size, my shoulder is killing me, I think my eye is probably turning black and blue, I'm naked and cold, but yeah, I guess I'm alright."

The barn must have been an old building. There weren't any windows, but there were large gaps between the boards in my area and pale moonlight filtered through. I put my face to the outside wall and tried to peer through one of the slats. I couldn't see much. I was about to ask more questions when the lights came on.

I took the opportunity to get a better look at my surroundings. It was definitely an animal stall. The walls went from the floor all the way to the ceiling. The door appeared to open in two parts, an upper and a lower half. The upper half stood open. I heard at least two sets of footfalls approaching my door. I moved backwards toward the back wall, not wanting to know what would come next.

Dr. Cosic and his men stepped into view. He stood there leering at me, appraising me from head to toe, smoking a cigarette. He wore a suit and tie. Not at all the friendly kitchen worker I had met only a few days before. The bastard. He'd murdered Delray. I wanted to tear him apart.

The two men he had introduced as his former students stood next to him, Chicago, only he wasn't wearing his hat, and the other one. All three of them leered at me. I wanted clothes very badly.

Cosic motioned to one of them to open the stall door. They took slow, unhurried steps into the stall. The students both carried wicked-looking automatic rifles, large banana clips with what I guessed to be more than 30 rounds each.

"Our business in this town must be finished, thanks to your young soldier," Cosic said. "We, however, are adaptable, you see. Now, we must move to another town. This will cost us money. We will get ransom for those two down there," he said, as he poked his head in the direction of his hostages. "But you? You are a more long-term investment." He dropped his cigarette and ground it out beneath his polished shoe. "Have you ever been to Russia, Sergeant Harper?"

I didn't respond.

"Well, I think you will like it there. There are not so many women like you in Russia." He strolled until he stood directly in front of me. He took a minute to run his gaze slowly up and down my nakedness. I wanted to pry his eyes out with my fingernails.

"You, we will sell. Not tomorrow, not next week," he shrugged. "We will sell you, once you are ready, and you will make good money for us. But first, you will make a trip to Russia and there, you will make your new home."

He nodded at me as if he'd completed the task he had set for himself, then turned and walked out of the stall, leaving me with his former students.

The men glanced at each other and smiled. Chicago handed his weapon over to the other one, then turned to look at me while he undid his belt, his eyes cold, his jaw set and determined. I thought

I was freezing before. His stare, his stroll toward me, my knowledge of what was to come next sent icy shards through my veins.

While Chicago pulled the belt out of his pants, the other guy leaned against the wall, propped Chicago's weapon there, then crossed his legs at the ankle, his arms folded over his chest. He tried to look bored but his eyes glinted with interest. My gaze darted around the stall, looking for something, any opportunity to defend myself. There was nothing there save for me, the two men and piles of hay.

The hay seemed to have a life of its own, wrapping around my ankles, making it difficult for me to dodge and move away from Chicago. He seemed to come at me through the obstacle as if it didn't exist. The hay was maddening in the way it slowed me down, made my movements awkward. Soon I stood backed against the wall, my arms trapped behind me.

As soon as he was in range, I braced myself against the wall, reared my leg up and kicked Chicago in the middle of his chest as hard as I could. He grinned and stumbled back, talking to the other guy in a calm voice. They laughed at me, their smiling faces a taunt I could barely stand.

He wrapped his fist in one end of his belt, drew his arm back and whipped me, hard lashes at my thighs and arms, left, then right, then left again, his grin growing, the stinging smacks echoing loud in the small stall.

It's exhausting, to be beaten, to hold all of that pain. It seemed to go on and on, one vicious slash after another until the strokes melded together into one long ripping throb. It felt as if I should be bleeding. When I could stand to look at my skin, the welts were wide and angry but there was no blood, only pain. Pain and humiliation that there was nothing I could do but bare it.

I refused to cry, refused to cry out. Soon we were both simply grunting. Chicago breathing heavy as if he'd run a race, a grunt punctuating each stroke. Me, breathing heavy, a grunt at each new lash of pain as the beating slowly but relentlessly sapped my strength. He didn't give up, didn't let up until I lay curled up in the hay, too tired to try to move out of the way any longer, too exhausted to think.

After that, they used me as they willed it.

I am a strong woman and not by accident. I had intentionally spent much of my adult career in self-defense training, running, lifting weights, training to take care of myself in any situation. If my hands had been free, if I'd been wearing clothes, perhaps I would have stood a better chance. As it was, I was helpless while they raped me.

They took turns, one always watching the other, a weapon always close to hand, as the other went at me. They smelled of tobacco and sweat, and their smell rubbed off on me. Even when they weren't touching me, I couldn't get rid of the feeling that they were still there, that odor ever present on my skin.

The tactic had its undeniable effect on me. The humiliation and pain of repeated, relentless attacks sapped my will, ground at my spirit. I hardly felt human. The details are too painful to conjure up. I'd give anything, anything to forget them.

Ian and Frank heard every moment of my torture through the thin wall of my stall. Over the next two days, each time men came for me, the British went through their own form of hell.

"Bloody leave her alone, you rank bastards," one of them yelled.

"Not again, you'll kill her," said the other.

They screamed and begged, but they were just as powerless as I was. Once, I heard one of them sobbing. It helped, somehow, to hear them cuss and plead for me. At the same time, knowing I had witnesses made it worse, far worse. I found myself trying to diminish the humiliation of their knowledge. I stifled screams and muffled my cries. Each time I whimpered, each grunt of pain, every slap and punch, I couldn't help but know that they were right next door, listening to it all.

I mentally named my tormentors. There was Chicago, because of the baseball cap he always wore. Fat Lip, for the big slobbery lips he insisted on putting on me. There were two other men that showed up later that first evening, each carrying weapons with equally large banana clips and each brutal in their treatment of me. One I called Shorty, the other Blondie for the most obvious reasons. They all wore radios on their belts and talked to each other often, checking in, constantly coordinating what would happen next. None of them ever spoke to me, not in English anyway, but they said plenty. While I didn't understand the words, I understood the sentiment as they hurled insults. Sometimes they laughed as they ravaged me, a wild banter between them with me in the middle feeling lost in my own head.

Between the four of them, they kept me tortured for hours on end. By the afternoon of the second day, I didn't think I could take much more. I felt ripped apart inside, every inch of me bruised. The few moments they left me alone, I cowered in the corner of the stall, unable to lay down on my battered body, afraid to close my eyes. Somehow knowing Ritza and who knows how many other women had survived a similar thing, gave me the knowledge that the abuse wouldn't kill me, but I knew I would never be the same. Shattered insides. Emotionally. Physically. How could I ever recover?

The news that Cosic planned to sell me eased some of my fears. It meant that I was property that had value and that he wouldn't kill me. The guards didn't seem worried about damaging the merchandise, so I also figured they wouldn't try to sell me until I was cleaned up a bit, and healed, which, considering what they were putting me through, could take days. I had to assume the plan was to break me, let me get healthy again, and then get the maximum dollar they could. To do that, they'd have to wait for all the swelling and bruising to go away. That meant I had some time.

Ever present in my mind was the fact that, if the British paid the ransom for the journalists—and I had to assume that would happen any day—Cosic and his men would have to move after they turned them over. Ian and Frank would tell others about me, about my torture and the intention to sell me. Cosic would have to move me somewhere after that, probably somewhere outside of Bosnia and away from any slim chance I had of rescue. If I was going to get away, it had to be before the British paid the ransom. I repeated that line in my head over and over until it began to feel like a child's song of hope. Before the British pay the ransom. Before the British pay the ransom. It was my deadline. Each time they pinned me down, as they grunted and pounded away at me, I lost myself in the metronome of the repetition as a constant reminder of my goal. Before the British pay the ransom, before the British pay the ransom.

I had no idea where we were, couldn't guess how far away we were from other homes or villages. All I knew was that I was in a barn. Barns usually meant farm fields, and in Bosnia, farm fields meant landmines. Every day, children and farmers died or became permanently maimed because of the millions of landmines scattered about. Even if I got out of the barn, danger could lurk in the fields surrounding the barn. I didn't care. I'd take my chances out there if I had to.

Like a wolf willing to chew off its own foot to escape a trap, I would rather choose to wander through a minefield than face the possibility of the perpetual odor of sweat and tobacco on my skin.

Thirty-one

I asked Ian to keep track of the time when the men came to my stall.

"Why," he asked. "What are you planning?"

"Just do it, would you?"

"You can't escape," Frank said. "You'll only get yourself killed."

"And staying alive while they go at me every day is better, is it?"

"Oh, luv," Ian said. "Don't talk that way."

"Shut up and keep track of the time, would you? And don't call me, luv."

It reminded me too much of Harry.

Most of the day, my hands remained tied with plastic flex ties. I figured, if I really worked at it, I could sever the plastic. That task seemed easy enough. Whatever I did, I'd have to make sure I could get all three of us out of there. If I left the journalists, and Cosic thought I could give their position away, he would kill them. How could I get us all out before the British worked out the ransom deal? If I couldn't figure it out before the exchange, Cosic would have me out of the country and I'd be sentenced to the same life as Ritza.

The men allowed me time to sleep, but I rarely did. They brought me food and water. I forced myself to eat and drink. A stinking bucket in the corner served as my toilet.

Sometimes I silently laughed at them. They didn't know me

and therefore didn't understand that the task Cosic had given them, to break me, was an impossible one. Despite the impossible nature of the thing, they kept up the unpleasantness regularly until they all seemed bored with it. In the moments when I allowed myself to consider it, I imagined they began to view it as a task, like walking the perimeter or cleaning their weapons. I fought less, my strength sapped, but that didn't mean I had given up. I would never go to Russia. I would never be a pliant slave in some brothel. I bided my time and repeated my goal.

Before the British pay the ransom.

They brought Clayton Hawes in to have a turn with me. He was pathetic and obviously intimidated at the prospect of performing in front of the watching younger men.

"I don't want no part of that whore," he said, hitching up his pants and walking away. I had a momentary feeling of relief but that didn't last long.

Late on the second day, Chicago sprayed me down with a garden hose. I couldn't have been easy to be near since I was covered in filth. He stood in the door of the stall with the hose, aiming the freezing water at me, laughing as I danced around. When he finished I cowered in the corner, shivering so hard I thought all of my teeth would shatter. I didn't think I would ever warm up, until Blondie and Shorty came to the door. In short order, I was covered in their filth again and repeating my hopeful chant. Before the British pay the ransom.

At first, Ian and Frank tried to say encouraging things; that people were looking for us, that help was on the way. I wasn't convinced that anyone would come. As stubborn as I knew Ramsey to be, I knew he would be the first to believe that I had fled an arrest for murder. McCallen wasn't around to vouch for me. I didn't know anyone else who could argue that running away wasn't in my nature.

At any moment, Cosic could decide it was time to move, to accept the ransom, to ship me off to Russia or some other place. I had to make a plan despite all the unknowns and I had to make it soon.

Sometimes, I'd ask the men to undo my hands, to let me relax my arms for a while. Now and then, when they were finished with me, they would undo the bounds for a time. It was just long enough to get complete circulation back in my arms, enough time for it to hurt like hell and wish I had never asked for the freedom. As soon as I felt normal again, they came in, wrestled me down and rebound my hands. They would laugh at this. I was sure they had experience in doing exactly this to others that had come before me because they seemed to know how long it took for the circulation to return to my limbs. Their cruelty made me more determined to get out of there.

The fact that they sometimes removed my bounds meant that the men kept their pockets full of flex-ties. At one point, several of them slipped out of Chicago's pocket onto the floor of my stall. I covered them with my body and then pushed straw on top to conceal them. I didn't know at the time how I would use them, but I kept working on a plan to get out of there and having extra ties seemed like a good idea.

Then, late on my second night, I heard a miraculous sound, an unmistakable sound. Sore and uncomfortable, I had known I wouldn't ever get to sleep. So, I lay there, listening to crickets and to one of the British quietly snoring next door, when I heard through the night air, the rattle of an M1 Abrams tank somewhere in the distance.

There's no other sound like it. The deep rumble, the high-pitched squeal when it turns and the rattling ching of the treads, like the sound of chains mashed together, were music to my ears. It was the sound of rescue.

I moved to the wall separating our cells and kicked it hard.

"Hey, you guys! Wake up." I whispered.

I heard them scramble about for a few seconds.

"What time is it, right now?" I hissed at them.

"God damn it. What is it with you and the time?"

"Just tell me the time, would you, please?"

"It's half past twelve."

"Good, that's good."

"Why? What was so bloody urgent?" Frank asked, that last couple words distorted by a noisy yawn.

"Hey, how are you guys tied up? Flex ties or what?

They whispered between each other for a second, as if they thought I was losing it. I took a deep breath and tried to calm myself. I needed to sound reasonable.

"Come on, just answer me, please."

They whispered some more but I could hear them clearly.

"If she tries to break out of here, she could get us killed," one of them whispered.

I leaned against the wall separating us.

"Look, if I don't get myself out of here, I'm going to be shipped off to god knows where and become some Russian mobster's sex toy. Think about that while you dream about the BBC paying your ransom and going back to London to sip tea. Believe me. I don't want to put either of you in danger."

I couldn't blame them for thinking of their own skins. We were all in extreme danger, but I needed their help. "Come on. Tell me how they have you secured."

"Well, we're both kind of shackled to the wall. There's a big metal ring in the wall and a thick rope is looped through our handcuffs..."

"Handcuffs? Metal handcuffs?"

"Yeah, handcuffs. The rope goes between the handcuffs through the metal ring and then over to Frank there, and the same thing with him."

I rolled that around in my head for a bit. I was sure I could figure out a way to cut my flex-tie. It was only plastic, but handcuffs were a different matter. The rope could be cut, but the handcuffs would have to stay on while we made our escape. I was glad Cosic had taken me in the spur of the moment. The plastic bindings would be much easier to deal with.

We talked about their situation and mine for a while. They could move around their cell easily with the length of rope they had. I could move anywhere as well, but with my hands behind my back, I was still very restricted. Not having clothes or shoes was a problem too. My captors always closed the upper half of the stall door when they shut me up for the night, but the locks were flimsy. Cosic and his boys obviously weren't too worried about me. Cosic had said women were silly to put themselves in harm's way. I was grateful for his underestimation of my abilities.

Once I got them started, Ian and Frank began talking about how long they'd been there, how uncomfortable they were. They told me that after their brief interview with Ritza and Captain Griffin, they had waited while Griffin and the girl left, not wanting to be seen leaving together. The reporters left twenty minutes later and walked right into the hands of Clayton Hawes, Chicago, and Fat Lip. They suspected one of the women in the brothel had tipped Cosic to their schedule.

They had been hustled into the back of a panel truck, injected with something to make them sleep and woke up here. Frank apparently had hurt his knee when thrown in the back of the truck.

"It was swollen up to twice its size when they first put us in here. They actually gave me some ice for it, the bastards," Frank complained. "It's a little better now, but I can barely stand on it."

Frank was kind of a whiner, but I was glad he told me about the knee. Any plan I made would have to consider his immobility.

Frank wanted to keep talking, but I needed him to be quiet so that I could listen to the night. I finally had to tell him I was going to sleep. Eventually, the quiet snoring started up again, and I concentrated. I heard voices outside from at least two different people. They moved around the barn, slowly as they talked. After a long while, I heard what I expected to hear and I kicked the wall again.

"Hey, what time is it now? Quick, tell me." I asked.

"What the hell is she on about?" Frank whispered.

"It's five in the morning," was the sleepy reply.

"Before I got here, did they always shut you up for the night at ten o'clock?"

"Yes, same as every night," Frank said.

I suddenly felt hopeful. This farm could have been sitting in

243

the middle of a minefield. I couldn't just go blindly into those fields without acknowledging the danger. Now that I had a solid direction to go, and a real goal to reach, I would take the risk. I would just have to hope that landmines weren't in my path.

The British didn't need to know what I planned. It would only get them worrying. I worried enough for all of us. I couldn't afford to fail.

Thirty-two

I wanted another night to listen, to confirm that the tank was part of a regular patrol that came in this direction at the same time, but I couldn't risk the wait. I had been Cosic's prisoner for three days by then. The BBC guys, for a solid week. I figured after a week, the ransom negotiations, if there were any, had to be wrapping up. If I was going to do anything about my situation, I had to do it soon, had to do it before the British paid the ransom. After that, my chances for escape diminished greatly, possibly becoming nonexistent.

That afternoon, Dr. Cosic came to my stall. I hadn't seen him over the days I'd been a prisoner, not in person anyway. I'd seen him in my dreams during the times when I imagined a variety of ways to exact revenge.

He stood in the doorway peering at me over the half door. I cowered and moved back against the wall as I did whenever any of them came. At some point in my captivity, I realized that if they weren't seeing any progress in breaking me, they might just kill me, deciding I wasn't worth the trouble.

Chicago and Fat Lip stood outside the stall watching as Cosic stepped in slowly, his hands in his pockets. He strolled up to me, raised his hand to my face. I shrunk away from his touch. He stroked my face, my hair, and spoke softly to me. I couldn't understand his words but he made gentle, soothing sounds as if he were coaxing an animal to obedience.

I wanted to slam my knee into his groin, to spit in his face and scream obscenities at him. I figured I'd be better off with a good performance, one that might convince him that they had accomplished the task they had set for themselves.

He said something to Chicago and Fat Lip. They argued with him angrily. Eventually he ordered them to do what he asked. Chicago stepped forward and cut the flex tie that bound my hands together. The immediate rush of circulation was sweet at first, and then grew painful as it always did. Cosic rubbed my arms saying soothing words, being gentle and kind, smiling at me even. I wanted to throttle him, could almost feel my fingers squeezing the breath out of him.

Apparently, it wasn't enough that he and his men could do what they wanted with me. The objective was to leave me a whimpering ball of willing flesh. His men had been brutal and constant. Cosic's job was to show kindness and in that way, earn my trust. By this time, I knew that struggling didn't help. No matter how hard I fought, no matter what small bites, scratches or kicks I managed to get in, eventually, they would overpower me. That didn't stop me from trying.

As soon as they freed my hands, I stopped the cowering act, the temptation to fight too great. I managed some very satisfying punches, a solid elbow to the ribs and almost managed to knee Cosic in the groin. Thinking back on it, I think he wanted me to fight like that, knew that removing my restraints would mean I'd fight harder. It was his excuse to call Chicago and Fat Lip to join him. By the time they finished kicking and punching me, I was barely conscious, completely out of energy, all the fight gone out of me. After that, Cosic was easily able to pin my arms down. His gentle torture seemed to last for hours.

I went to that place in my head I had been constructing over the hours of torture. The smells in the barn helped me go there. I rode a horse on a beach of white sand, splashing through waves of blue ocean water. Sea gulls dipped and called. I rode the horse until my thighs, my whole body was sore from the effort. The sun burned my skin, the sound of the waves crashed in my ears. In the distance, rolling hills promised a place, lush and peaceful. I set my sights on that place, the horse's mane gripped in my fists. It was a place far from the reality of my situation, but never quite far enough.

When Cosic finally finished with me, he kneeled down, cupped my chin in his hand, and made me look him in the eye. "Yes, you are very special. I almost want to keep you for myself." I looked back at him. He was feeling triumphant. What a foolish man. The thought that anyone could believe me capable of murder had shocked me. Staring into Cosic's dark eyes, I had no doubt that killing him would not be beyond my capabilities.

He said something to the others. Again they argued but Cosic was the boss and they eventually agreed to do whatever he demanded.

Cosic, the Bosnian slaver, strolled out looking self-satisfied, closing the half-door behind him and not looking back. My hands were still free and I had an overwhelming feeling of triumph. Chicago started to close the upper half of the door but stopped. He strode in, taking a flex cuff from his back pocket.

"NO!" I screamed. "Please don't. I've been good. I've been good." I begged. But Cosic didn't come back to stop it. I gave up the struggle. Chicago bound my hands again. It didn't matter. The plastic wouldn't stop me.

I lay there for a time, imagining Cosic's death. I envisioned putting a bullet through his brain, driving over him in a humvee, slamming my fist in his face repeatedly. I needed my anger to stay focused on my plan.

Later, as soon as they shut my door for the night, I started on the plastic tie. Moonlight slanted in though the old walls of the barn. The dim blue light helped me with what I was trying to do inside, but would be dangerous for me outside. I had hoped for a cloudy night.

I had studied the walls during the daylight hours. In several places, large flat nail heads stuck out from the old walls. One nail near the door looked particularly sharp. As soon as I heard my captors leave, I started rubbing the plastic tie across the nail head.

The nail was partway up the wall, so I had to turn my back on it, crouch down, and just rub back and forth on it, anyway that I could. I missed quite a few times and scratched up my wrists instead, but I could barely feel any pain with the adrenalin pumping through my veins.

My shoulders ached with the strain, my knees quickly grew sore from crouching, but I kept at that nail. Finally, the plastic started to stretch and grow thinner. When it was broken, I felt complete and utter joy. The painful feeling of blood recirculation was easier to take.

I asked Ian what time it was. I hadn't told them what I planned to do. If they heard me working on my bindings, they hadn't said anything. I knew they'd hear me when I started working on the door, but I didn't much care what they thought. I had to think about my own escape.

"It's quarter past ten. What are you doing?"

I didn't answer him. It had taken me fifteen minutes to sever the tie. I hoped I could get the stall door open in much less time.

The top of the stall door had one of those metal sliding locks on it. Nothing much more secure than a bathroom stall door. I had just enough light to see the thin metal bar through the gap in the door. I slipped one of the flex-ties I had concealed earlier through the gap and jiggled the sliding lock. My hands were shaking and my heart pounded in my ears. I worked at the lock furiously. I didn't want to spend more than twenty minutes on this part of the task. Sweat dripped into my eyes. I grit my teeth with the effort, but I kept at it.

Again, Ian asked me what I was doing. Frank sounded worried, saying I was going to get myself, and them, killed.

"Please be quiet, both of you, and trust me," I whispered.

I kept working at the lock.

The plastic was too flexible. I tried to envision the small metal nipple that I would have to lift and move in order to release the lock. I sucked in a breath when I felt it finally start to slide. Once I maneuvered the nipple out of the locked position, the metal bar glided slowly but easily to unlock the door. The top of the stall door swung open as if on its own.

I imagined Cosic never considered that I might try to escape. His dismissive attitude about women had worked in my favor. Plastic flex ties and the simple lock might have been enough for the victims he had kidnapped in the past, but he had underestimated me. Taking me must have been a spur of the moment decision on his part. He hadn't planned on needing an extra set of handcuffs or a decent lock.

I swung the door open wider, the creak of the hinges alarmingly loud to my ears. I prayed that whoever was on patrol outside didn't hear it. I stuck my head out and scanned the barn area. It was empty, as I expected it to be. I reached over the lower door. The lock opened easily and I stepped out of my stall.

It would have been a miracle to find a pair of pants or shoes lying around inside the barn, but my fantasies did not come true. I would have to do this naked.

I closed the stall door and looked toward the end of the hall to the door where I usually heard the men enter. I glanced in the opposite direction and was relieved to see another door on that end. I made a guess that they entered by the door closest to the house, so I planned to use the opposite one.

"Hey, Ian, what time is it now?"

"You got out!" he whispered. I heard him stand up and move to his stall door.

"Ian, damn it, what time is it exactly." I pleaded.

"It's just after eleven, but what…"

How could it have taken me forty-five minutes to open the door? My heart slammed in my chest. I had to get moving.

Ian kept asking questions, but I moved toward the door that I thought was away from the house and more concealed. It wasn't locked, but I had no idea what I would find once outside.

I opened the door a crack, peeked out, and listened. Silence, except for night insects. There was too much moonlight. If anyone looked in this direction, they would easily see me. I prepared to step outside and froze. The crackle of a radio cut through the night air. It came from somewhere behind me, but some distance away. I held my breath and listened. The guard talked into the radio as he moved away, his voice growing fainter. I let out my breath. There was at least one more guard somewhere out there. Seconds were too precious. I had to get moving.

I opened the door, stepped out of the barn, pressed myself against the wall, and let my eyes adjust to the new darkness. I took my first look at my surroundings. About a hundred yards away from the side of the barn stood a field of thick, tall grass. Or a minefield. Either way, that's where I was going. If I headed straight through the grass, I would eventually run into the road, and the patrol with the noisy tank. At least, that's what I hoped. If the patrol I heard didn't come back in this direction regularly, my efforts would be wasted. No time for second-guessing.

Lowering myself to the ground, I low crawled on my belly, using my elbows and knees to pull myself forward. The ground was gravelly and rough. I stayed low, ignoring the rocks that dug into my skin. My body had been through much worse in the last few days.

I was committed now. If I were caught outside the barn, I would be done for and maybe cost Ian and Frank their lives as well. I moved as fast as I could, keeping my eyes on my objective, and didn't waste a moment looking around. When I hit the grass line, I dove in, then waited, motionless, listening for any sounds of alarm.

After several seconds of calm, I looked back to the barn and saw a low, stone house just a few yards away from the barn. Behind the barn stood a shelter with stacks of hay, and an old tractor parked inside. A small light illuminated an area over a side door of the house. A car sat parked in the small dirt driveway. As I watched, two men walked around the side of the house, carrying weapons, one puffing smoke from a cigarette. They stopped and leaned on one of the cars, casually chatting. Obviously, my movements had gone undetected. I had to keep it that way.

If I had been standing, the grass would have come up to my chest. I crawled on my hands and knees for another hundred yards or so. Listening for an alarm. Crawled some more. After a time, I stood up and ran.

The grass brutalized my skin. The tall blades left paper-thin cuts all over me, lashing me as I sprinted by. My feet landed on broken stalks that stabbed into my heels. I ignored the discomfort. I hadn't counted on the grass. Running had always been part of my plan, but I had no idea I'd have to run through this. I tried to part the way with my arms. Tried lifting my legs high. Nothing made running through the obstacle easy, but I kept going. Each time my foot hit the ground I prayed I wouldn't trip a landmine. I had less than an hour, minutes to get to the road. I focused on that. I didn't have any idea how far the road was. Noise travels easily at night. The road could be close, or it could be several miles away. I had about five hours before they would find my stall empty. I planned to use every moment of that time to reach the road. If the patrol didn't come along, I'd have to find some other way to get word back to McGovern.

Sweat ran into my eyes. My feet grew more damaged with every step I took. I was a runner but this was unlike any running I'd ever done. I tried not to think about distance and time. I just ran. My lungs burned. Dust from the grass made my eyes and nose sting. The sharp edges of the tall stalks shredded my flesh.

Suddenly, I stumbled through a wall of the grass and my feet hit pavement. The tar was still warm from the daytime sun. I stopped, panting. I put my hands on my knees and doubled over, my chest heaving as I struggled to catch my breath. I had reached a road, but I didn't know if it was the right road. I looked around frantically, walking in circles, trying to find something that would indicate that I had reached my goal, and I found it. Deeply grooved, radiated hash marks imprinted on a soft part of the road. The 70-ton tank often left evidence that it had passed an area and I almost collapsed in relief at seeing the sign.

Then I heard it and felt it. The road vibrated under my sore feet. I saw the headlights of the humvees in the convoy, and the dark shape of the tank, the gun pointing straight down the road.

I stood in the middle of the road, waving my arms, smiling. My nakedness should have embarrassed me, but worries about propriety went out the window. The humvee stopped just in front of me, the headlights blinding. Someone climbed out of the back seat.

"Sergeant Harper?"

The glare of the headlights made it impossible to see who the large, dark silhouette was. "Oh my god," he said. He ran toward me but he moved too fast. I instinctively cowered, backing up, my hand up to stop him.

"It's okay," he said, skidding to a stop. "It's me, Corporal Graham."

"Graham?"

"Yeah," he said, walking toward me slowly now, his arms out to prove he was harmless. "We met in the mess hall, remember?"

He stopped then laid his weapon on the ground and shrugged out of his web gear, dumping it all on the ground as he slowly moved toward me. He unzipped his jacket, and held it open for me to step into.

"Corporal Graham," I said, and remembered the young man who had perfectly executed ten pushups in the mess hall.

"Yeah," he said. "It's okay." I stepped toward him and slipped my arms into the sleeves. He let go of the jacket. I zipped it up, turning back to him, my head down, trying to hide the tear that had slipped out. I pulled up the jacket collar and pressed my nose into it, inhaling deeply. Fresh outdoors and a pine scent filled my nostrils. I wiped my face with the back of my hand.

"What the fuck, Sergeant Harper," Graham said.

"Corporal Graham, you have no idea how glad I am to see you."

= = = = = = = = = =

It took me a while, but I was finally able to get them to move a couple of miles down the road to lessen any chance that Cosic and his boys would hear and be alarmed by the commotion. Lieutenant George, leading the patrol, called the TOC on the radio. Colonel Raybourn eventually came on, sounding tired. They went back and forth over the secure radio about what to do.

Sitting in one of the humvees, wearing Graham's jacket, I explained yet again, what had happened to me, that the two British reporters were in danger, and that we needed to move quickly.

"There are only five of them, sir, including Cosic. They each have automatic weapons. That's about all I can tell you," I explained.

"No matter how many men they have, they won't be able to withstand a tank attack," Raybourn said.

"Sir, I'm begging you. If I take this patrol back there, yes, we'd have overwhelming force. There's no denying that. But Cosic's men are walking patrol and on guard. They will hear us coming from miles away. If they feel we're on the move to attack, they could kill their hostages or move them. Move them someplace where we may never find them."

Talking about the possible death of the reporters made Raybourn consider getting the British forces involved. If the American forces led this rescue attempt and the journalists were killed, it would be a diplomatic nightmare.

"The Vice President is spending the night on McGovern tonight. We can't go into this thing half-cocked. I will get in touch with the British headquarters immediately. You'll just have to hold tight until we hear from them."

"Sir, we are running out of time."

"We're not doing this without British support. Hold tight. That's an order."

Waiting was almost worse torture than what I'd suffered in that barn. Time continued to slip away. We had already wasted over an hour with Raybourn. Getting another set of officers involved could take hours as well. They would argue about who would lead, how the operation would be conducted. Meanwhile, the night continued to move closer to dawn.

Part of me wanted to go in there with guns blazing, get this thing over with, but I knew Cosic wouldn't hesitate to kill the British. I also knew that if they found me missing in the morning, they would cut their losses quickly. They would either kill their hostages immediately, or move them somewhere we couldn't find them.

It was excruciating to wait. I paced and cursed and hoped that the officers in charge would get their shit together and get out here to save those men.

Graham brought me a cup of coffee from a thermos. I enjoyed the blissful taste while I listened to him and his soldiers tell their stories about the Vice Presidential visit. I had missed it. All that time preparing and I hadn't been there to see Gore. Still, I wanted to keep them talking, to take my mind off the waiting, but it didn't help.

I could tell by the way they all looked at me, that I was a mess. One of my eyes was swollen shut, my lips so damaged it was hard to talk. I stank. Standing around with a group of men who were freshly showered, made me feel worse. Somehow, their ordinariness made it easier for me to consider what the rapidly diminishing time forced me to consider. I only had one choice. It became difficult for me to breathe.

"We can't let you go," the lieutenant said. "Colonel Raybourn has ordered us to wait here until they make a plan."

"Listen to me, sir, because I've waited as long as I can, and I don't have any time left. This is only going to happen one way. You will take me back to the exact spot where you picked me up or I will walk back there right now on my own."

It was already well after four. Dawn was only about an hour away. I had sketched a layout of the barn and house. I gave them directions to find it. I knew that sneaking back into the barn in broad daylight was insane. I needed the cover of darkness and I needed to be back in my stall before they came for me in the morning, or all of this would have been for nothing.

As much as I knew I needed to get back, I was also totally and completely petrified. How long would I have to wait for rescue? What if Cosic decided to move me in the morning? What if they shipped me off to some Russian province in hours? And how could I survive one more rape, one more session in the hands of those bastards? I didn't know if I could hold on to my sanity. My body vibrated in fear, but there were no more options to consider.

"Can't you give it another hour, Sergeant Harper?" Graham said. "We could follow you. Get the location."

"You don't need to follow me. Just plot the grid coordinate from the place you found me and follow a straight line for about five miles. I've left an unmistakable trail in the grass that leads you right to them. You want to save me? Then get the people in the TOC to do what I've said. Otherwise, two men will die."

The young lieutenant stood there looking indecisive. I didn't have time for indecision. He was in a tough spot, but he knew I was right.

He turned to Graham, "Let's go."

I sighed in relief and climbed into the vehicle.

In minutes, we were back to the spot where they had found me in the road.

"Thanks, Graham and thanks, sir. Tell Colonel Raybourn it was all my doing."

"Oh, don't worry, Sergeant Harper. I plan on it." The lieutenant said, smiling, but I could see the worry on his face.

I got out of the humvee and stood there, looking at the path I had created through the grass. For a moment, I hesitated. Tears threatened to flow. I had to work to cut them off. My whole body shook. I put my hands on my knees and bent over, trying to catch my breath. I wiped my face, then sank down to one knee. I tried to collect myself.

"You don't have to go back," I heard Lieutenant George say. He stood behind me. I could feel him there, about to reach out and touch me, to offer some support. I didn't want his hands anywhere near me, and besides, he was wrong. I did have to go back.

I took a deep breath, stood up, shrugged out of the Graham's jacket, letting it fall to the ground and sprinted into the grass.

Thirty-three

I lay on my stomach, looking through the tall grass at the barn and the house. Dawn looked like a promise peaking over the horizon. I had lost the cover of darkness. Low crawling wouldn't help me now. My only chance was to hope no one paid attention. No lights were on in the house. I was just about to make my move, when Fat Lip walked around the side of the barn. My heart thudded in my chest as he made a circular stroll, ambling around the yard and back toward the house. I waited. As soon as he turned the corner, I made my dash and slipped silently into the barn.

"What the fuck are you doing back here?" Ian demanded in a harsh whisper.

I walked around outside my stall, looking at the farm implements scattered around the old barn. I took time selecting a weapon. Eventually I found a small pickax that fit very nicely in my hand and took it with me back into my stall, shoving it under a pile of hay.

There was no time to get the upper half of the door relocked. I had no idea how I would explain all the grass cuts and my ruined feet. I tried to make myself as dirty as possible, rubbing dirt from the floor of the stall all over myself, hoping I could cover up some of the damage. It would have to do. Then I slipped a flex tie over my wrists and settled back to wait.

Ian and Frank kept whispering questions, but I ignored them. I couldn't speak to them, couldn't explain about the indecision and the time it took for the people in charge to see how desperate the situation was. I had failed. The failure sapped all of my energy, all of my hope. I couldn't talk about it.

When Chicago and Fat Lip arrived to check on us, they argued between themselves for a bit. I didn't understand what they were saying, but I figured they were blaming each other for leaving the upper half of my door unlocked. Their accusations grew intense and threatening. I wanted them to go to blows over it, to shoot each other even. Instead, they stood at my door, shouting back and forth. Eventually, Chicago slammed the door shut, locked it and they stalked away, too angry with each other to abuse me. They never seemed to consider that I may have unlocked the door. When they were safely out of earshot, I started laughing. It may have sounded a bit demented since I couldn't seem to stop.

"What's so damn funny?" Frank asked.

"They walked away," I said, between bouts of quiet laughter.

"What's so funny about that?"

My laughter dried up. "I don't like what they do to me when they stick around."

"Oh. Sorry, luv."

"Don't call me, luv."

I kept thinking about Raybourn and how the man couldn't come to a decision, his bureaucratic brain unable to understand the consequences of a failure to act. He'd probably been angry that I had returned, but I didn't care. He could get angry all he wanted. It was his fault. His indecision had left me no choice.

Each time the men came into the barn, to feed us, to check on us, I worried they were about to move us, or to release the British. I felt a dread that my efforts the night before were for nothing. No one would come, or they would come too late.

The day seemed never ending, my nerves on edge. The sounds of activity outside the barn set my imagination on overload. Doors opened and closed, a truck came and went. Talking. Movement. Everything about the sounds told me something was about to happen. Either they were about to move us, or they were close to making the ransom exchange.

When it grew dark, I lay down, burrowing into the hay for warmth, fearful that my sprint into the grass had been for nothing. No one would rescue us. Ian and Frank would be taken away and I would be alone. I went to sleep thinking about how big Russia was. How would I ever find my way home again?

========

When I woke up, it was to the sound of rustling footsteps in the straw. My stall was ink dark. I sat up, opened my eyes wide, and waited for them to adjust to the darkness. I could hear someone moving toward me. A dark figure, crouched low, slowly came into focus as it drew closer. I froze, my eyes wide, trying to see. Then a gentle hand went over my mouth and I felt lips close to my ear.

"Quiet, luv. Don't want the keepers to get wise."

It was Harry. I almost sobbed in relief as he knelt down in front of me, his face rubbed in black camouflage paint, a black knit watch cap pulled down over his ears, an automatic weapon settled comfortably across his chest. The most visible thing about him were the whites of his eyes and the flash of his teeth as he smiled at me. He brought his index finger to his lips telling me to be silent, his eyebrows raised questioning if I would comply. I nodded vigorously, tears flowing freely down my face. He removed his hand from my mouth and I could see the horrified look he attempted to hide at my appearance.

'Don't worry, Harry," I whispered. "I'm okay now." I said with an awkward grin, my mouth and face too swollen to smile.

He nodded, then gestured for me to turn around. He cut my hands free, re-sheathed his knife and then shrugged out of his backpack. I was impressed with the smooth and silent way he completed each task, his movements causing only a whisper of fabric, the pounding of my own blood in my ears seemed to shatter the stillness he created.

He unzipped the backpack and pulled something out. My tears threatened to flow again at the sight of the black coveralls. He stood me up, then helped me put the coveralls on, lifting my feet to slip them into the legs, my hand on his shoulder for support, his eyes averted from my nakedness. He felt sturdy, solid. He slowly raised the zipper on the coveralls that were too baggy and loose, but I didn't care. To be relieved of my nakedness was a major step toward feeling human again. I couldn't help but smile. When Harry met my gaze, his eyes were glassy. He blinked to clear them. There were so many things I wanted to say to him, but there was no time. I'd never been so happy to see anyone in my life.

He repeated the gesture of his finger to his lips then motioned for me to stay still, stay where I was.

I grabbed his hand. "No way. I'm not staying here," I whispered.

He leaned in to put his lips next to my ear. "We'll come back..."

But I didn't let him finish and shook my head. "Not happening."

He stared at me for a long moment and must have seen my determination. When he nodded, I wanted to clap my hands in glee like a child who finally got the toy she always wanted, but I contained my joy and prepared to follow him.

I mimicked his crouch as he moved forward, his weapon now pressed into the hollow of his shoulder as he sighted down the barrel. When I tapped him on the back, he stopped and turned toward me, his lips pressed together in an angry scowl. I pointed to the pistol he wore in the holster strapped to his thigh. He shook his head no, his eyes wide as if I'd suggested something outrageous. I nodded my head, yes.

"Bloody hell, woman." His words came out in a hiss. I wanted to giggle, but I knew that would only make him more determined to leave me behind. He unsnapped the holster, pulled the pistol out and handed it to me, grip first. The feel of the nine millimeter in my hand felt fantastic, heady, as if I had control of my destiny again. I released the magazine, saw that the clip was fully loaded, slipped it back into place, chambered a round by pulling back on the slide and releasing it and loved the satisfying sound it made. I looked at Harry and grinned.

He flashed his teeth at me for a second through the black paint he wore then put the all-business look back on his face. He turned and led me out of the stall. Once outside the door I saw the rest of the squad.

They all looked the same, camo'd up, their faces streaked in black, watch caps pulled low on their foreheads, crouched and silent, weapons sited and at the ready. The satisfaction I felt in knowing that Cosic and his men were about to be trounced was delicious.

At Harry's signal, we all moved down the hall. While Harry had been with me, two men had released Frank and Ian. I saw them as we moved by the door, clutching at each other, eyes wide and frightened.

Harry opened the barn door, took a quick look, then signaled to move out both to the right and left. Since I was the first out behind him, I crouched and ran toward the right corner of the house and felt more than heard others following me, some directly behind, others going to the left.

The night was warm and bathed in an abundance of moonlight, making it easy for my already dark-accustomed eyes to see. The fabric of the awkward fitting coveralls scratched against my oversensitive skin and I winced at the feel of sharp gravel under my bare feet, but I was free. The reality of it felt dreamlike. I said it to myself to make it feel more real. "I'm alive, I'm free," I whispered. And now I was after the bad guys who had hurt me, who had killed Delray. The weight of the pistol in my hands gave me reassurance that all of that was true and not a dream.

My back pressed to the wall of the house, I tried to slow my breathing. I glanced at the two men who had followed me. They both nodded their readiness. My heart raced with adrenalin, the joy of being out of the barn, knowing the bastards who had tortured me for so long were about to get theirs, made me feel light, as if I could float away if I weren't careful.

I peeked around the corner and saw nothing. I signaled it was clear, and the men moved past, crouch-walking forward while I covered them. From the other side of the house, weapons fire, the staccato bleat of multiple rounds from at least two weapons. The guards must have been moving around the other side of the house, but my team stayed focused ahead of us, on our own task at hand.

Then Fat Lip came running at us, tossing a cigarette away. He skidded to a stop when he saw us and fumbled as he tried to bring his weapon up, but he was late. The man closest to him fired twice and Fat Lip's chest opened up in an inky dark blossom. He fell backwards, his arms and legs splayed wide and unmoving.

We moved forward while one of the soldiers stopped to check if Fat Lip was alive. I could tell, looking down at him, that he wouldn't be raping anyone again, the bastard. The sound of footsteps in gravel drew my attention. I raised my weapon and moved toward the sound and saw Chicago trying to sneak out the backdoor of the house. He wore loose-fitting sweatpants with no shirt, his hair tousled as if he'd been woken from sleep, his weapon clutched in one hand. He looked in the opposite direction from me and started to run toward the high grass.

"Stop!" I said, but he didn't. He spun toward me, bringing his weapon up, but I already had him in my sights. I dropped to one knee. The first shot went wide right, only grazing his arm, spinning him slightly. He managed to squeeze off a round but it went well over my head, the zip of the shot sounding too close for comfort, but Chicago was slow, late. That cost him. The second two shots I fired killed him. He hit the ground and I heard life leave him in a hiss of air. One instant, he was alive, a rapist and slaver. The next second, death appeared in his eyes that stayed partially open like a latch that won't catch.

It was suddenly too hard to breath. I'd never taken a life before. I knew firing on a weapons range would never feel the same after that. I imagined I would always see Chicago, that startled look on his face as the second round hit him, the grunt he made each time he was hit and the sound of his last breath. Better that, I reasoned, than the fate Chicago had planned for me.

The soldiers checked his pulse as a formality. He looked so young, lying there, handsome even, the rapist bastard. I waited for a triumphant feeling of revenge to come, but it didn't. It never would.

Noise erupted inside the house then, running feet, furniture crashing, weapons fire, controlled and precise. The two soldiers and I stayed outside, watching the back door. One of them jogged around the side of the house, and came back signaling that no one else was around.

Then Harry's voice beckoned us.

"All clear here," he said from the front of the house.

"Clear," one of the soldiers with me said. I had thought the soldiers were all British, but when I didn't detect an accent from the guy who responded, I gave him a closer inspection and realized I'd been wrong.

"Captain Griffin?" I asked.

He removed his black knit cap and smiled at me. The man who tried to save Ritza, the General's Bulgarian prisoner, and the man who always hid behind his clipboard was part of this commando raid. It was a surprising thing for him to do.

He held out his hand for me to shake.

"Glad we were able to find you Sergeant Harper."

"Not as glad as I am that you did."

We made our way to the front of the house where Harry stood with Cosic. I smiled when I saw his hands bound with flex ties.

He wore cotton-striped pajamas. He'd lost one of his slippers in the struggle. His hair stood on end, his eyes bloodshot and puffy. I looked at him in his proper bedclothes, this pimp and slave trader, and I wanted so very much to kill him. I thought my thirst for vengeance had been spent on Chicago, but the sight of his smirking face flipped a switch on something dark and powerful inside me. In the next instant, I found myself standing next to him, with my weapon pointed at his temple.

The pathetic maggot sank to his knees immediately, crying and begging incoherently. My aim followed him down to the ground with the weapon zeroed at his temple, not sure whether I wanted to blow his brains out or remove his privates. Both seemed equally satisfactory. I breathed hard, could hear my own heartbeat as I envisioned his head snapping back, the blood flowing from his temple, and I wondered truly, how I would feel afterwards if I pulled the trigger.

Then I heard Harry's voice as if from a long distance away.

"I totally understand how enticing killing him might seem right at this precise moment, luv, but let us remember that…"

"Do you know what this animal did to me?"

I was surprised at the cold, even sound of my voice. Cosic went perfectly still, holding his breath. His life was on a very thin thread. Tears rolled down his cheeks. I laughed. I liked the power I felt over him. I sounded a bit crazy, even to my own ears.

I thought my hands should be shaking or that I should feel hesitant especially since I'd already killed one man, but none of that happened. I simply felt cold, hard hatred.

I heard a rustling as if someone were trying to sneak up on me. I swung the weapon around and pointed it at Griffin. Everyone froze.

"Don't fuck around," I said, too calm, too cold. My vision began to grow narrow, as if someone were dimming the lights. My words seemed to come from someone else. I returned my aim to Cosic's head but my hand wasn't quite as steady as before. "This animal dies. Right here, right now," I said, trying to focus.

"Wait, luv! What about all them other girls?" Harry said in a rush. "If you end him now, we won't know what we need to rescue all the other damsels what need rescuing."

I hadn't thought of that. People like Ritza. Maybe Mishka's sister. The earth tilted slightly and I took a step to steady myself.

"On the other hand," Harry continued, "if we was to take him into custody, we find out where all the other ladies are that he has done this very same rotten bloody thing to, you see? We free them … you hear me? We free them, we put this beast on trial in Her Majesty's court and then, then after all that, you get to see him hang."

"Bullshit, Harry. You guys don't hang people anymore."

Harry took a step toward me. "Well, no," he said."But we should ... shouldn't we?" He took another step, staring into my eyes, I wanted to be lost in his gaze, wanted to fall into that gaze. My knees felt buttery, mushy. He laid his hand over mine, lowered the pistol, then gently pried it from my hands.

"I don't think I was really going to shoot him," I whispered, my words a bit slurred as if I were drunk. "I just wanted to make him feel ... "

"Make him feel what, luv?"

But before I could answer, the earth tilted again and I passed out.

Thirty-four

It took me a while to realize I was in a bed, in a tent and wearing surgical scrubs. The last thing I remembered before I passed out, was staring into Harry's green eyes and I felt a pang of sadness at his absence. Still, my situation had improved considerably. I took a moment to revel in the change, smiling to myself. Every part of my body ached. I noticed there was an IV tube in one arm and that I wore a catheter. My head throbbed with my heartbeat, but it was glorious to be alive and out of that barn. Someone came over and looked down at me, said my name, but my eyes were too heavy to keep them open a second longer. I went back to sleep with a contented sigh.

Sometime later, I woke up with a start, my heart clattering away like a badly rehearsed flamingo dancer playing castanets. I clutched the sheets in my fists. For a moment, the smell of hay and Chicago's tobacco-laced breath filled my nostrils. I could almost feel his hands on me.

After several minutes, once I convinced myself that my new surroundings were real, the staccato beat of my heart slowed and the deafening roar of blood pounding in my head diminished. Nightmares had been rare for me. I couldn't remember the last time I'd had one, but now, I had plenty of material to use. I clenched my teeth against the prospect of revisiting that barn in my dreams night after night.

My attention wandered to something less threatening. What little of the place I could see from my bed told me I was in a mobile hospital ward; the walls of the large tent flapped gently in the wind. A soft yellow light filtered through the mesh windows. From the size of the place, I figured it had to be the hospital located somewhere near Tuzla. A few other soldiers lay in beds in the ward, spaced apart from each other for some privacy. I lay there, looking around at things, watching the comings and goings and feeling as if I could sleep for a thousand years, when someone in surgical scrubs realized that my eyes were open.

"Hey, Sergeant Harper," he said, grinning. "It's good to see you awake."

He was a nice looking young man, with a mustache that didn't comply with regulations. His nametag read Specialist Folson. He told me I was doing great and that a steady stream of people had been asking about me since I had arrived there.

"How long have I been here?" I asked.

He looked to the ceiling for the answer then said with confidence, "Two days. Two days, plus today so, almost three."

"How could I have slept so long?"

"You've been through severe trauma. Your body needed time to heal. It's a good thing," he said. "Take every chance you have to do more of it."

Later, the doctor arrived, did some simple checks and gave me the rundown of my injuries.

"Your cheekbone had a small fracture. That's why your eye is still swollen. Do you have a headache?"

"Are you kidding? " I said. "It's like a marching band practicing inside my head and, between you and me, they have no rhythm at all."

He tried to keep from smiling but it didn't work. "Unfortunately, that will persist for sometime I'm afraid. The good news is your eyesight hasn't been affected, so you shouldn't need surgery. At least we don't think so, so far. We'll continue to monitor that. It is going to take some time for ... well, for us to assess the situation. You don't have any serious internal injuries, but we'll monitor that as well. The catheter comes out today so be sure to let me know if you have any trouble urinating."

He told me what tests they had done, what tests they were going to do. Some sexually transmitted diseases were detectable immediately, he told me, like Chlamydia and gonorrhea. Others would take more time and more tests.

"We've pumped you full of antibiotics and hopefully that will take care of most of the worry."

He cleared his throat then forged ahead.

"We've given you a pregnancy test. It was negative. I can provide you with a series of medications commonly called the morning after pill. You have the option of taking them now. There will be side effects. You'll probably feel sick to your stomach for a day or two, but after that, you can rest assured that you aren't pregnant. If you don't want to take them, we'll redo the pregnancy test in a week."

He waited for me to make my decision, but I didn't need to think long on it. I held my hand out. He passed me a small Dixie cup with a couple of pills in it.

Sometime later, I insisted and Folson, after resisting as long as he could, handed me a small mirror. I saw what I expected. One eye, the one that had been swollen shut, had improved a bit, but my cheek was a shock—huge, purple and swollen to the point where I could barely see past it. What little of my eye I could see was red with blood. The other side of my face had what looked like a rug burn all across it. I remembered how that got there, when Blondie dragged me by one leg across the stall. I shuddered at the memory.

All of the bruises still looked fresh even though they were several days old. My hair was impossible, bits of straw and grass tangled in the curly tendrils. In total, I looked like I'd been through hell which seemed appropriate since I had been through hell and more. It was time to take charge.

"That's it," I said. "I've got to have a shower."

"Are you sure you're ready?"

"Damn right I am."

Folson brought me flip-flops, a shower puff, some bath gel, a towel and a toothbrush. Getting out of bed was a long slow process, painful at every move. Even the water, weak as the pressure was, hurt in places. I scrubbed and scrubbed, the water going from hot, to warm to ice cold. I didn't care. I scrubbed and wondered how long it would be before I would ever feel clean enough again. I brushed my teeth until my gums bled.

Eventually I dried off and wrestled a comb through my hair, my arms growing tired and numb several times before I could work my way through all of the tangles. I climbed back into bed and sleep came instantly.

When I opened my eyes, Ramsey and Santos were there. They stood off in a corner, talking to one of my doctors. I wanted to close my eyes again, pretend I hadn't seen them, but Ramsey noticed. The man had an uncanny ability to see everything.

If I had expected an apology, and I admit I might have had a silly notion that one was due, I was disappointed.

"Master Sergeant Harper, we'll need to debrief you," Ramsey said.

"Hello, Mr. Ramsey. Mr. Santos. I'm fine, thank you. How are you?"

His ears turned pink then color washed up his neck to his face. He glanced at Santos. "We wouldn't require it if it wasn't absolutely necessary."

"Is civility necessary?"

"Okay, I get that you might be angry."

"That I might be angry? You're a comedian, Mr. Ramsey. I had no idea how funny you could be."

He looked to the floor, put his hands on his hips, took a deep breath then was finally able to look at me again. It amused me, that admitting he was wrong bothered him so much. He still refused to admit it.

"I have good news. The DNA test results came back. Your DNA did come up positive for some of the trace evidence, however most of the samples match those of the Bosnian we have in custody, Cosic."

"Shocker," I said. "Is that what you call good news? Of course, I'd only think it was good news if I had the slightest fucking fear the DNA was mine in the first place."

I was getting myself worked up. The temper he had accused me of having, the trigger switch of rage I felt, was hard to turn off. Sure, I had a volatile temper. But I hadn't killed Delray. For a while there, he'd almost had me believing that I had done it.

"You're attitude isn't helping things."

"My attitude?" I ground my teeth and forced myself to be calm, my temple throbbed and my body still ached all over. I clenched my fists, stared at my knuckles that were still all scratched and purple. Ramsey and Santos had been doing their job. They just hadn't been very good at it.

"Okay, here's this," I said. "And pay attention. I'm not subjecting myself to any debriefing until I get a full apology from you and from Mr. Santos verbally and in writing. If I don't get apologies, I'll demand a lawyer. I know I'm no longer your suspect, but considering how incompetent this investigation has been so far, how could I know that you wouldn't screw it up again? So, if you want the information I have, you'd better admit you were wrong and apologize, or my new lawyer could drag things out for days, weeks, maybe even months before you get what you need."

Ramsey tried to stare me down but I didn't blink. He glanced at Santos then shrugged. "Okay. Sorry."

"Seriously?"

"We were wrong."

"He was wrong," Santos said, pointing at Ramsey, his smirk infectious. "I, as you may recall, wasn't convinced."

"Okay, I was wrong," Ramsey said, his hands shoved deep into his pockets. "I admit it. But that's it. And I'm not writing any damn apology letter. Take it or leave it."

He knew I didn't have much choice but to leave it. There were too many women, all of the interpreters that had suddenly disappeared from McGovern Base, who were out there somewhere waiting to be rescued just as I had been. I gave in. I made the painful move into a wheelchair and Santos wheeled me into an examination area where we spent hours and hours going over everything. Telling it meant reliving it. The men weren't wanted for rape, but the repeated sexual assaults were evidence of the human trafficking ring they had established. I felt I had to give them all the details, anything that could help other women in similar situations, especially the women still under Cosic's influence. Despite how painful it was, I gave Ramsey and Santos all of the details. Every stinking visit to my stall, every slap, punch and kick, every rape, every humiliation, every nasty bit of it. After awhile, it was too much.

"That's it," I said. "I'm done." My hands shook, my body trembled. I'd showered but I could still smell horses, sweat and tobacco. "I'm not going there anymore. I'm sorry."

"It's okay," Ramsey said. He'd grown quiet while I told the story the second and third time, barely asking questions anymore. He'd stopped looking at me, couldn't meet my gaze.

"I have a question for you, now," I said.

"Go ahead."

"General Paterson. What will happen with him?"

"General Paterson is no longer in command, as you might expect. He's back in Germany now."

"But he'll face criminal charges?"

"Oh yes. Believe me. He will face a long list of charges and specifications. He knowingly participated in the sex slave trade. He has a lot to answer for."

"Good," I said. "Good. Are we done?"

"Yes. We appreciate what you've been able to tell us. We're ... we, ah."

Ramsey stopped and pinched his nose between his eyes, his face red. After a long pause, he leveled his gaze at me.

"Master Sergeant Harper. I'm very sorry that I mistakenly considered you a suspect in Specialist Delray's murder. Throughout this entire ordeal, you've displayed nothing but integrity and courage." He rose to his feet and stared at me. "I'm proud to serve with you."

He snapped to attention and saluted me, Santos followed his lead.

The move shocked me for a moment, then, once I realized what they were doing, I had to fight back tears. I was still a trembling mess, but managed to return their salutes. They held them for what felt like forever, staring at me.

Ramsey left after that, but Santos wheeled me back to my bed, silently getting me there, helping me climb back under the covers, ignoring my shakiness. Just before he left, Santos paused. "How did you do it?" he asked. "Was there something you used, some thought or prayer that helped you make it through all of that?"

I'd thought about that a lot. The answer was something I planned to remember each time my thoughts strayed back to that barn. "They were using tactics. The isolation, the beatings, even the rape. They were just tactics and rape was their most powerful weapon. As a soldier, I can understand the use of tactics."

"A weapon. Thinking about it that way helped?"

"Yes. They wounded me with their weapon. But I survived it. I'll be okay."

= = = = = = = = = =

Later that evening, after I'd hobbled back from a trip to the latrine, I found that someone had left me a small vase of red and yellow poppies beside my bed. Next to the vase sat a soft brown teddy bear with a shiny big balloon that said, "Get Well Soon," tied to one of its paws and a card. Several people had signed the card with Bosnian sounding names, hasty scribbles and little notes of support by each one. I didn't recognize most of the names, save for one. Mishka. "We have found my sister, thanks to you. I owe you everything! Xxoo."

"Are you okay, Sergeant Harper," Folson asked. "Should I get you something?" My laughter and tears alarmed me too, but I managed to shake my head no. I curled up with the teddy bear, and after a good long cry while Folson paced back and forth with a worried look on his face, I went to sleep.

The next time I woke, I found Harry sitting next to my bed. He must have been sitting there a while, his eyes roaming the tent, a forgotten bunch of wild flowers clutched in his beefy paws. When he glanced back at me and saw that I was awake, he gave a little start in surprise, rose from his chair, leaned down, and kissed me on the forehead, his lips lingering there. He seemed uncomfortable, nervous. He sat down again and scooted his chair closer until he was right next to the bed. He cleared his throat.

"They argued for hours over who would lead the raid, the British or the Americans. Your Colonel Raybourn—he almost made a real dog's dinner of it, the spazzy bastard. Well, he finally backed down."

I ran my hand over his head, held his cheek in my hand.

"It is so lovely to see you," I said.

"Me too, luv. You're looking better."

"Ha. I look like crap. You don't have to pretend."

"You've got a bit of a keeker there, but it will go away."

He said it with a smile, but he couldn't look at me for more than a couple of seconds. He took my hand and wrapped it in his, more to steady his own trembling than mine. He kissed the back of my hand, then the palm. He sniffled and shrugged a shoulder to wipe moisture from his face. He covered his emotions with talking.

"We, ah … well, we never believed you scarpered, Steele and me, but we didn't know how to convince anyone of anything else. It was a full day before I even learned you were missing. They all treated Steele like a nipper and wouldn't listen to him. He was practically going barkers. I came onto the American camp during Gore's visit. Did you know that Steele has some relative, an uncle I think, who was part of your Vice President's security team?"

I shook my head no, but it was easy to imagine. If the family genes replicated that size, then it was easy to picture a secret service assignment for a member of Steele's family.

"Steele got his uncle to have a dekko at Delray's snaps, and told him everything about your soldier, about you and the missing girls. When this secret service bloke went to Ramsey—that chap is completely gormy, that Ramsey—well, he had no choice. Ramsey had to take it seriously. He still pissed about over it, grilled the young sergeant for hours, but in the end, the pictures showed everything. She had snaps of the men working for Cosic pushing the BBC boys into the back of a lorry, the same lorry they eventually traced to the big Texas bloke, Clayton Hawes. It was all in the pictures. One of Cosic's men clocked Delray with her camera. The snaps had him looking dead at the camera, pointing. They matched the image of that lorry to the one in the sniper photos, so we knew who to look for, but the Bosnians had already legged it. Ramsey and the police eventually sussed it out and nicked Hawes, but he wouldn't blather. He acted like a nancy, more petrified of what Cosic would do to him than the legal trouble he faced."

"Harry, I can barely understand a word you're saying," I said chuckling, but that didn't stop him. He abruptly stood up, the frustration showing in his clenched jaw and the color that rose in his cheeks.

"They finally put it all together and nicked Hawes that evening, that very evening you legged it to the patrol." He opened his mouth as if to say something, then pressed his lips together. Finally, the words exploded out of him. "Damn it, Lauren. Why in the bleeding hell did you go back? When I heard you had done it I was gutted." He stood at the foot of my bed, his fists clenched.

"I had to go back, Harry. They would have killed them if they found me missing."

"Christ, woman, do you know how barking mad that made us? Raybourn nearly had a coronary. Hell, I nearly had a coronary. They mucked about all higgledy-piggledy after that."

"Raybourn was too slow. He couldn't make a damn decision. I had to do something. I couldn't wait any longer."

Harry looked down at me, shaking his head. He sat down again and picked up my hand, squeezing it. He stared at our interlaced fingers then ran a hand down his face and eventually he continued his story, quieter, as if the memories exhausted him.

"Then they started arguing about who would lead the raid, and who would be back up. It was such a bleedin' cock up. I couldn't believe it when they kept at it. I finally lost it, and for the first time in my military career I raised my voice and threatened an officer."

"Oh, Harry. What did you say?"

"I told that bloody, mealy-mouthed Raybourn to make a bloody decision and to bodge together a team on the quick, full stop. He needed to think about you. How you risked your life to escape. That you bleedin' went back to save the two men with you. I told him, if after all of that, you ended up getting killed because of his indecision, I'd be back to rip his bleeding head off. I'd still like to sort him out, the spac."

He shook with anger at the memory, his knee bouncing up and down nervously. I'd never seen Harry so wound up. I gently lay a hand on his thigh. He leaned his forehead on our clasped hands and took several deep breaths. I ran my hand over his crew cut, and stroked his cheek with the back of my fingers.

"I was never so happy to see anyone in my life. When I realized it was you in that stall…"

He slowly unclenched himself, his eyes closed. After a while, he gazed at me again. He stroked the top of my head, petting me, soothing me. It was comforting and sweet and for the first time in what seemed like forever, I felt completely safe.

"That major, the one in charge of the interpreters, Townson. He claims he didn't have a baldy notion the women were being conned into slavery. Says he thought Cosic was helping them, but he had earned a quid or two for the work he did. Him and Hawes both. Hawes helped Cosic with transporting the women and other logistics. He claims he wanted out of it, but it was already too late. Cosic, Hawes and Townson are nicked now and Bob's your uncle."

Harry paused and scanned the tent, his eyes glistening. He was talking a lot, but I got the impression he wasn't saying what he really wanted to say. I waited. He'd get to it in his own time.

"It took us a long while, too long, to suss out what happened." Harry stopped and shook his head, looking away. "Those BBC blokes, they told us what happened, what they did to you," he said, his gaze directed at the floor.

"Oh, that," I scooted myself up in bed, and reached over and traced the crooked line of his broken nose and the strong arch of his eyebrows across his face.

"Harry Fogg with two Gs, please don't play the pity party for me. I'm going to be doing enough of that myself."

I couldn't pretend the experience would be easy to forget or that I wasn't having nightmares. At times, I drew comfort from thinking of it in as military a fashion as possible, as tactics used and wounds received in an operation. But I could still feel the cold steel of the nine millimeter in my fist, the way it bucked as I fired, that look on Chicago's face as he went down, and the smells of sweat, horse and tobacco would always bring me back to that barn, but there was only one way to get over what had happened. Time and distance, my mother would say. Time and distance.

"I think ... at this point, all I can feel is joy at being free. In time, I'll start remembering the details. Pity will be the last thing I'll want to get from anyone, especially you."

"Oh, I don't pity you, Lauren," he said, shaking his head. "The reporters said you gave 'em hell. They said you were smart and brave. And that mad dash into the night through the tall grass, absolutely starkers!" He shook his head. "I can't wait to tell me mum about it, I tell you."

"Your mother?" I asked, chuckling.

"Of course! Well, you'll have to come meet me mum," he said, as if it were the most natural suggestion in the world. "I'll have you know that my mother parachuted into France during the German occupation. Led some of the French resistance fighters, she did," he said proudly. "She'd have some stories I think you'd like to hear, I'm sure."

"I'd love to meet her, Harry. She sounds like a brave woman."

He nodded his head, squeezing my hand. "I used to think she was the bravest woman in the world, I did. Now, I'm not so sure."

He grew quiet, his gaze taking in all the damage to my face. "You're a hell of a soldier, Master Sergeant Harper," he said quietly. "A beautiful, brave and lovely soldier. Permission to kiss you now?" he asked.

I smiled, and felt how swollen and sore my face remained.

"Permission granted, but be careful."

He leaned down and kissed me, gently, tentatively. It wasn't a proper kiss. My lips were too swollen for that, but the sentiment was there. His kiss felt full of promise. I wanted more. When he broke the kiss, he locked eyes with me and then proved he wasn't easily distracted.

"So, when should I tell me mum you're comin'?"

Turn the page for an excerpt from the next book in
the Master Sergeant Harper Mystery series.
On sale now.

The Sapper's Plot

Available from most online retailers.
www.mldoyleauthor.com

VINE HILL ROAD PRESS

Sap-per, n. U.S. Army engineer specialized in digging and building fortifications, constructing combat expedient bridges, roads and air fields and handles the disposal of bombs, mines etc.

Chapter 1

Someone retched loudly behind me and, in sympathy, my own stomach clenched in a painful heave. Sweat trickled down the middle of my back and pooled around the clasp of my bra before it continued its downward trail, the slow progress made my skin feel like a thousand bugs crawled on it. The high-pitched warble of insects sent a constant undulating note into the air and contributed to that crawly feeling on my skin. Aside from the jungle thrum and the horrible human noises that went on and on, no one made a sound. Everyone around me stood frozen in place.

Like everyone else, I kept staring at the cement slab, hoping something would begin to make sense. The more I stared, the more a creeping sense of pressure built on my lungs. Breathing was already difficult in the thick jungle humidity. Looking at the thing buried in cement intensified my near panicked desire for fresh air.

We stood in the frame of what was intended to be the foundation of a simple, two-room school building. The engineers had completed the wooden frame a couple of days before, and today, were scheduled to pour the cement slab.

Someone had already been busy with the cement and left a horror in their wake.

A section of concrete had been poured and smoothed in the center of the frame. In the middle of the smooth surface, rose a sudden swelling, a mound that sloped to the outline of a shoulder. Dark green camouflage fabric poked through the cement and the unit patch, usually sewn onto the right shoulder of the uniform, sat clearly visible on the sleeve. At just above the elbow, the arm disappeared again until it resurfaced a little further away. Four fingers stood frozen, sticking out of the hardened floor. More flat concrete led the eye to a protruding knee, the green camouflage pattern decorated with flecks of dried cement.

Whoever had poured the cement, had taken the time to smooth around the mounds, even smoothing between the shoulder and hand, between the hand and the knee, making the floor appear exactly the way it should have, save for the gruesome corpse frozen in the center.

The expert trowel work gave me the willies. The killer had left a message with the smoothing of the cement, clearly an ugly message, the meaning unknown. I didn't think I wanted to understand what it meant.

"Sick son of a bitch," I mumbled to myself.

Soldiers and people from the local village stood around staring at the body. The news team I had escorted to the site, Tony Cordovan and his videographer, Juka Dropic, stood close behind me. One of them breathed loudly, his breath whistling through his nose.

Cordovan and Dropic were the reason I'd been ordered on this mission. An investigative news team from Minneapolis, they claimed they wanted hometown coverage of the humanitarian mission and the National Guard soldiers from Minnesota, but the news team had a reputation for finding scandal where it didn't exist. Their request to come along had alerted Army leadership to the potential for bad press in the middle of the jungle. My orders were to keep an eye on them and try to figure out what they were after.

The orders had come at the last minute and I'd been furious to get them. Everyone knew I'd just returned from a deployment, a mission that had almost cost me my life. They all knew I needed rest, but I'd been ordered here anyway. The thing that really pissed me off was that I'd been forced to cancel the vacation plans I'd had with Sergeant Major Harry Fogg of the British Royal Army, plans I'd looked forward to for months and a period of relaxation I needed. Badly.

And now, evidently I'd brought the news crew to a murder scene. The suck factor of this last minute mission continued to increase exponentially.

Aside from the musky smell of the jungle, a decidedly pungent odor hung in the air, like someone had doused a dung heap in cheap perfume. I took shallow breaths and when that didn't work, pulled up the collar of my uniform to cover my nose and mouth. That didn't work either.

The man who had been loudly retching finally gained control of his stomach, but now his sobbing filled the air.

"Bobby! Oh god, Bobby!" he cried.

He crouched on the ground inches from the body. With his arms wrapped around his knees, he rocked back and forth, eyes wide and mouth open in a silent wail.

I wondered how he knew who it was under the concrete, until the glint of a gold ring caught my attention. A large stone surrounded by a signet-type setting identified the hand now frozen in death.

Looking at that ring, the hand and the placement of the knee, another bit of information became clear. Bobby had been fighting. He had been alive when someone poured the concrete on him.

The impressions of small paw prints and the thin pronged prints of birds were scattered around the corpse, evidence the jungle's scavengers had already been at it. On closer inspection, white bone sticking out of the ravaged flesh of his hand proved almost too much for my already upset belly.

I spun away from the repulsiveness and walked smack into Dropic. Mumbling an apology, I made my way to our vehicle, past several soldiers, most of them looking as green as I felt. Leaning on the hood of our truck I took deep shaking breaths. The memory of the smell lingered in my nose. Breathing through my mouth didn't help, only intensified my regret that I'd eaten breakfast hours earlier. After a few moments, I was able to stand, walk to the passenger side and sit down in the vehicle, my legs hanging outside the door. I grabbed my water bottle from the floor of the truck and took deep gulps of lukewarm liquid, then poured more into my palm and splashed my face a few times.

When my breathing slowed down, I glanced up and caught a glimpse of myself in the truck's side-view mirror. My caramel-colored skin looked dusty brown and unhealthy, my hair had started the day in the usual way, as a long, wildly curling mane, French-braided while it was still soaking wet. The tail was shoved up under the braid so that it was off my collar and secured with a fat barrette. Despite my efforts, fuzzy wisps of dark hair stuck up around my head, making my face look narrow and drawn. The lines of red in my brown eyes and puffy bags underneath didn't help. I looked like crap.

I'd started the day in a freshly starched and laundered uniform. The pants had almost stood by themselves and made a sound like separating Velcro when I forced my legs into them. Now, my summer-weight jacket was already soaked through with sweat and the only thing holding the pants up was the black web belt I wore. Even my boots, which I had, out of habit, spit-shined the night before, were already covered in a thick coating of dust.

The news team along with our driver, Sergeant Alfred Mora, and I had packed sleeping bags, food and equipment to keep us for a week into the back of our Humvee and left Soto Cano Air Base along with the engineers just as the morning birds began to chirp.

Taking the advice of the combat engineering unit's First Sergeant, Donald Dodd, we tagged along with their convoy following the long line of vehicles for almost two hours to make it to Los Flores, a tiny mountain village in a remote region of Honduras.

"It doesn't matter if you've got an eight-digit grid coordinate," Dodd had said with a mouth full of tobacco chew and his boonie cap, the floppy brimmed hat made for jungle use, pushed back on his head. He pointed at the dot on the map that indicated our intended destination. "See, all along here, Sergeant Harper? There aren't any roads going in or out of there, ya see? You could be bouncing around that jungle for days and never find the place." He spit a long stream of tobacco juice on the ground to emphasize his point, avoiding my eyes and looking apologetic at his need to spit.

At first, Dodd had tried to talk me out of going along, using every excuse, including the remoteness of the location and even that I would be the only woman at the engineering site. Eventually, he'd understood that I wouldn't be deterred and that I would be bringing the news crew along whether he liked it or not. He hid his displeasure well, but every time he looked at me or the reporters, I could see irritation lurking behind his gaze.

Once we left Soto Cano, our convoy traveled on asphalt roads for only forty-five minutes before the roads turned to dirt. Fifteen minutes later, even the dirt road petered out. The rest of the slow and bumpy route had followed dried creek beds, mule trails and no trail at all save for tire marks, evidence that vehicles had traveled this way in previous trips. Pickup trucks, a wrecker, a five-ton truck and a hodgepodge of other vehicles made the slow journey through the jungle to this remote village. Two deuce n' half's, aptly named for their two-and-a-half-ton capacity, carried most of the engineering unit soldiers, the combat Sappers who would be building a school house instead of their usual mission of blowing things up, digging defensive positions and the like.

Driving behind one of the Deuces, I watched the soldiers bouncing around in the back, grateful for my seat in our Humvee. We were seat-belted in, but I still had one hand braced on the dashboard, one hand holding onto an overhead pole, and my ears closed to the comments and complaints from our passengers.

We began the ride from the base camp with the windows open and the steamy Honduran air whipping around inside the vehicle.

Once we hit the off-road portion of the trip, we zipped up the plastic flaps that served as windows for protection from tree branches that slapped and scratched us along the way. Cordovan had trouble getting his window closed. He fiddled with it for several minutes but couldn't get the zipper to budge. Eventually he was whacked by a snapping branch and his face now carried a scratch across his cheek.

As we loaded the vehicle in the morning, I'd noticed, that while Dropic's gear was smart, well-used, outdoorsman gear, Cordovan's was sparkling new department store stuff, purchased more for the label than its durability. Even the hiking boots he wore, while high-priced Gortex footwear, would probably barely last the one trip. It was further confirmation that the reporter was out of his element, had left his comfortable city reporting behind to gain access to the story he was after.

His bio and the tapes of his reports I had studied told me that Tony Cordovan had a reputation for investigating white collar crime, government misdeeds and city scandals confined to more civilized surroundings. Now here he was, in the heat of the jungle. Whatever brought him out here had to be something significant, something controversial, or Cordovan wouldn't have made the trip. It was worrisome.

Not to mention that I'd just delivered them to a murder scene.

A young sergeant in the vehicle next to mine talked over the radio to the headquarters' Tactical Operations Center in Soto Cano. Several solders stood around listening to the exchange. The officer in charge of the TOC had practically been asleep when I signed out with them that morning; only one other person had been on duty at the time. I imagined they were scrambling to figure out what to do about this sudden turn of events.

"Secure the area and wait for instructions," was the response on the radio.

"How we supposed to secure the god damn area when we don't have any weapons? What a load of crap..." the young sergeant said in exasperation to the men standing around him. Into the radio he said, "Roger, that. Out."

The state of alert on a nation-building exercise usually remained low. We hadn't come here with defense in mind. Weapons were not authorized. We only wore helmets while traveling in vehicles, no flack vests, and only military police, the few sent to Honduras, were issued weapons. As far as I knew, there weren't any MPs at this remote construction site so there was little chance a single American weapon was available. There weren't any fences around the site, no defensive positions, no guards, and it appeared the only communication link we had with the main base was through the radios in the vehicles. Secure the area? With what?

The young sergeant climbed out of the Humvee, slammed the door behind him and cursed all the way back to the murder scene.

The sound of footsteps on the gravel behind where I sat in the vehicle caught my attention. Dropic walked to the back of the truck and I cursed under my breath, knowing what he was about to do. In confirmation, I heard the rip of the zipper as he opened the rear storage compartment. Further shuffling confirmed he was pulling his video gear out of the truck.

Unlike most Bosnians I'd met, Dropic, was a large man in size and voice, who wore his hair below his shirt collar, his beard short and untrimmed, his cargo pants loose and wrinkled, his photographer's vest pockets filled with spare batteries, clamps and cables, and a wide infectious grin that masked his impatience with his TV personality partner. Dropic's video camera and tripod looked small and lightweight in his beefy paws.

Why did he have to be Bosnian?

I was afraid of him. It was irrational, I knew. He hadn't threatened me. In fact, he'd tried to be funny, charming even. Still, his voice, his accent drenched me in memories that left my insides feeling liquid. Dropic was just a guy trying to do his job and had nothing to do with the brutal nightmares I carried with me after my time in his war-torn country. He didn't resemble the men who had attacked me, the men who had brutalized me, held me prisoner and almost enslaved me.

He didn't resemble the man I had killed.

My rational mind knew all these things, but it didn't matter. Upon meeting him, his voice, his accent had stirred up memories still too vivid, too raw to ignore. It didn't help that he smoked the same damn cigarettes they had smoked. The smell of the unfiltered Camels, the sight of the red package in his hands was enough to make me tremble. God, I hated the smell of those things.

The exhaustion I felt now, the exhaustion that seemed to have settled in my bones so deep I sometimes felt like I could curl up and sleep for weeks, stemmed mostly from the fact that, almost nightly, I'd jerk awake at three a.m. with the smell of horse, hay and those damn cigarettes in my nostrils, the nightmares so vivid I relived the experience over and over again.

None of that was Dropic's fault, but every time I heard his accent, every time I smelled the cigarette smoke that seemed to cling to him like a second skin, I couldn't help but blame him for it. Why the hell did he have to be Bosnian?

I moved to the back of the truck where Dropic hiked his battery utility belt around his waist and snapped the fastener in place. I steeled myself for the confrontation, freezing my liquid insides to hard ice.

"That is an American soldier. You will not shoot video of his body." I said.

The steady and commanding sound of my voice surprised me and stoked my confidence. When he ignored me, some of that confidence leaked out. He continued to gather his bulky equipment. He attached a small light to the top of the camera and plugged the attaching wires in place. His glance flicked to me for a moment, then he reached into his bag and grabbed a handheld microphone. I crossed my arms over my chest, trying to still my shakes. He wasn't going to make this easy. At a murder scene like this, I thought it unlikely that any solder would be willing to talk to him, but evidently he intended to try to get them to talk. A dark smirk played at the corner of his mouth as he hefted the gear from the truck. I stopped him with a hand on his arm and felt his considerable muscles tense. His smirk became a glare. He looked eager and ready to argue his point.

"You can't stop me," he said.

"Yes, I can."

"What happened to freedom of the press?"

"This isn't America."

He opened his mouth to say something, then stopped, realizing what I said was true. After a moment, he shook his head as if to brush an insect away and tried to step around me. I stepped in front of him, putting my hand in the middle of his chest.

"Shooting video of dead American soldiers is not permitted. Ever."

"You can't cover this up," Dropic said in frustration. "This is news."

"It won't be in a week."

He towered over me, his jaw clenched in frustration. If he had bothered to look closer, he would have seen my knees tremble. I tried to push the brutal visions out of my head, the ones from Bosnia. He sounded so much like them. His intimidating presence felt like them and the way he towered over me, made me feel trapped, as trapped as I had been under their brutal care. If he moved at all, I feared I would flinch. I widened my stance and managed to stand my ground.

Dropic slowly absorbed the truth of what I said. He had come here in my vehicle. He didn't have remote satellite uplink equipment with him and there was little chance he would find the technology needed in this isolated place. He would have to physically drive the video somewhere to feed it to the vast news machine. There was no way for him to get his video out without my help, and I wasn't going to help him.

He pressed his lips together and leaned over me as if he wanted to get physical but restrained himself. His nostrils flared in frustration, his nose hairs whistled and I got a strong whiff of his tobacco breath. It took every ounce of my will to stare back at him. He finally called to Cordovan over my shoulder.

"I should feel homesick. She's acting like we're in Tito's Yugoslavia or something. She's won't let me get the footage."

Cordovan strolled over, his safari jacket looking crisp despite the damp jungle heat. Somehow he had rearranged his black hair to its perfectly coifed state. I felt rumpled and dirty next to his faultless appearance. Up close, I noticed his black eyes were slightly bloodshot, the skin around them puffy and sagging. Those slight imperfections made me feel a little better.

Cordovan surprised me by shaking his head.

"Don't overreact, Juka. We don't need shots of the body. That's an American soldier buried under there. Have some respect."

"Have some respect?" Dropic repeated incredulously. "Who are you trying to kid?"

I felt a bit incredulous myself. The false note of sincerity in Cordovan's voice, the solemn look on his face, the way he strolled over with his hands buried in the pockets of his crisply ironed jeans, it seemed all too casual.

"I'm sure Sergeant Harper is concerned about the family. Seeing that video would be horrible for them," Cordovan said. He shuddered to demonstrate his empathy.

I narrowed my eyes at him not believing a word of it but if he intended to stop Dropic from shooting the video, I wasn't going to complain. The body wasn't going anywhere for a while. Maybe he figured they could get the footage later.

"You can't control the news," Dropic barked at me. "You people never seem to learn. Government's crumble over such things. And don't forget, Mai Lai, Watergate, Lewinski…"

"That's enough, Juka," Cordovan interrupted, angrily. "She's not covering up a murder. Just preventing you from shooting video we probably wouldn't show on the air anyway."

Dropic stopped, his mouth open in shock. He looked at the gear in his hands, and I got the impression he wanted to throw everything down. Finally, he stormed away in the opposite direction of the crime scene hauling his gear with him. I was grateful for his departure and used the excuse of brushing hair out of my face to see if my hands were still shaking. They were. I cursed under my breath. Falling apart every time I talked to the Bosnian was not an option.

"Thank you," I said to Cordovan, surprised my voice was steady.

He shrugged. "I didn't do it for you. I simply don't approve of that kind of sensational video."

I had researched Cordovan's action news reports. The times he had chased people from place to place, the glare of the camera lights making the subject look guilty no matter what they may have done. The doors slammed in his face, the hands in front of the lens. I wondered what he was up to.

They had agreed to follow my ground rules, signing the formal agreement before they left Minneapolis. Break the rules and they would be denied access to the military controlled construction site. Perhaps Cordovan was simply following the rules. Perhaps, whatever had originally brought them to this place was bigger than a body buried in cement. I didn't like it.

He turned back to the scene at the foundation.

"Do you think he was alive when they poured the cement on him?"

"I think so, yes."

"Looking at that," he shook his head. "Makes it hard for me to breath."

"Yes."

"How could someone do such a thing?"

There was no way to explain it.

"So much for this band of brothers idea," Cordovan said. "Soldiers killing each other like that."

I thought he had taken a leap to assume a soldier did it, but I kept my mouth shut. Cordovan peered at me waiting for a response. When he didn't get one, he scanned the crowd of villagers. "They have probably never seen anything like this." Twenty or so villagers had gathered along the forest line to watch the events at the clearing where their new schoolhouse was to be built.

The adults seemed of uniform height, just over five feet. The men wore checked or stripped button-down cotton shirts over dusty dungarees, floppy straw hats pulled down on their heads.

Their faces were a mass of brown, weathered wrinkles.

The women, their hair pulled up or plaited down their backs, wore cotton dresses with aprons and knee socks, their feet in worn sneakers. Barefoot children stared wide-eyed, some hugging the legs of their mothers.

"Doesn't leave much of a good impression, does it?" he asked.

Honduras had seen its share of civil war, war with neighboring El Salvador, rebel groups and guerilla warfare. I didn't think violence was such a stranger here.

I gazed around the crowd. One boy of about six wore a t-shirt with a grinning Bart Simpson on the front. A teenager, maybe fifteen, wore a Lakers jersey, his hands shoved into the back pockets of the jeans he wore low slung around his hips. I hadn't seen any satellite dishes, but the village had generators so it was possible they had internet access somewhere. There could even be videogame consoles in some of the homes. Movies, music and video games meant they had been exposed to plenty of barbarity.

"It's not as remote as you might think," I said. "I bet some of these kids could quote you lines from your favorite action movies,"

Cordovan shrugged. "That may be true. But do you think any of them have met Americans in person before? It's a shame to think that we're simply reinforcing the violent Hollywood stereotype."

As uncomfortable as it made me, his assessment was probably right. These missions were meant to leave positive impressions, provide humanitarian relief, make friends. We weren't making any friends today.

Someone behind us cleared his throat. Cordovan and I turned to find three men standing with hats in hand, obviously waiting to speak with us. The man in front stood out in the crowd. While most of the villagers were dark brown and weathered from sun or their hard work, or both, this man's skin was much lighter, almost white and smooth, as if his life had been easier, certainly with far less time in the sun than anyone else around us. He wasn't noticeably taller, but he stood erect, as if he weren't afraid to look life in the face.

He introduced himself and the other two men to us in Spanish. I could understand the names at least. Senor Bonilla was the one doing all the talking and introductions. When we shook hands, I noticed his were soft and clean. Senor Bonilla was not a laborer.

Senors Rioja and Egberto barely looked me in the eye. Their clothes were well worn but seemed to be their Sunday best as if they had dressed for the occasion. They had taken extra effort to comb their hair and clean up their cowboy boots, but dirt remained under their fingernails and unlike Bonilla, their hands were hard, cracked and calloused. Working men.

I wasn't sure what made Rioja and Egberto more nervous, meeting Cordovan and me, or being around the confident Senor Bonilla. Bonilla did a lot of talking, gesturing at them at the village, doing a little bowing to Cordovan. I figured someone would clue me in if it were necessary. Bonilla directed a question at me.

"I'm sorry, I don't speak Spanish."

The three men looked surprised. Cordovan made apologies for my lack of the language. I was accustomed to people assuming I was Hispanic, my brown skin and dark, curly hair, led many to make the wrong assumption. I felt no inclination to outline my heritage for the men.

"Mr. Bonilla is a sort of mayor of the village," Cordovan finally explained. "He is welcoming us and offering his assistance. He expresses his regret at this unfortunate death." Cordovan looked at me, as if waiting for me to respond.

"Tell him thanks for the condolences. I'm sure his assistance will be appreciated when the investigators arrive," I said.

Cordovan translated, then seemed to wait for more from me.

"I'm sorry that this tragedy has interrupted the important work we're doing for your village," I said.

Again, once he completed the translation, Cordovan turned to me as if there should be more for me to say. I had to be careful. My authority extended to escorting the media team, not representing the humanitarian mission to the village leadership. It wasn't my place, and I didn't like Cordovan shoving me into the position.

I glanced at the men who waited patiently. Rioja and Egberto looked down or away from me as soon as our eyes met. Bonilla, however, made his own appraisal. He checked out my boots, my body and stared at the name tapes on my uniform. When his eyes met mine again, he smiled darkly. I decided I didn't like the soft-handed man.

"Please tell Mr. Bonilla that I'm just a visitor to his lovely village, with no authority to speak for the Americans. If he needs some assistance from the Army, I can help find the right officer for him to speak to."

Cordovan translated. He poured out the charm, going on and on in flowery sounding speech, saying far more then I had. Bonilla glanced at me a couple of times during the translation and then finally locked eyes with me for a long moment. Something told me he had understood my English and the inaccurate translation Cordovan delivered revealed something to him.

Curious, I thought.

Raised voices dragged my attention back to the scene on the slab. The man who had been crying earlier, was now yelling and gesturing threateningly at Sergeant Dodd. Two soldiers grabbed his arms to restrain him but he jerked away from them and took a wild swing at Dodd's jaw.

Crap! We already had a dead body. We didn't need to watch this unit implode on itself because of it, and right in front of an audience of villagers. I excused myself from the group and moved quickly to the scene. Since I wasn't part of the unit and had a separate mission, I had hoped I could stay on the sidelines of this drama. Every step I took toward the fight felt like I was moving toward a place I didn't want to be.

Army Acronyms –
Military jargon is filled with acronyms. It is impossible to list all of them here but I've attempted to include those acronyms used in this story. If you find any I've missed, contact me on my website at www.mldoyleauthor.com

201 File – Army personnel file containing a soldier's training, awards, promotions, transfers from the date of first entry and throughout the soldier's career.

BDU – Battle Dress Uniform; a woodland pattern camouflage uniform. No longer worn by U.S. Army forces. Replaced with the ACU – Army Combat Uniform.

CID – Criminal Investigation Division; Unit tasked with the investigating federal crimes and serious violations of military law by members of the Army.

EOC – Emergency Operations Center; a twenty-four-hour center of support for emergency situations, activated when a situation is serious enough to warrant the input of multiple staff offices.

EOD – Explosive Ordnance Detachment; a detachment charged with identifying unexploded ordnance, deactivating explosives and clearing minefields and a bunch of other stuff you have to be a bit crazy to do.

General Order Number One (GO1) – A military order used to outline prohibited activities which are thought to threaten good order and discipline during major military deployments. Activities can include drinking alcohol, gambling, procuring the services of prostitutes and many others. The list of prohibited activities is adjusted at the discretion of the officer in charge to fit the deployment or mission.

Humvee or HMMWV – High Mobility Multipurpose Wheeled Vehicle; a four-wheel drive vehicle produced by GM which serves as the main vehicle for the US Military. The wide-bodied, fat-tired vehicle can be produced with a turret, be up-armored and have a wide range of other modifications depending on usage.

LZ – Landing zone; a place where a helicopter can safely land. Sometimes a permanent location or one designated hastily to accommodate emergency landings.

M16 – U.S. armed forces military rifle which fires 5.56 NATO rounds at semi-automatic or fully automatic rate.
MP – Military police.

NATO – North Atlantic Treaty Organization; an alliance of countries from North America and Europe used to seek peaceful solutions to member country conflicts.
or
NATO- Normal Army Tea Order; British slang for tea served white with two sugars.

NCO – Non-commissioned officer; grades of soldiers from corporal through sergeant major, sometimes called the backbone of the Army for their leadership skills, a most responsible for carrying out the day-to-day mission of an operation.

OPORD – Operations Order; a document outlining a plan, the objective, the associated tasks, equipment and staffing necessary to complete a mission.

PAO – Public Affairs Officer; an officer charged with providing advice and guidance to the commander on media and communication matters.

PMCS – Preventive Maintenance Checks and Services; a series of checks and services performed on military equipment before, during and after a mission to ensure the equipment is and stays in working order.

PSD – Personal Security Detachment; like bodyguards, soldiers charged with the safety and security of one individual, usually a high-ranking officer.

QRF – Quick Reaction Force; a standby force used by commanders to respond to emergencies.

SAW – Squad Automatic Weapon or section automatic weapon; a weapon used to provide heavier automatic firepower to squads or sections. The type of weapon varies but is usually fed with an ammunition belt and can be carried or mounted on a vehicle or tripod.

TDY – Temporary Duty Travel; orders authorizing movement of military service members and civilians from one travel location to another for a short tour of duty.

TOC – Tactical Operations Center; the headquarters and center used to provide tactical support to the commander.

UCMJ – Uniform Code of Military Justice; the foundation for military law.

Acknowledgements

My years at the keyboard have taught me that I simply cannot write in a vacuum. My first writing group was born from a class I took at The Loft in St. Paul, MN. I lost touch with most of the members but more than a decade later, I can still thank Kathy Haley for being the one who shepherded us together and for continuing to read the stories I've cobbled together. Her advice has always been spot on and well appreciated.

The most recent cast of characters, the Novel Experience, is born from members of the Maryland Writer's Association. At the core are Gale Deitch and Cindy Young-Turner, authors to watch. You should also keep an eye out for Jonathan Allen, Brian Connors, Mark Willen, Victor Brown, Alma Lopez and C. J. Cooper.

Thanks to all of my beta readers, especially Loreen Doyle-Littles, Larry Doyle, Eileen McIntire, Ali Bettencourt, Colleen Riley, Barry Guertin, Kristin L. Wilson and the wonderful and talented Zander Vyne.

I'd also like to thank Liz Trupin-Pulli, for being so patient, trying her best and helping me navigate through this world of publishing.

A very special thanks go to Laura Michelle Hurst for the hook up and most especially Jaymie Hurst. You couldn't possibly know how valuable your responses to my ever expanding list of questions served in the shaping of my British character. Not to mention, it was just a heck of a lot of fun to learn so much from you.

My biggest thanks go to my family for being there for me. Rebecca Doyle, Reuben, Ramsey, Kyle and my niece Lauren. I didn't have to go too far to find a good name for my main character!

Most of all, to my mother, Ruth. Thanks for always having your nose buried in a book. I wish you were here to see this.

About the Author

M. L. Doyle has served in the U.S. Army at home and abroad for more than three decades as both a soldier and civilian. She is the co-author of two memoirs which chronicle the lives of prominent women in uniform. Her award winning fiction also features women who wear combat boots.

A native Minnesotan, Mary currently resides in Baltimore where she is furiously penning more adventures.

You can also look for Mary's adult romance series, *The Limited Partnerships Series*, which is written under the pen name Louise Kokesh. The series is available as four novellas. The omnibus is also now available.

Mary would love to hear comments from readers. Please like her M.L. Doyle Author page on Facebook. You can also reach her on her website at www.mldoyleauthor.com.